Kim.................................. and took one of her hands in his. .............rstand that you are accepting my offer, Harriet?" he said softly.

Before she could protest, he stripped off her glove and set his lips in the soft center of her palm, the unexpected heat sending shivers of ecstasy through her whole body. The warmth of his hot breath on her exposed wrist made her dizzy with longings she dared not examine too closely.

"Harriet?" Kimbalton's voice was soft, but his hooded eyes held a predatory gleam, and they were fixed on her lips. He held her open hand against his chest and Harriet distinctly felt the hammering of his heart.

Harriet felt her mouth go dry. She could not speak. And she realized that though it had been hard to say yes to this libertine lord's shocking proposal, it now would be even harder to say no to his still more shocking demands. . . .

# SIGNET REGENCY ROMANCE
## Coming in June 1995

---

*Sandra Heath*
Magic at Midnight

*Emily Hendrickson*
The Abandoned Rake

*Mary Balogh*
Lord Carew's Bride

---

# Roses for Harriet

*by*

Patricia Oliver

A SIGNET BOOK

SIGNET
Published by the Penguin Group
Penguin Books USA Inc., 375 Hudson Street,
New York, New York 10014, U.S.A.
Penguin Books Ltd, 27 Wrights Lane,
London W8 5TZ, England
Penguin Books Australia Ltd, Ringwood,
Victoria, Australia
Penguin Books Canada Ltd, 10 Alcorn Avenue,
Toronto, Ontario, Canada M4V 3B2
Penguin Books (N.Z.) Ltd, 182–190 Wairau Road,
Auckland 10, New Zealand

Penguin Books Ltd, Registered Offices:
Harmondsworth, Middlesex, England

First published by Signet, an imprint of Dutton Signet,
a division of Penguin Books USA Inc.

First Printing, May, 1995
10  9  8  7  6  5  4  3  2  1

Ⓟ  REGISTERED TRADEMARK—MARCA REGISTRADA

Printed in the United States of America

# Contents

# PROLOGUE

# The Bartered Bride

"Gad, it feels wonderful to be back in England again," the Earl of Kimbalton remarked dryly, his voice heavy with sarcasm. "Slap me if I hadn't forgotten how deucedly damp the place becomes in the autumn."

This observation was greeted by a genial grunt from the other occupant of the room, who lingered at the table littered with the remains of a hearty English meal of braised pigeon pie, roast venison, a round of beef, and sundry side dishes of curried eggs, ham, and rabbit stew.

The earl stood at the window of the only private parlor to be had at the Stag Horn Inn and stared morosely at the steady downpour churning up a sea of mud in the inn yard. The unmistakable sound of wine, poured by an unsteady hand, sloshing into a pewter mug caused him to turn his back on the dismal view and cast a jaundiced eye at his traveling companion.

"Easy on, old man," Lord Kimbalton said, noting that the wine flagon they had shared with their midday meal was more than two-thirds empty. "You'll be too foxed to travel when the weather clears if you drink much more of old Barton's prime brew."

"Oh, it ain't going to," the younger gentleman replied carelessly. "I have it on the authority of Barton himself that this storm will last well into the night." He took a long pull at his mug and grinned at the earl, a devil-may-care twinkle in his blue eyes. "So make up your mind to it, Giles. We are stranded here for the rest of the afternoon. Don't look so glum, old boy, the fair Ophelia will undoubtedly be there when you get to London." His grin widened mischievously. "As will your illustrious Mama, Giles. Now that alone would make me take the next *paquebot* back to Calais."

Lord Kimbalton's well-shaped lips flickered in an answering smile. Peter was right, he thought. His sweet Ophelia would definitely be waiting eagerly to welcome him back to their cosy lovenest in London. Viscount Bridgeport was also right about his mother, Giles acknowledged with a grimace of resignation. The most recent letter from Lady Kimbalton, delivered a week ago by the viscount himself in his capacity as unofficial courier between the Foreign Office in London and the Foreign Minister in Paris, demanded—in the hysterical tones the countess had adopted upon the death of her eldest son almost a year ago—that Giles return home immediately to fulfill his obligations as head of the family.

"Don't think I haven't considered doing exactly that," Lord Kimbalton remarked, his smile broadening. "Particularly in view of this dismal English weather. But I lack your careless disregard for tradition, my dear Peter. Besides which, I would never dare to cross Mama," he added with a rare flash of humor. "She is quite capable of traveling to Paris herself to demand that Castlereagh release me immediately from my duties. So I may as well submit gracefully to the inevitable." He moved to the table and poured himself some wine.

"Parson's mousetrap ain't *inevitable*, Giles," the viscount exclaimed, his handsome, boyish face alight with amusement. "Don't throw in the towel so easily, old man. I've been dodging the noose successfully for years. All it needs is a little resolution."

"That's all very well for you to say, Peter. With three younger brothers to step into your shoes, there is no need for you to take a wife at all unless it suits you."

"Which it ain't likely to," came the laughing response. "I must say it was most inconsiderate of your brother to be out cavorting in the hunting field instead of getting himself legshackled to some suitable chit and filling the nursery at Kimbalton Abbey with a hoard of little Montagues." The viscount's lips quirked distastefully at the notion, and Giles eyed his friend with amusement.

"As I understand it, Brian was in the company of Lady Mary Standish at the time, a chit expressly selected by my dear Mama as her future daughter-in-law. From what my mother tells me, they were in daily expectations of announcing the happy event."

"Not if I know anything about your wily brother, Giles," the viscount exclaimed. "Brian was no more enamored of the idea of getting riveted for life than you are, my lad. And I'd wager a monkey that if he was contemplating getting buckled, it would not be to Lady Mary Standish. Dashed cold fish that girl, believe me. Not your brother's style at all, come to think of it."

Giles gazed at his friend thoughtfully. Before Brian's untimely death, his own life had been arranged entirely to his satisfaction. Looking back on it now, he could see that it had been almost too perfect. His relationship with his mother had been cordial, his friends were numerous enough to fill his days with lighthearted entertainment, and his nights—Giles smiled at the recollection of his nights—filled with the fair Ophelia. Before meeting the enchanting Mrs. Ophelia Brooks at Vauxhall Gardens one summer evening four years ago, Giles had enjoyed the favors of many high-flyers, but none of them could hold a candle to the pale beauty who had captivated and held his interest since then. No, he thought with a stab of nostalgia, Ophelia had been the perfect mistress—somewhat reluctant at first to accept the protection he offered, but well worth the effort he had expended in overcoming her scruples.

The earl took another draught of the wine, his thoughts returning to his brother. Brian's death had changed everything, of course. The countess had turned overnight into one of the Furies, harrowing him mercilessly along the road to matrimony and respectability. Giles shuddered at the memory of the living Hell his comfortable existence had become. To escape this maternal persecution, he had been driven to obtain an appointment to the staff of the Foreign Minister, Lord Castlereagh, and had fled London—fled even the lovely Ophelia—to enter the world of politics in Paris.

After three exciting months on Castlereagh's staff at the British Embassy in Paris during the summer and autumn of 1815, Giles had had little enough time for his personal affairs. The atmosphere of intrigue and political unrest among the foreign powers gathered in the French capital for the signing of the peace treaty had kept him constantly on the alert, demanding his personal attention to details that would normally be entrusted to junior officials. He had grown to enjoy the uneasy shifting and maneuvering that went on beneath the glittering surface of diplomatic circles. He had abandoned Paris reluctantly, driven by a nagging sense of duty he would have disclaimed as nonsensical a year ago. Much as he hated to admit it, his Mama was right; it was time to marry and secure the future of the Montagues at Kimbalton Abbey.

Lord Kimbalton resumed his seat at the table and picked

idly at the crumbs of a gooseberry pie on his plate. "You may be right, Peter. I remember thinking at the time that Mama was putting her blunt on the wrong horse. Lady Mary is hardly one of the dark beauties my brother favored, and her die-away airs would not have suited Brian at all."

"Well, at least you won't have to worry about that silly chit being thrown at your head, Giles. She married her cousin James last spring. But don't fret, old man. No doubt Lady Kimbalton has another brainless baggage picked out for you."

Giles glanced at his companion in some annoyance. "You mistake the matter, Bridgeport. Mama knows better than to back me into a corner as she did Brian. Besides, her taste in females is execrable."

The viscount let out a hoot of laughter. "True, but if you do not wish to find yourself leg-shackled to a simpering ninny-hammer without two thoughts in her head to rub together, I suggest you look about you for a candidate more to your liking, Giles. Once these things are set in motion, you know, they're deuced hard to wriggle out of."

The earl set his mug down so sharply, the wine sloshed onto the checkered tablecloth. He had not given the matter of finding a suitable bride much thought once he had made up his mind to acquiesce to his mother's demands. He had assumed that he would be obliged to go through the tedious motions of attending the endless rounds of social events to examine the latest crop of marriageable females. He repressed a shudder. What if Peter were right, and Lady Kimbalton had already made his selection for him? Giles had no difficulty in imagining what that choice would be. His mother's taste ran to simpering misses barely out of the schoolroom, just the type of female calculated to set the earl's teeth on edge.

"I draw the line at getting riveted to a chit in her first Season," he declared testily, reaching for the flagon of wine to refill his mug. "I require a wife who will take up residence at Kimbalton Abbey and leave me to pursue my own amusements in London. A woman who knows her place and will not expect me to dangle at her apron strings like some moonstruck knock-in-the-cradle. A woman of good sense, in other words. One who has not been perverted by an unseemly exposure to books, yet who is possessed of a lively intelligence, and . . ."

He stopped abruptly to glare at his companion, who showed every sign of dissolving into laughter again. "Do you *know* such a woman, Bridgeport?" he growled.

The viscount could no longer contain his mirth. "No, I don't, old man," he admitted, after his laughter had subsided. "But if I did, I would damned well marry the lass myself. You're dreaming, Giles, if you think that such a paragon exists."

Giles found himself grinning in spite of himself. "You may be right, my friend, but I swear I would give a thousand pounds to find a suitable wife without having to endure the torture of Wednesday evenings at Almack's, that inevitable interview with an obsequious father, the endless wedding preparations, and the hordes of guests my mother will doubtless muster to witness my immolation on the altar of St. George's." He grimaced with distaste. "Come to think of it, salvation from such a fate would be worth two thousand pounds to me—and cheap at the price."

The viscount sat up and set his elbows on the table. "This paragon would naturally be expected to turn a blind eye on your liaison with Mrs. Brooks, I suppose?"

The earl shrugged his elegant shoulders. "That goes without saying," he replied. "I have no intention of terminating my comfortable connection with Ophelia to accommodate a wife. She would have to accept that."

"And what about age?" the viscount continued, his handsome face unnaturally serious. "How old should this paragon be? Obviously not in her first blush of youth, I assume."

It was the earl's turn to laugh. "I really don't care, as long as she is not much above twenty-five or-six."

"And looks? Is she to be a beauty, too? Something resembling the divine Ophelia, perhaps?"

"That would be impossible," Giles said shortly. "No, I don't want a beauty. Beautiful women tend to be temperamental, as your recent escapade with Madame Dupont should have taught you, Peter. They want to be forever flaunting themselves before the *haute monde*. No, no beauties, thank you. Comely, wholesome, healthy, yes. And innocent, of course. That goes without saying."

Giles took a long pull at his wine and set the mug down carefully, his eyes never wavering from the viscount's face. He knew that Bridgeport was periodically short of the ready, being addicted to the gaming tables. He smiled to himself, thinking that if anyone could produce a suitable candidate to fit the stringent demands he had just laid down, Peter would be that man. The earl himself had ceased to pay much attention to

the waves of new females who flooded London each year in
hopes of making a suitable match. Peter Egerton, on the other
hand, was a notorious womanizer and probably knew all the
available females in London, a goodly number of them on
more than casual terms.

"Well?" he inquired, suddenly impatient to know if such a
female as he had envisaged as his countess really existed.

"Are you serious about the two thousand pounds?"

"Of course I am. Never more serious in my life." The earl
paused, gazing intently at his companion. "Do you know such
a female, Peter?"

The viscount gave his head a shake, as though pulling himself out of a reverie. "Yes," he replied slowly. "I think I do."

"Then why haven't you married her yourself?" Giles chided
him. "I never took you for a slow-top, lad."

A slow smile spread over the viscount's face. "I couldn't do
that, old man," he said, his voice laced with amusement. "You
see, she's my sister."

The silence which followed this unexpected pronouncement
stretched out for several moments while Giles Montague gathered his wits together.

"Your sister?" he repeated.

"Yes, my only sister."

"I didn't know you had a sister."

"Well, I do. Lady Harriet Egerton."

"Why haven't I ever met her?"

"Harriet has no fondness for London. She lives in Sussex
with an old aunt of ours. Lady Sophronia Egerton. My father's
sister."

"Sounds promising. I gather she's on the shelf?"

"In a manner of speaking," the viscount admitted. "But to
see her you would never guess it."

"She's not your age, I trust."

"Oh, no," the viscount responded with a wide grin. "She's
twenty-five. And comely, wholesome, and healthy," he added,
his white teeth flashing in an engaging smile. "No bad habits
that I know of. Except gardening, of course. Mad about roses
is Harriet. Takes after my mother."

The earl dismissed this with a wave of his hand. "And
looks?" he asked abruptly. "What about looks?"

"No beauty, to be sure," the viscount replied. "But then you
said—"

"Yes, I know what I said. But I don't want an antidote either."

The viscount chuckled. "No fear of that, Giles. Harriet may not be an Incomparable, but she's no antidote, I can assure you."

The earl regarded his friend for several moments. "Would she be agreeable to such an arrangement, do you suppose?"

Peter shrugged his broad shoulders. "There's no telling what a female will do," he said with a widening grin. "But I could put it to her if you like. Just say the word, my friend, and the whole thing could be settled without your dear Mama catching a whiff of it."

Giles rose and strode over to the window. The rain was coming down in sheets, and a brisk wind had come up, shaking the last brightly colored leaves of an old sycamore tree down into the thick mud of the inn yard. Barton had been right. There would be no leaving Dover until the morrow, if indeed the storm blew itself out by then.

Bridgeport's words rang in his ears. Lady Harriet Egerton. The name had a familiar, comfortable sound to it, he thought. A female with one bad habit: gardening, Peter had said. Well, he could not afford to be intransigent about this arrangement, Giles told himself. Especially if the female in question was the sister of a good and trusted friend. At least he would know what he was getting, and the choice would be his. Giles did not for a moment believe that would be the case if Lady Kimbalton had anything to do with the matter.

With any luck at all, he could be betrothed to this Lady Harriet when he next confronted his mother. Perhaps even married. The notion appealed to him. The sooner he concluded this first step to setting up his nursery, the sooner Lady Kimbalton would cease to persecute him. That notion appealed to him even more. And why not? he thought. A special license might be obtained in Brighton, and they could be in Brighton by tomorrow afternoon. If the weather cleared. If the wench was willing. If she were not—as Peter had promised—an antidote.

Suddenly he thought of Ophelia, and a wave of nostalgia shook him. If he had his way, he would be posting up to London at this very minute, rain or no rain. It had been altogether too long since he had held the fragile Beauty in his arms, but a few more days would make little difference now, he reasoned. And once he had put this business of getting himself leg-shackled to Lady Harriet Egerton behind him, he could spend the rest of the year, and all the years to come, doing what pleased him, with whomever he chose.

The more he considered it, the more convinced Giles became that he had found the ideal solution to his dilemma. Of course, Lady Harriet was bound to accept the arrangement he would propose to her. What female would turn down the chance to be a countess? he thought. A wealthy countess. And once the knot was tied, he could be comfortable again. Without stopping to consider how this might be achieved, Giles spun away from the window, a complacent grin on his face. A dutiful wife at Kimbalton Abbey, a beautiful mistress in London. What more could a man want?

Lord Kimbalton strode back to the table and glanced at his empty mug. "Let's call for some brandy, Peter," he said, his dark mood a thing of the past. "We have the whole afternoon to wile away, my lad, and your sister's health to toast. The future Countess Kimbalton. If she'll have me, that is."

"Welcome to the family, Giles." The viscount held up his half-filled mug, a broad grin on his face.

# CHAPTER ONE

# The Small Spinster

"Ouch!" Lady Harriet Egerton drew back sharply from the rose-tree she had been trimming of its spent flowers. "The devil fly away with these thorns," she added angrily, thrusting her punctured thumb in her mouth and sucking on it vigorously.

"Good Gad, child!" she heard her Aunt Sophronia exclaim sharply from her comfortable seat on the terrace overlooking the extensive rose-gardens where Harriet had spent the better part of the afternoon. "If you would only wear gloves when you dabble with those pesky plants, you would not have to resort to stable language every time one of them got its hooks into you."

Lady Harriet laughed ruefully. She had engaged in this same argument often enough in the five years she had lived at Lark Manor with her lovable, irascible, and highly voluble Aunt Sophronia to pay little heed to the old lady's strictures. "I always get pricked when I'm careless, Aunt. I fear my mind was full of plans for that new rose-bed Turpin has prepared for me over by the herb-garden. Shall we plant more red climbers along the wall, do you suppose? Or would you prefer the new pale yellows we used under the library window?"

"Pshaw!" Lady Sophronia exclaimed impatiently. "Don't you think, child, that there are more than enough rose-trees on this estate? You'll be wanting to dig up the vegetable plot next, and then where will Mrs. Collins get her rhubarb for those pies you enjoy so much?"

Harriet sighed and snipped off another fat red rose-hip and dropped it into the wicker basket at her feet. "Don't you mean the rhubarb jelly *you* like so much, Aunt?" She glanced affectionately at the woman ensconced in a rickety chaise-longue of dubious vintage, her thin shoulders muffled warmly in her shawl in spite of the mild warmth of the early autumn sun. Her aunt was also getting on in years, she mused, uneasy at the thought. Today she looked definitely peaked.

"Are you warm enough, Aunt?" Harriet inquired, careful to keep the anxiety from her voice.

"Lud, child!" the old lady snapped in response. "Don't coddle me, Harriet. You know I cannot abide being molly-coddled. I still have enough wits to call for a rug if I need one." Her crimped curls bounced with the force of her indignation. "Although I would doubtless be dead and buried before that old windsucker of a butler could bring it to me. Where is that rascally fellow anyway? I declare it is well past tea-time, and I am more than a mite peckish." She glanced impatiently towards the double doors which led into the house. "Ah, there he is, the old rumstick," she added in a loud whisper as the doors swung slowly open and the maligned Harvey appeared, laboriously pushing a tea-cart before him.

"I thought I told you to let one of the footmen do that, Harvey," Lady Sophronia trumpeted accusingly. "It's high time you admitted that you are getting too old for these exertions, you know. It's not as if there were no other servants in the house."

The butler came to a halt beside Lady Sophronia's chair. "I am more than able to fulfill my duties, milady," he replied stiffly, looking down his long, thin nose at his accuser.

"Nobody said you were not, Harvey," Lady Harriet cut in, anxious to put an end to this running battle between her outspoken aunt and her grandmother's aging butler, whom she had inherited with the small manor house five years ago upon her grandmother's death. "But it would do no harm to allow James or Thomas to carry that heavy tray up from the kitchens."

"Very well, milady," the butler responded from between thin, humorless lips. "Will there be anything further, milady?"

"No, thank you, Harvey." Lady Harriet watched the butler's stooped figure move slowly back into the house, and sighed. She knew full well that Harvey was as determined to stick to his old ways as her aunt was in her attempts to change them. She had long ago placed her money on the crotchety old butler.

Lady Harriet arranged the tea-cart closer to her aunt, and

was about to sit down herself when she heard a cough from the open door behind her.

"Begging your pardon, milady," the butler said in his dry, toneless voice. "There are two gentlemen asking for you, milady. Shall I show them out here?"

"Gentlemen?" Lady Sophronia repeated, her spirits lifting as if by magic. "Yes, indeed, Harvey—"

"No," Harriet cut in ruthlessly. "We are not receiving this afternoon, Harvey. Please deny us." She watched the butler disappear into the house and turned to pick up the silver teapot, conscious of her aunt's astonished stare.

"Have your wits gone begging, child?" Lady Sophronia demanded. "Didn't you hear what Harvey said? Two gentlemen have come to call on you, and you send them away as though you had a whole army of eligible suitors beating a path to your door. How do you expect to catch a husband, Harriet Egerton, if you—"

"I have no wish to *catch* a husband, Aunt, as I believe I have told you any number of times these past five years. And if you are so anxious to drink your tea in the company of old Squire Russell and that pimply, tongue-tied son of his, then I shall certainly instruct Harvey to admit them."

"How do you know it was Squire Russell?"

"I don't," Harriet confessed with a grin. "But who else could it be, dearest? How many really eligible gentlemen do we know in these parts, can you tell me? Besides," she added prosaically, "I must look a positive fright." She passed a delicate Wedgwood cup to her aunt and raised her own to her lips.

"Harry!" a loud male voice interrupted the peaceful scene, causing Harriet to splash her tea on the serviceable blue kerseymere gown she used for gardening. "Here you are, lass. What's all this nonsense about denying yourself to your own brother? Shame on you, sweetheart."

Harriet sprang to her feet at the sound of the well-loved voice and gazed with a welcoming smile on her face as Peter Egerton strode across the stone-flagged terrace and grasped her in a hug, which lifted her off her feet and swung her around dizzily.

"Peter!" she cried breathlessly, reaching up to wrap her arms about his neck. "Put me down at once, you madman. You catch me in my gardening clothes, dearest, and you are bound to get this beautiful coat covered with mud. Whyever didn't you send word you were coming?"

"I didn't know, love, that's why." He grinned at her engagingly, and Harriet realized that he probably hadn't thought of it at all. Familiar with the feckless habits of her devil-may-care brother, she was not surprised. Her feet back on firm ground, Harriet watched with amusement as the viscount turned to plant a smacking kiss on his aunt's soft cheek.

"And what have we here?" he teased that blushing lady. "Cleopatra lounging in all her glory on the banks of the Nile, sipping China tea? Aunt, you are truly blooming. Breaking all the hearts in the neighborhood, I've no doubt."

"You silly boy," Lady Sophronia responded, giving him a playful smack on the sleeve. "Leave off this nonsense at once, or you will get no rhubarb pie, sir."

Harriet heard her brother groan in mock distress and smiled at his foolery. Peter had always been her aunt's favorite nephew, and Harriet was glad to see that his arrival had cheered the old lady as nothing else could. A sudden movement drew her eyes away from this tender family scene, and she gasped audibly.

A stranger stood in the open doorway, gazing with hooded eyes and a faintly mocking expression at the group around the tea-cart. Harriet felt her breath catch in her throat as the man's stare locked with her own. She was conscious of being examined as though she were a prime piece of horseflesh to be sold off at Tattersall's. The impression was fleeting, but so acute it made her uncomfortable. When the stranger's gaze slid down her figure with disconcerting impertinence, Harriet turned to her brother, her back stiff with indignation.

"Peter," she said sharply, mortified as much by the stranger's open appraisal as by her brother's careless incivility. "Who is this . . ."—she paused deliberately, her gaze flicking coldly over the stranger—". . . this gentleman?"

The viscount whirled around and waved casually at the stranger. "Come on out, Giles. As you see, we stand on no ceremony here." He turned to Lady Sophronia. "Aunt, meet Giles Montague, the Earl of Kimbalton, one of my closest friends, just returned with me from Paris. Giles, this is my very favorite aunt, Lady Sophronia Egerton. She is blessed with a sharp tongue but a tender heart."

Harriet watched as the dark stranger—a stranger no more—made an elaborately elegant leg to her aunt, throwing that susceptible lady into a flutter of delighted embarrassment. She stood, tense and rigid, waiting for the chance to give the impertinent rogue the set-down of his life if he dared to cross the line of propriety by so much as a hair's-breadth. She was vaguely disappointed when he did not give her that satisfaction.

"And this is my little sister, Lady Harriet Egerton," she heard Peter say, a teasing note in his voice. But her attention was riveted on the tall man, who turned to her and took her hand politely in his. He raised it to his lips, in a salute so brief and correct that Harriet could not—much as she would have liked to—find any fault with it. Yet beneath the stiff formality, Harriet felt a current of something much less innocuous, something she could not put a name to, a sensation of intimacy that could not possibly be there. *Should* not be there, she told herself crossly. Yet it was. She saw it in his eyes.

"Lady Harriet," the earl murmured, his slate-gray eyes abruptly hooded and bland, as though nothing of any import had passed between them at all.

But Harriet knew differently—if her senses had not misled her. "My lord," she heard herself respond in a reed of a voice, her expression carefully schooled to conceal her consternation at the odd vibrations she was receiving from this strange, rather arrogant man who had stepped into her life, and would doubtless step out of it without a backward glance, unaware of the chaotic sensations his passage had stirred in a spinster's breast.

"Would you care to take tea with us, my lord?" Harriet forced herself to say, before turning away to smile lightly at her brother. "Since Aunt Sophronia has already mentioned that Mrs. Collins is serving rhubarb pie this afternoon, I need hardly ask you, Peter, I assume?" She was surprised when Peter grinned broadly.

"Giles knows all about Mrs. Collins's rhubarb pies, love. I warrant he is as anxious as I am to try some. In fact, I have told Giles all about you, Harriet. And Aunt Sophronia, too, of course. He was intrigued to learn about your passion for the cultivation of roses. Quite taken with the idea, weren't you, Giles?" The viscount glanced at his friend and laughed, as if at some private joke.

Lady Harriet turned in surprise to the earl, catching what appeared to be a flicker of annoyance in the glance Lord Kimbalton exchanged with her brother.

"You are a connoisseur of roses, my lord?" she inquired with a trace of warmth. But the spark of interest which had flared briefly at the possibility of finding a kindred spirit in the tall stranger withered at the gleam of mockery that she encountered in the gray depths of his eyes.

"Your brother is exaggerating the facts, Lady Harriet," the earl said coolly. "I can hardly lay claim to such talents. Flowers hold no particular interest for me except as convenient tributes to the ladies." He smiled cynically, casting another speaking glance at the viscount, who appeared to be enjoying his friend's predicament.

"And, of course, for the dead," the earl added baldly, fixing his gaze once more on Harriet, as if daring her to find fault with his logic.

Harriet dropped her gaze to the tea-tray, wondering if her wits had gone begging. How could she possibly have expected to find a glimmer of affinity between herself and this taciturn, rather arrogant oaf? she wondered. Furthermore, she thought, arranging two more cups on the tray and reaching for the squat silver tea-pot, why would she wish to?

When no acceptable answer presented itself, Lady Harriet poured the tea with a flourish, banishing such idle, disturbing thoughts from her head.

When Giles followed his friend out onto the terrace at Lark Manor, he had not known quite what to expect. Comely, wholesome, and healthy did not convey a very accurate picture of a female, he realized rather belatedly. Neither did the Lady Harriet's penchant for roses, which the viscount had described in tiresome detail during their short journey from Brighton up the fifteen miles or so to Ditchling. As he paused in the doorway, catching his first glimpse of Lady Harriet as her brother swung her around in a boisterous hug, he was suddenly uncomfortably aware of the special license tucked carelessly into his coat pocket. He must have been foxed indeed, he thought, to have allowed himself to be carried away by Peter's enthusiasm.

Back at the Stag Horn Inn at Dover, the plan had sounded both practical and simple to execute. In one fell swoop, the viscount had put it, Giles could be free of both his mother's persistent intrusion in his life and the need to go through the tedious round of activities associated with the marriage of one of London's wealthiest gentlemen of rank. The argument had definite merit, or so it seemed at the time, and Giles had allowed himself to be persuaded to obtain the license in Brighton. Just to be on the safe side, the viscount had joked. If all went well, the earl could be married and on his way to London to take up his bachelor existence again. And should the lady prove unpalatable, Peter had assured him, he had lost nothing but the price of the license and two days of Ophelia's delicious company.

Yes, Giles thought, watching as Lady Harriet clutched her brother round the neck and laughed happily up at him. Lord Bridgeport had a glib tongue in his head, that was for sure. But the special license suddenly seemed rather embarrassingly premature, and the lady abruptly ceased to be a convenient candidate for his countess, and became an enigma. For the first time since the viscount had mentioned his sister as the solution to his friend's matrimonial obligations, Giles asked himself if perhaps Lady Harriet was quite the kind of female he had anticipated.

For one thing, she was rather smaller than he liked. Her honey-colored curls barely reached her brother's shoulder, and Giles knew himself to be quite two inches taller than his friend. Her hair was simply dressed and held off her face by a blue ribbon. Her face—what little he could see of it—was unremarkable, but her smile was sweet, at least the smile she lavished on that rogue of a brother of hers. And her eyes? Giles wondered idly what the color of Lady Harriet's eyes might be.

Then suddenly she was gazing straight at him, and he knew. They were a brilliant hazel with flecks of gold, and they stared at him in shock and faint annoyance. Her happy smile faded abruptly, small mouth thinning into a disapproving line, chin lifting in a mute challenge. When she did not lower her gaze, Giles allowed a hint of mockery to distort his own faint smile. The devil take the woman, he thought. Had she no sense of modesty at all? Lady Harriet was obviously in need of a lesson in how the Earl of Kimbalton dealt with impertinent females. Deliberately, Giles let his eyes run over her small figure, pausing at the swell of her firm, womanly breasts before traveling down her slender form and back again, coming to rest on the thin, compressed mouth. His mocking smile broadened, and he felt mildly vindicated when Lady Harriet flushed and turned away to address her brother.

She was as tense as a hair trigger when he stepped forward to take her limp hand in his. If he knew anything about females, Giles thought cynically, this little spinster was coiled to strike him with rapier swiftness if he showed anything but the strictest decorum. His bland formality was obviously unexpected, for Giles caught the flicker of disappointment in her hazel eyes before she dropped them.

Giles did not remember much of the conversation over the tea-table. His attention was held by Lady Harriet, whom he observed covertly as she deftly played hostess to her unexpected guests. Gone was the flash of temper he had detected upon their first exchange of glances, and there was no longer any hint of annoyance in her bland expression. It was as though she had drawn a polite veil over her features, rendering them vacuous and indistinguishable from the dozens of other simpering faces he encountered at any London gathering. Faces belonging to females he steadfastly ignored, he reminded himself grimly. But for some odd reason, Giles found himself unable to ignore Lady Harriet.

There was more to this wench than he had expected, Giles mused, leaning forward to accept a second cup of tea from his hostess and meeting her eyes over the delicate blue porcelain. Vacuous was the only term he could think of to describe that brief glance, and the slight smile—which hovered on the edge of a simper—that accompanied it held just the correct degree of politeness to please the most difficult arbiter of social etiquette. Yet Giles had caught an intimate glimpse of the woman behind the mask, and it amused him to speculate what else Lady Harriet was hiding behind that insipid expression.

If he were wise, Giles told himself wryly, he would be alarmed at the discovery that the unruffled countenance of his hostess concealed anything other than the usual clutter of inconsequential female concerns that one would expect of an untutored mind. Kimbalton was not given—as were some of his contemporaries—to the cultivation of his female acquaintances for their intellect rather than for the more tangible pleasures they provided. Even his lovely Ophelia, he realized suddenly, who pleased him more than any woman he could remember, knew little or nothing of the real Giles

Montague, and shared none of his interests outside the bed-room.

Need it be any different with a wife? he wondered, mar-veling at the sudden transformation of his hostess from staid spinster to giggling chit as Lady Harriet exchanged affection-ate banter with her brother. Giles had never given the matter much thought, assuming that, like his father before him, he would marry only under duress, and then to a woman who would share only a fraction of his time and little or nothing of his mind. Was Lady Harriet such a woman? he mused. Even upon such short acquaintance, his instincts warned him that the female he had come prepared to wed without a second thought might not quite fit the specifications he had enumer-ated so carefully to the viscount.

Then he remembered the special license in his pocket, and Giles gave a mental shrug. What did it matter after all which female he selected? he thought. Better his own selection, even if she was—as this diminutive spinster appeared to be—not quite as perfect as he could have wished, than accept his mother's choice of bride. The memory of Lady Kimbal-ton's penchant for witless chits fresh out of the schoolroom made him shudder. It was all the earl needed to strengthen his resolve to get the matter behind him as quickly as possi-ble.

Lady Harriet will have to do, Giles thought grimly. All that remained was to obtain her acceptance of his offer. And what if she had yet to show any sign of partiality? He brushed the thought aside impatiently. Actually, he liked her the better for not being overeager to put herself forward. But once Peter had broached the subject of their visit, which he had promised to do first thing in the morning, the marriage would be as good as accomplished.

In the meantime, he mused, catching Lady Harriet's glance across the empty tea-cups, a little light flirtation would not be amiss. He smiled gently into her hazel eyes, amused at the faint blush that mantled her cheeks as she looked away. Yes, the elusive Lady Harriet was no different from any other fe-male of his acquaintance, he thought smugly. She would do very nicely.

Giles felt a surge of relief. Life stretched out before him once more, serene and comfortable. He relaxed, enjoying the warm September sunlight on his back. Peter had been right after all. The whole affair would be settled without his mother catching wind of it.

That thought, more than any other, gave Giles a great deal of satisfaction.

Lady Harriet did not sleep as well as usual that night, and dawn found her dressed in her new green riding habit, striding down to the stables for her morning gallop. She had hesitated briefly when her abigail laid out her new habit rather than the well-used brown one she usually wore.

"That old brown thing ain't hardly decent anymore, milady," Lucy had declared with her brusque, country directness. "I quake to think what his lordship would think if he was to chance upon you in that shabby old rag."

"My brother has seen me in it dozens of times," Harriet protested, deliberately misunderstanding the reference.

"Master Peter ain't the one I have in mind, milady, as well you know," the abigail scolded. "It ain't every day we have a strapping, handsome gentleman staying at Lark Manor. And an earl, too, as Cook told me last night. Full of juice, no doubt, and prime for the picking. But you won't stand a donkey's chance in that brown rag, milady. So you listen to me—"

"Oh, very well, Lucy," Harriet cut in, realizing only belatedly that she actually did want to wear the green habit this morning.

"And let me fix your hair in a cluster of curls again, milady. You looked fit for a king last night, even if I do say so myself."

"Certainly not," Harriet protested. "I'm going for a canter on Red Rogue, not for a sedate drive in Hyde Park. My hair would be hanging down my back in less time than it takes that horse to get out of the gate."

"Well, at least wear your new green shako, milady. Ever so fetching it looks. Bound to catch his lordship's eye, too. Looks like a downy one that earl. Used to seeing his females rigged up to the nines, no doubt."

Unaccountably cast down by the abigail's acute observation on Lord Kimbalton's taste in females, Harriet slashed at a perfectly innocent dandelion with her riding quirt. Lucy may have guessed correctly in that regard, but she was off the mark in others. The earl was not really handsome at all, she thought, at least not in the dashing, romantic sense of the word. His features were too harshly chiseled for beauty, and his expression, arrogant and faintly cynical, held no hint of the humor and *joie de vivre* that made her brother's blond good looks doubly attractive to the ladies. His lips, though admittedly well shaped, had the distressing habit of curling up at one corner in a perpetual sneer. Doubtless a sign of a sour disposition, Harriet decided uncharitably. And if an unwary female were so foolish as to imagine that the dark curls tumbling in attractive disarray over his lordship's collar and around his shapely ears betrayed a softness beneath that harsh exterior, she would, Harriet had no doubt at all, be sadly disappointed.

No, Harriet told herself once again, the earl was unappealing in every sense. Discounting his impressive height and the broad shoulders, which filled his exquisitely cut coat of expensive superfine with nary a wrinkle, a female with half her wits about her must be disgusted at Lord Kimbalton's intolerable rudeness. She herself still smarted from the way his gray eyes had slid up and down her form, examining every inch of her with lazy interest. Her pulses still hummed with outrage.

Had he perchance found her wanting?

Harriet came to an abrupt halt, her quirt tapping her skirts impatiently. Where had such a cork-brained notion come from? she wondered. And what did she care what the arrogant rogue thought of her? Suddenly she wished she had worn her old brown habit, just to affirm her complete disinterest in the earl's opinion of her. Hadn't she been wearing her dusty blue kerseymere yesterday? She must have looked an absolute fright, with her hair untidy from bending over the rose-trees, and her half-boots coated with mud. But that had not prevented the scoundrel from flirting with her over the tea-table, had it? Or had she imagined that, too? she wondered. Was she turning into one of those pathetic, aging spinsters, so starved for a man's approval that they turned every male glance into an implied compliment, every gesture into a mark of regard, every word into a declaration of secret passion?

Harriet shuddered. What farradiddle was this? she thought angrily. While it was true that at eighteen, during her first and only London Season, she hadn't made the slightest impression in the *beau monde* or among the eligible gentlemen her anxious stepmother had pointed out to her, Harriet had not lacked suitors among the local gentry. It had been Anabella, her fa-

ther's beautiful second wife, who had discouraged Harriet
from considering such paltry alliances, as Lady Bridgeport
had called them. And Harriet had been only too happy to stay
on at Egerton Hall with her amiable stepmother and her three
rambunctious half brothers after the sudden death of her father.

But her Aunt Sophronia had never cared for the sweet, ineffectual Anabella, and when Harriet's dear grandmother had
left her Lark Manor, she had been seduced by the idea of
sharing her own establishment with her aunt. She had also
been glad of the opportunity to give full rein to her interest in
roses, an interest she had shared with both her mother and
grandmother. She had been exceptionally happy here, revel-
ing in the independence her grandmother's bequest had provided. So why this sudden emotional upheaval over a
perfectly odious earl with no manners to speak of? she wondered.

Angrily, Harriet flailed her quirt again and one of the last
asters of the season lost its pink head.

"Are you always so violent in the mornings, Lady Harriet?"
an amused voice drawled from close behind her. "Perhaps I
should not have ventured out so early. I would not like to lose
my head at your hands."

Harriet jumped at the sound of his voice, wondering if her
fevered brain had conjured his odious presence out of thin air.
Slowly, she turned around, her expression carefully under control. "Good morning, my lord," she said dryly, ignoring his
facetious comment. "Surely my rag-mannered brother has not
left you to your own devices?"

"No doubt Peter was confident you would take care of me."
The words were innocuous enough, Harriet decided, but the
intonation of the earl's voice gave quite another meaning to
them. As if to confirm her suspicions, Lord Kimbalton's
mouth twitched into a faint smile, and his gray eyes dared her
to misunderstand him.

A cold fury swept over Harriet at this deliberate provocation, and her grip on the quirt tightened until she could feel
her knuckles pull. How she longed to give this smirking jack-
anapes a monumental set-down. Keeping a tight rein on her
temper, Harriet allowed her eyes to rove over the earl's tall
frame, from the crown of his bare head, down past the impec-
cably tied cravat, over the brown tweed riding jacket, flicking
quickly past the skin-tight buckskins, and pausing to admire

the high gloss of his expensive boots. Slowly and deliberately, she raised her eyes to his face, noting with some satisfaction that the smirk was gone, replaced by a frown of annoyance.

Harriet pulled her stiff lips into a smile. "Forgive me for pointing out the obvious, my lord," she began coolly, "but you appear quite big enough to take care of yourself." Then, appalled at her own rudeness, she added a half-hearted invitation. "However, I see you are dressed for riding. If you are so inclined, my lord, perhaps we can find a mount in the stables up to your weight. Follow me," she could not resist throwing in as she turned on her heel and strode down the path, her fingers quivering with frustration on the handle of her quirt.

The sound of his boots crunching on the gravel path behind her told Harriet all too plainly that he was not to be fobbed off so easily. Instinctively, she quickened her pace, but the earl made no attempt to catch up with her. She entered the stable-yard in a defiant swirl of skirts, and was relieved to see that Higgins, her head groom, was putting the finishing touches to Red Rogue's bridle.

"Good morning, Higgins," she said, stopping beside the big roan gelding and running a gloved hand down his sleek neck. "How is this Rogue feeling this morning? Ready for a good run?"

"Aye, milady. That 'e is. Likes this cool weather 'e does, and no mistake. Shall ye be wantin' young Jake to take the edge off 'im for ye, milady?"

"You are getting soft in the head, Higgins," Harriet retorted. Higgins had been a groom at Egerton Hall in her father's days, and had put Harriet on her very first pony. He had been happy to come with her to Lark Manor five years ago, but tended to forget that she was no longer a child. "When have you known me in need of such coddling? Answer me that."

Then, suddenly conscious of the groom's curious glance over her shoulder, Harriet turned to survey the earl. "What I do need, Higgins, is a horse that will carry his lordship. I was thinking of Greybeard, perhaps, or even Thunderbolt. What do you think?"

Higgins tugged his forelock and cast an experienced eye over the earl's tall frame. "Ah, I think Greybeard is more than capable of takin' yer weight, milord."

"Do not be put off by his name, my lord," Harriet interrupted, seeing her guest's lip begin to curl. "Greybeard was
my aunt's idea of a joke when I bought the colt five years ago.
He does not live up to his name, believe me."

Higgins gave a humorous snort. "Right ye are, milady. A bit
of a 'andful 'e is at times, to be sure."

"Bring them both out, Higgins, and let his lordship take his
pick. No doubt my brother will be down shortly, so you can
have both animals saddled."

As if in response to her command, the viscount himself
strolled into the yard. "I had forgotten what deucedly early
hours you keep in the country, Harry. A man cannot get a decent night's sleep, what with all the birds setting up a devilish
racket before the sun's even up."

"You should abandon the murky hells of London and visit
me more often, Peter," Harriet chided him, her mood lighten-
ing at the sight of her brother.

"I need to speak to you about something important, Harry,"
the viscount said unexpectedly. "Can you not ride later?"

"Certainly not," she replied with a laugh. "Whatever it is
will have to wait until later. Now, do make yourself useful
while you are here, Peter. Come and give me a hand up, will
you?" She turned to take up Red Rogue's reins, preparing to
mount.

"Allow me, Lady Harriet," an amused voice said close behind her, and Harriet realized that the earl, rather than her
careless brother, stood ready to throw her up into the saddle.

Disconcerted at Lord Kimbalton's obtuseness, Harriet
turned to glare at him. Did the wretch not see she wanted nothing to do with him? she fumed to herself. "There is no need to
inconvenience yourself, my lord," she said stiffly.

"Oh, I insist," came the smug reply.

Harriet glanced down impatiently at his linked fingers waiting to take the weight of her foot, and grimaced.

"If you imagine for one moment that I can raise my foot that
high, my lord," she said ungraciously, "then you must be daydreaming."

"How about this, my lady?" he countered, lowering his
hands to the correct height.

Unable to find any further excuses, Harriet gingerly placed
her foot in the earl's large hands and allowed him to throw her
effortlessly into the saddle. Controlling Red Rogue's sidling

with a firm hand, Harriet looked down into his gray eyes, un-accountably annoyed at the derision she saw there.

"Thank you, my lord," she said coolly, wheeling her horse about. "I trust you will enjoy your ride." The flicker of annoyance in his eyes before he hooded them made Harriet chuckle to herself as she cantered out of the stable-yard and turned towards the distant woods. With any luck she would not have to encounter either her feckless brother or his bothersome guest until they gathered at the breakfast table. And if she were to ride over to Ditchling, three miles to the south, she might take her breakfast with Lydia Coulton at the vicarage and avoid the tiresome gentlemen altogether.

Giving in to this uncharacteristic contrariness, Lady Harriet followed her inclination, so it was well past midmorning when, feeling a twinge of guilt at her prolonged absence, she turned Red Rogue's head towards Lark Manor once more.

# CHAPTER TWO

# A Convenient Arrangement

Feeling rather satisfied with herself, Harriet had quite forgotten her brother's desire to speak with her until she descended into the front hall later that morning. She had changed her riding habit for a light wool morning gown of warm gold that matched the flecks in her hazel eyes. She was on her way to the small sitting room at the back of the house where Aunt Sophronia invariably sat with her embroidery, enjoying the morning sun, when a familiar dry cough made her pause.

"What is it, Harvey?" she inquired, turning to face the stooped butler as he shuffled out from behind the stairs.

"Begging your pardon, milady. His lordship is waiting for you in the library. Very anxious to speak with you, he is."

For a dreadful moment, Harriet thought the old butler was referring to Lord Kimbalton. She had half opened her mouth to instruct Harvey that she would be unavailable for the rest of the day, when she remembered Peter's request earlier that morning.

"Thank you, Harvey," she murmured, redirecting her steps towards the library. She had a pretty good idea that her charming brother intended to cajole her out of another *loan,* one of several he had obtained from her over the years and conveniently forgotten to repay. Harriet smiled. She loved her brother dearly, and sympathized with his desire to live up to the standards of the circle of friends he frequented. And he could have done so easily, she knew, if their father had not allowed his estate to fall into disrepair.

Lord Bridgeport had preferred politics to farming, and spent much of his time in London and on the Continent on one diplomatic assignment or another. As a result, the income from Egerton Hall had dwindled alarmingly over the years, and upon the viscount's death six years ago, Peter had stepped into his inheritance only to find it sadly depleted. He had taken immediate steps to remedy the damage—for that Harriet could not fault him—but for the past few years the income from the estate had been diverted into rebuilding and restocking the tenant farms. Peter had also been extraordinarily generous with their stepmother and her three young sons. In fact, Harriet knew that the new viscount had drawn very little on the estate for himself since it had come into his hands. She respected him for this and could not find it in her heart to begrudge him a small loan occasionally, when he found himself with pockets to let.

So it was with an affectionate smile on her lips that she entered the library to find her brother sprawled in a leather armchair, a worried frown on his usually sunny countenance.

"Harry!" he exclaimed, bounding out of his chair with lithe grace. "Where the deuce have you been, lass? I have been kicking my heels here for hours."

"I decided to ride over to the vicarage this morning. Lydia has been after me to help her with the church bazaar again this year, so I thought we might discuss it over breakfast." She paused to smile teasingly at him. "Did you have a pleasant ride, love?"

"Oh, it was all right," he answered distractedly. "Giles found old Greybeard very much to his liking, however," he added, his face brightening. "Is the horse for sale, by any chance?"

"No, he is *not*," she replied sharply. "And just how long does that man intend to stay, Peter?" she added with a hint of petulance quite unlike her. "If he is in the market for a horse, he is looking in the wrong place, let me tell you."

Peter gave her a curious look. Knowing her brother as she did, Harriet thought he looked rather guilty. But what he could have done to bother his rather lackadaisical conscience, she could not guess.

"No, Harry," he replied soberly. "Giles is not looking for a horse, although, as I said, he did rather take a fancy to Greybeard. Sure you won't sell the brute?"

"He is *not* a brute," she answered hotly. "And he is *not* for sale. Greybeard is showing considerable promise as a hunter, and I wish to try him in the field this autumn."

"That's exactly what Giles said," the viscount remarked. "Took him over a few hedges and liked the feel of him." He grinned boyishly at her. "You could get any price you had a mind to ask, you know. Giles has mighty deep pockets, especially when he sets his mind on something."

"I can well imagine it," Harriet said sarcastically. "But his lordship can take his deep pockets elsewhere. I have no need of his blunt." She saw the guilty expression flash across her brother's face again and paused, gazing at him intently. But the look was gone, replaced by his normal teasing grin.

"I trust you have not interrupted my morning tasks to talk horse-trading with me, love," she said lightly. "If it is what I think it is, you have only to ask, and it is granted, my dear. Please don't stand on points with me, Peter. Surely you know me better than that?"

Instead of the rueful laugh she had expected, the viscount turned to stroll over to the window, and Harriet was now certain that her brother was apprehensive over something he hesitated to speak of.

"No," he said slowly, after a slight pause. "It is not horses or even a loan I wish to talk about, Harriet." He turned to meet her surprised gaze, his blue eyes serious for once. "It is you, my dear," he admitted with a crocked grin. "Have you ever considered marriage, Harriet?"

The question was so unexpected that Harriet had a hard time focusing her thoughts. "Marriage?" she repeated stupidly. "Of course I have considered marriage, you silly boy. When I was eighteen or nineteen I was quite taken with the idea, in case you don't recall. But you remember what happened to me in London. I did not take, as our dear Anabella put it. In spite of all your efforts on my behalf, dear, none of your friends took a second glance at me." She smiled to take any bitterness out of the words. "But I have not been without suitors, as you well know. Squire Russell is quite determined to have me for his tongue-tied son. And that blond Adonis, Sir James Rathbone, over on the other side of Ditchling, is a regular caller—although I rather think his mother disapproves of me. But he does have a veritable passion for roses," she added teasingly.

Her brother smiled sheepishly. "Does that mean you will not consider anyone who does not share your passion for flowers, Harry?"

Harriet stared at him in surprise, then a gurgle of laughter escaped her. "How absurd you are, Peter," she said. "I can hardly expect many gentlemen to be interested in such things now, can I? It would be nice if it were so, but I am not unreasonable, you know."

"Then you would consider a suitor with no taste for gardening?"

Harriet gazed at him suspiciously. "I am not about to consider any suitor at all, not even Sir James, if that is what you mean."

"No, my dear," the viscount said hastily. "Actually, I had a much more eligible candidate in mind. One with rank, address, good looks. In short, a gentleman of the first stare of elegance. And—"

"Do not tell me," Harriet interrupted sharply, her heart thumping uncomfortably at the suspicion that had crossed her mind. "A man with deep pockets, no doubt. Is that what you were about to say, brother?" She glared at him steadily, willing him to deny the dreadful thought that hung suspended at the edge of her consciousness.

The viscount came across and took both her hands in his. "Come and sit down, Harry," he pleaded, drawing her towards the dark leather settee and taking a seat beside her. "You are right, of course. I am speaking of Giles."

Harriet's breath caught in her throat, effectively impeding the retort that hovered on her lips. A thousand thoughts jostled through her mind, none of them making any sense at all. Finally, she pulled her scattered wits together. "And what makes you think you have the right to parade eligible suitors through my drawing room?" she snapped, her temper simmering.

"I am your brother, Harry, and naturally I am interested in seeing you comfortably settled in the world. And Giles is not just any eligible suitor. He is my special friend, and since he has decided that he must marry as soon as possible, I saw no harm in bringing him here." His voice trailed off, as if there was a good deal more he was not telling her. "You should be glad I thought of you, Harry. Giles is dead set against allowing his mother to choose his bride. She favors schoolroom chits with their heads full of romantical nonsense, and Giles cannot abide such female farradiddle. It was pure chance that I thought of you, Harry. A stroke of genius, if you ask me." He gazed at her hopefully, a twinkle of amusement in his blue eyes. "Giles thought so, too," he added innocently, as if the earl's approval made everything all right.

Harriet rose slowly to her feet, her face pale with fury and mortification. "Do you mean to tell me that Kimbalton *knows* why you brought him to Lark Manor?" she hissed between clenched teeth. "Am I to understand that he is here to inspect me as though I were some new addition to his stables?"

"Harry, do not fly up into the boughs, dearest," the viscount stammered, scrambling to his feet and possessing himself of her cold fingers. "I meant it for the best, you know."

Casting him a withering glance, Harriet jerked her hands free and strode over to the window. She saw nothing of the neat park dotted with elms and sycamores in all their autumn splendor. Nor did she notice the two under-gardeners digging up the extension she had planned to add to the already ample rose bed beside the gravel drive. She let out the breath she didn't know she had been holding and turned to face her brother.

"How *could* you, Peter?" she demanded, her voice quavering with distress. "And without a word to me. You are unspeakable! How ever am I to face the man knowing that you . . . that he . . ." She hesitated, unable to cope with the enormity of the situation. "And I am not even in the market for a husband," she wailed. "I'm five-and-twenty, Peter, well and truly on the shelf."

"Nonsense, Harry. You are a fine-looking woman, and I swear you don't look a day over twenty."

Harriet sniffed. "That doesn't change the fact that I am not in my first youth," she insisted. "A man like Kimbalton could have his pick of the London Belles." Probably has had his pick of them, she thought viciously.

"Giles doesn't want a London Belle, my dear," the viscount said gently. "He wants a sensible female who will make his life comfortable."

Although she certainly thought of herself as eminently sensible, Harriet was unaccountably miffed at being considered so by the Earl of Kimbalton. "How convenient for him," she said icily. "I trust he will find one to his liking. But he will have to look elsewhere, I am afraid."

"Now, don't be stubborn, Harry," the viscount urged. "Just think. You could be mistress of Kimbalton Abbey, a showplace if ever I saw one. And a countess into the bargain. You shouldn't let your peevish temper blind you to these obvious advantages, my love. The Montagues have been at the Abbey for over six hundred years, Harry. Think on it."

When she did not answer, Peter drew her gently down beside him on the settee. "Such arrangements are common in our circles, Harry, don't deny it. I thought you had more sense than to turn up your nose at such a windfall."

"I am very well as I am," she insisted stubbornly.

"Of course, you are, love. But do you wish to spend the rest of your life alone, dearest?"

"I am not alone. I have Aunt Sophy."

"But for how long, Harry? Aunt won't last forever, you know."

"Then I shall live with you when you marry, Peter, and play favorite aunt to all your little ones."

The viscount laughed. "I would not count on that anytime soon, if ever," he teased. "I have no stomach for marriage, as you know." He paused, rubbing her cold fingers absently between his own. "Would you not rather have little ones of your own, sweetheart? You could easily do so, you know."

Harriet turned her face away and sighed. Her wretch of a brother had hit upon the only flaw in the ideal life she had created for herself here at Lark Manor. She could have no children of her own.

"Kimbalton does not strike me as a man enamored of country life," she murmured, as if talking to herself. After the words had left her mouth, Harriet realized that Peter would see it as a softening of her resolve. "I refuse to live in London," she declared.

Peter laughed again. "That is just the point, Harry. Giles prefers London, so he would not be forever underfoot." He sobered again and glanced at her anxiously. "There is more to this arrangement which you should know, Harry," he began, and Harriet could hear the nervousness in his voice. "All I ask is that you promise not to bite my head off until you hear all the facts. Agreed?"

Harriet looked at her brother's boyish, handsome face for several minutes before nodding reluctantly.

"Very well. Tell me everything, Peter." She sighed. "I suspect that your precious Kimbalton is looking for the kind of wife I can never be, so do not get your hopes up, love."

"But you cannot deny that Giles is a highly eligible *parti*, can you, Harry?"

Harriet laughed ruefully. "He is that, all right," she admitted, wondering what had happened to all her previous reservations about the earl. "He is indeed a most eligible *parti*."

* * *

By the time she reached the top of Oak Hill, Harriet was out of breath from the long walk, half of which she had covered at a run. She flung herself down against one of the old trees which had given the spot its name, and leaned back thankfully against the gnarled trunk. For a while she was safe, she thought, letting her eyes wander over the familiar countryside around her. The neatness of the patchwork fields and meadows, dotted with occasional brown Jersey cows, and the tranquility of the winding lanes and pathways that crisscrossed the land for as far as the eye could see, had a calming effect on her ragged nerves. She sighed and relaxed, thankful at having escaped from the house without anyone detecting her sudden flight. She had a momentous decision to make, and Harriet did not want either her brother—much as she loved him and valued his concern for her welfare—or Kimbalton to force her into a choice she might regret.

An hour later, Harriet was much calmer, and her thoughts less chaotic, but a comfortable solution to her dilemma still eluded her. One minute, she would convince herself that life as the Countess of Kimbalton would offer her much of what she now enjoyed, with the added advantage of a family of her own. No sooner had her mind decided that marriage to the earl—even an arranged, coldblooded one as her brother had proposed—was the only sensible thing to do, than her heart would protest that the earl, for all his obvious advantages of rank and wealth, would never be the kind of devoted husband she had dreamed of in the foolishness of her first and only disastrous London Season.

The nostalgia of a young girl's unfulfilled dreams overcame Harriet in a sudden rush of longing so intense that her throat constricted. She was being missish beyond bearing, she told herself disgustedly, brushing impatiently at a tear that threatened to spill down her cheek. Harriet Egerton never cried—at least she had not done so since her father died six years ago—and she refused to start now. And what for? she wondered. A man whose only concern was to get himself leg-shackled to a wife who would guarantee his future comfort.

Exhausted at the fruitlessness of these meditations, Harriet drew her knees up and hugged them, pulling her skirts down over her ankles. She rested her chin on her knees and stared out at the tranquil Sussex cows browsing under the mild September sun as though they hadn't a care in the world. Which of course they hadn't, she told herself crossly. They were content with their lot, or appeared to be. Lord Kimbalton wanted a female with the same disposition as a cow, one who would fulfill the role he doubtless had designed for her without fuss or bother. And without any argument, Harriet guessed. He did not look like the kind of man who would tolerate any deviation from his rules. Well, that clearly left her out of the running, Harriet told herself firmly, for she did not see herself as blindly accepting any man's rules without question.

She sighed and tucked a tendril of her honey gold hair back into the chignon she wore. Should she listen to this romantical voice that seemed to register only the odious qualities about the earl? Or should she pay attention to the practical voice, which listed the many undeniable advantages to the union Peter had proposed?

Harriet sighed again and glanced up at the sky. The position of the sun told her that she had been up here longer than she had planned. The dratted man had made her miss nuncheon, and now she would have to go down to the kitchen to beg leftovers from the taciturn cook, Mrs. Porter.

"The devil take it," she muttered disgustedly.

A throaty chuckle startled her out of her reverie, and Harriet swung round to see the object of her dilemma standing nonchalantly behind her, a wicker basket in one hand, a rug in the other.

"Perhaps this picnic your cook has prepared for us will sweeten your temper, Lady Harriet," Lord Kimbalton drawled, placing the basket down beside her and shaking out the plaid rug.

"Are you calling me sour-tempered, my lord?" she shot back defensively. "And how did you persuade Cook to put up a picnic basket?"

"Very easily, I assure you," he said coolly, spreading the rug on the grass and lounging comfortably beside her, propped up on one elbow. "The esteemed Mrs. Porter hails from Hampshire. Near Petersfield, in fact, which is close to Kimbalton Abbey. I merely inquired whether a certain Jeremy Porter, my father's old game warden, was one of her brothers, and she was only too happy to oblige me. She remembered me as a lad, it appears."

Running a jaundiced eye over the earl's large frame spread out on the rug beside her, Harriet had difficulty imagining

Lord Kimbalton as a young lad. He was unquestionably large and solid—too large, actually, she thought, almost overpoweringly so. Taller even than her brother, with shoulders that strained at the seams of his corduroy hunting jacket, buckskin breeches defining the powerful muscles of his thighs, the earl made Harriet acutely aware of her own lack of stature. She felt unexpectedly vulnerable in the face of such blatant masculine power, exposed to forces she could neither control nor fully comprehend. Would she be able to deflect the inexorable male logic Kimbalton was sure to use against her to obtain his ends? she wondered, quickly suppressing a tremor of panic.

Harriet deliberately withdrew her gaze from this unsettling stranger who had brought sudden chaos into her life, and let her eyes focus on the distant brown cows, some of whom were resting beside a small pond, chewing their cud with the monotonous rhythm peculiar to their species. She felt her momentary panic ebb away, and her lips relax into a faint smile. If his lordship had sought her out to bully her into accepting his outrageous proposition, he was in for a surprise, she thought. Harriet Egerton was not the kind of female to accept masculine logic unquestioningly.

When she felt comfortable again, Harriet turned to meet the earl's eyes, one eyebrow lifting in silent query. If his lordship wished to broach the subject of his unexpected presence at Lark Manor, she thought perversely, he would get no help from her.

After several moments, Lord Kimbalton absently plucked a blade of grass and chewed on it. "I understand your brother has mentioned the purpose of my visit here." His gray eyes never left her face, and Harriet had the distinct impression that he was trying to gauge her reaction.

"Oh, yes, indeed," she replied blandly.

After a further pause, when Harriet said nothing more, the earl threw away his grass leaf and plucked another. "And what exactly did Peter say to cause you to run out of the house as though the hounds of Hell were at your heels?"

"Perhaps they were," Harriet replied lightly, and laughed at the flash of puzzlement she detected in his eyes. "Actually, my brother had a rather odd, fantastical tale to tell, one to which I had great difficulty giving any credence at all."

The earl stopped chewing abruptly, a frown drawing his

eyebrows down menacingly. "And what tale might this be?" he said sharply.

Harriet laughed again. She was beginning to enjoy herself. He was so easily provoked. The slightest hint of criticism or opposition was enough to bring those dark brows down into a glower. She settled back more comfortably against the trunk and smiled at him.

"Some fairy tale or other about a wealthy nobleman scouring the rural corners of England for a suitable bride. A dutiful, obedient female she would have to be, of course, who would reside quietly in her lord's ancestral home and provide him with heirs. All this without the least fuss and bother, naturally, and without inconveniencing the lord, who prefers to disport himself in London with some enchantress or other." Harriet paused, enjoying the mixed emotions—none of them pleasant—which flickered across Lord Kimbalton's face.

"Quite an amusing tale, would you not say, my lord?" she added mendaciously.

After an uncomfortable pause, the earl threw his grass away and cleared his throat. "I cannot believe your brother would invent such a fanciful tale," he growled at last.

"Of course, he did not," Harriet admitted, taking pity on him. "But you must admit it makes a wonderful fairy tale, my lord. It has all the ingredients of a medieval fable. Of course, it does lack a wicked witch or wizard to add a certain sense of impending danger—"

"I fail to see how you mistook me for a character out of a fairy tale," the earl interrupted impatiently.

"Oh, I did not," Harriet protested quickly, unable to hide her smile at the notion of Lord Kimbalton masquerading as a fairy prince. "That is why I thought it was all a hum, at first. Peter has always amused himself at my expense," she confessed. "I still find it difficult to believe the whole thing is not a Banbury tale."

"It is no such thing, I can assure you," the earl stated rather shortly.

"So Peter insisted; however, I still think it odd that . . ." Her voice trailed off as Harriet realized that there was no polite way to tell a man as starched-up as Lord Kimbalton that his behavior bordered on the ridiculous.

"I find nothing odd about it at all," he snapped, his brows coming together in a deep frown of annoyance. "Men of my rank have a duty to find a suitable wife to continue the line. An unpleasant reality, of course, but one I cannot ignore. Much as I would prefer to," he added coldly.

Taken aback by the coldhearted bluntness and pomposity of this remark, Harriet paused briefly to control the unwise retort that had risen to her lips. "I should think you could find a much better selection of females in London, my lord," she remarked with equal coolness. "I would imagine London ladies to be more your style," she added daringly.

He glanced at her sharply. "They are," he drawled with deliberate provocation. "But not for a wife."

Startled at the implications of this indecorous remark, and conscious of her heightened color, Harriet fixed her eyes on the cows again. How dare he make such unmistakable references to his illicit liaisons in the Metropolis? she fumed. Who did he think he was talking to, anyway? She glared frostily past the reclining earl, wishing that he had chosen any other part of the English countryside for his matrimonial search, but the sight of the placid bovines worked its subtle effect, and suddenly Harriet's sense of humor got the better of her. She felt a gurgle of laughter rise in her throat, which she made no attempt to quell.

"I fear you have been misled, my lord," she managed to say when her laughter subsided. "There are no suitable females in rural Sussex, at least none that I know of."

Lord Kimbalton shrugged his broad shoulders nonchalantly. "I find you eminently suitable, Lady Harriet," he said evenly, his gray eyes daring her to argue the point.

It was just as she had imagined, Harriet thought, shaken by the calm conviction in his voice. He had already made up his mind, and she was to have no choice in the matter. She returned the earl's stare, wondering what she could say to dissuade him from this madness. Asking herself, almost in the same breath, whether she really wished to dissuade him. Of one thing she was certain, however. She was anything but *suitable*.

"How can you say such a thing, my lord?" she demanded, torn between laughter and outrage. "You know nothing about me, yet after barely twenty-four hours at Lark Manor, you can make such a momentous decision. I find that rather remarkable," she finished lamely.

Lord Kimbalton merely smiled. "Have you considered that I

might be a remarkable man, my dear?" he suggested gently, a cynical curl tugging at his mouth.

"Remarkably foolish," Harriet retorted before she could stop herself. His use of the endearment raised her hackles. "And had you considered that I might have had a squint and a harelip?" she added scathingly.

"You have neither, I am relieved to say. Your brother's description convinced me that you would suit my purposes admirably."

He had fallen into odious pomposity again, Harriet realized. His conceit was monstrous, and she could not resist the urge to deflate it. "Ah, but I doubt Peter told you anything about my fiendish temper, my lord," she said sweetly. "And the deplorable fact that I am unimpressed by either rank or wealth, having been raised with both since birth." She stared blandly into the cool gray eyes, and raised her small nose a fraction before throwing out her challenge. "I fail to see that you have anything else to offer that might tempt me."

Paralyzed by her own daring, Harriet raised her delicate brows and smiled with what she hoped was polite commiseration. "I regret that Peter has brought you on a wild-goose-chase, my lord. No doubt when you remove to London tomorrow—"

"I have no intention of removing to London until you and I have concluded our business together, Lady Harriet," the earl interrupted with suppressed irritation.

Harriet was sure that at any moment now Lord Kimbalton would grind his teeth. With a little assistance from her, he might conceivably be brought to admit defeat. "Indeed?" she said politely. "And what *business* is this, my lord?"

The muscles on his square jaw bunched alarmingly. "I am making you an offer of marriage, Lady Harriet," he said between clenched teeth, his voice dangerously calm.

Harriet smiled her most vacuous smile. "And very charmingly, too, my lord. I am immensely flattered, believe me," she added coyly. Glancing around in search of a diversion, her eyes fell on the picnic basket. "Oh, what can I be thinking of?" she exclaimed in mock dismay. "You will think me the veriest wigeon. We have not yet explored Mrs. Porter's delicacies after you went to all the trouble of carrying them up here. And you must be starved, my lord. I certainly am." So saying, Harriet flipped the cloth from the basket and peered inside. "Ah, rabbit pie," she exclaimed gleefully, lifting out a dish and placing it on the rug. "And some of Mrs. Porter's damson tarts. And what is this? A bottle of wine!" She unwound the serviette from the bottle and inspected it eagerly. "Homemade plum wine," she exclaimed. "A rare treat indeed, my lord. However did you—"

Harriet was interrupted by what sounded perilously like a growl, and she glanced up apprehensively. Had she gone too far and given the poor man an apoplexy? she wondered. The earl's face had turned dark under his tan, and his eyes glittered dangerously.

"You do not like plum wine, my lord?" she asked anxiously.

"The devil fly away with the wine," the earl snapped angrily, his patience evidently at an end. "Your brother seems to think that you consider me an eligible *parti*." He paused, his annoyance giving place to a thin smile, which immediately spurred Harriet to another unwise response.

"Oh, Peter is right, my lord. But you hardly need me to tell you that, sir," she added archly. "Very eligible indeed," she repeated. "But not necessarily in my style, my lord. At least not unless you have something other than wealth and rank to offer me to compensate for that lack."

By the thunderous scowl that instantly clouded his face, Harriet realized that being told he lacked anything was a novel experience for the Earl of Kimbalton. She felt a glow of satisfaction. Perhaps now the odious man would take umbrage and stalk off, leaving her to enjoy Mrs. Porter's rabbit pie in peace.

"Will you try a glass of Mrs. Porter's plum wine, my lord?" she asked demurely, as though she had not just refused an offer from a gentleman who undoubtedly believed himself to be the catch of the Season. "I can recommend it highly," she continued, pouring the fragrant liquid into a glass and handing it to the earl.

"I did not come all the way up here to drink wine," he said coldly. "Nor did I expect to be insulted."

"Insulted?" Harriet exclaimed, unable to keep the amusement out of her voice. "I take that to mean that you did not expect to be crossed, my lord," she added coolly. "Are you sure you won't try the wine?"

The earl waved the glass aside impatiently. "Your brother assured me you were a sensible female, Lady Harriet. I am beginning to have my doubts, however."

"I consider myself a sensible female, my lord," Harriet replied lightly. "But the truth is, I find my present circumstances very comfortable indeed, and see no reason to uproot myself without any real incentive."

The earl's lips thinned into a smile, warning Harriet that he was not about to give up so easily. "Peter tells me that you are anxious to have a family of your own, my dear," he said smoothly, his eyes mocking her. "Since that is my own purpose in seeking a wife—my *only* purpose, I should add—it seems to be mere foolishness on your part to sit around waiting for Prince Charming to ride up and claim you. Life is far less fanciful, my dear, let me assure you."

Harriet felt her color rise at the earl's plain speaking. How could Peter have betrayed her most intimate secret to this odious man? she wondered, promising her brother a sound trimming when next they met. For now, her anger settled on the earl for his lack of delicacy in bringing up a subject which he must have known would embarrass her.

"You are quite off the mark there, my lord," she countered coolly. "It so happens that my Prince Charming has already ridden up to claim me. Several times, I might add. And if I had been as anxious for a family of my own as you seem to think, I would have accepted Sir James Rathbone's offer anytime these past three years." She derived no little satisfaction at the black frown that settled once again on the earl's face. "I might yet do so, of course," she added mendaciously, unable to resist the temptation to goad him. "When Sir James gets wind of your presence at Lark Manor, my lord, he is bound to come *vent-à-terre* to throw himself at my feet again."

She smiled smugly as the earl's frown became a glower, and a rush of perverseness made her reckless. "Sir James is the embodiment of every young girl's dreams, I might add," she could not resist saying. "He is a blond Apollo with the bluest eyes . . ." Harriet let her voice taper off in a fair imitation of a maiden sighing for her true love. She was enjoying herself and considered that a little embroidering of the truth might put the odious earl firmly in his place. "And he actually does ride a white horse." She smiled dreamily. "If I know Sir James at all, he will be here this afternoon in time for tea. Undoubtedly under the misguided impression that I am in danger of succumbing to your nefarious charms, my lord." She accompanied this outrageous remark with a simpering smile calculated to provoke instant revulsion in Lord Kimbalton's breast.

The earl swore under his breath and reached for the glass Harriet was still holding. He snatched it out of her hand and drained the contents in one long gulp. He held out the glass to be refilled, and Harriet's heart lurched uncomfortably at the savage light in the gray eyes boring into hers.

"Your Prince Charming sounds like a regular sapskull," the earl remarked contemptuously, as soon as Harriet had poured the wine and served herself a glass. "Am I to understand, my dear," he continued in a harsh tone, "that you find me unattractive?"

The question took Harriet by surprise, and she paused in the act of raising the glass to her lips to stare at the earl curiously. "What could my opinion of you possibly matter, my lord?" she said. "Besides, Peter told me you are looking for a sensible, practical female for a wife. It seems to me that if I did indeed find you attractive, I would be neither sensible nor practical. Under the circumstances, of course," she added hastily, unwilling to admit that under other circumstances, Lord Kimbalton might be extremely attractive indeed. But then he would not be offering to make her his countess, would he? she reasoned. His offer would be of quite a different nature entirely. The notion made her uncomfortably warm.

When he made no reply, Harriet felt impelled to remind Lord Kimbalton of his own words. "You did mention that it was a *business* arrangement you had in mind, my lord. And under those circumstances, perhaps it is fortunate that I do not find you particularly attractive," she added daringly, watching the now familiar scowl darken his features, and his eyes take on the color of rain-lashed slate.

"I meant *convenient*," he growled. "A *convenient* arrangement."

"Well, in any case, an infatuated wife is the last thing you would want, I should think. I imagine that such a creature would be extremely *inconvenient*, and could possibly make a great nuisance of herself into the bargain." Harriet held her breath, fully expecting the Earl of Kimbalton to wash his hands of her after that piece of frankly indelicate logic.

The earl drained his glass, and when he met her eyes again, Harriet was surprised to see a look of cynical amusement had replaced the scowl. "You have an excellent grasp of the situation, my dear," he drawled, holding out his glass to be refilled. "Dare I hope that you are prepared to take my offer seriously?"

Harriet sighed. Obviously, the odious man was not to be dissuaded from his purpose. She supposed she should feel flattered that the grand Earl of Kimbalton found her suitable for the elevated position he was offering her, but Harriet was conscious only of a vague sense of dissatisfaction. Probably she was being unduly missish about the whole affair, she thought. Besides, she was well past the age of romantical nonsense, and for all his good looks, Sir James Rathbone was not and never would be the Prince Charming she had facetiously painted him. And Peter was right—however much she hated to admit it—when he had pointed out the honors which would accrue to her as the Countess of Kimbalton. Any truly sensible female would not have hesitated a moment, and Harriet prided herself on her good sense. And yet . . . She glanced again into the amused gray eyes, which seemed to read her mind.

"You may dare anything you wish, my lord," she said evasively. "But your conditions are admittedly rather severe."

"Which ones do you object to, my lady?" His eyes became suddenly hooded, and Harriet guessed which one in particular the earl had in mind.

"Not the one you are obviously thinking of, my lord." She laughed at the look of annoyance which flashed across his face. "It is none of my concern what company you keep in London," she added airily, with more confidence than she felt. "However, I do think I am entitled to a tour of your ancestral home before coming to any decision. Lark Manor has been a comfortable home to me, and I would not exchange it for anything less."

The earl smiled.

It was a slow, confident, knowing smile, Harriet noticed, conscious of the knot of apprehension forming in her stomach. A smile which relaxed his habitually cynical, severe expression and erased the lines around his eyes, making him almost handsome in a hard, arrogant kind of way. The rogue imagined he had won, she thought, and regretted her frankness.

"I would insist upon a large garden," she continued, anxious to wipe the complacent smile from his face. "And lots and lots of rose-trees. A hothouse, herb garden, a pond with fish and water lilies—"

"Kimbalton Abbey has all of that and much more, my dear Harriet," the earl interrupted. He raised his glass. "I propose a toast, Lady Harriet," he said. "To a most harmonious and convenient agreement between us."

Harriet shook her head. "That would be most premature, my lord," she declared, suddenly aware that she was about to bargain away her freedom. "I suggest we drink instead to Kimbalton Abbey," she added, raising her glass. "May it please me."

Lord Kimbalton gazed at her for several moments, a speculative gleam in his eyes. Then he raised his glass.

"May it please you, my dear."

# CHAPTER THREE

# Prince Charming

The wench was as good as won, Giles thought cynically as he followed Lady Harriet's slim figure down the narrow path from Oak Hill to the lane leading back to Lark Manor. He was well pleased with the results of his conversation with the skittish Lady Harriet. Although she had displayed an annoying penchant for provoking him with her disconcertingly frank remarks, he had the distinct impression that her aversion to him was not as strong as she would have him believe. He smiled grimly as the lady in question climbed nimbly over a stile without so much as a glance in his direction. So the wench was independent, was she? Accustomed as he was to females of all ages fawning over him and seizing any pretext to hang on his arm with their scheming little hands, Giles found Lady Harriet a refreshing challenge to his reputation as a connoisseur of women.

But for all her prevarication and avowals of disinterest in his rank and wealth, Giles did not doubt for a moment that she would succumb to the temptation of becoming the Countess of Kimbalton. What female in her right mind would refuse such a plum? Giles smiled wolfishly as his eyes followed every self-confident motion of the diminutive woman who had the audacity to tell him to his face that she did not find him particularly attractive. Her very words, he recalled, repressing a surge of anger at the insult. *Not particularly attractive*, she had said, and what else? Something about his having nothing to tempt her to accept his offer besides rank and wealth.

Sweet Jesus, but the wench had a nerve, he thought, clenching the handle of the wicker basket so tightly that he heard it crack in his fist. And all that farradiddle about some insignificant baronet who rode around on a white horse. Doubtless a piece of feminine nonsense designed to throw dust in his eyes. Well, Lady Harriet had badly misjudged him if she thought such schoolroom tricks would work on the Earl of Kimbalton, he mused, stepping over the stile and lengthening his stride to catch up with the object of his wrath.

Lady Harriet came to a halt in the middle of the lane and turned to smile at him. "Am I going too fast for you, my lord?" she inquired with the false sweetness he was beginning to recognize as a prelude to a set-down. "I had forgotten that you cannot be accustomed to long country walks. I know from my own brief sojourn there that nobody walks in London. My stepmother insisted upon calling for the carriage to pay a call on the other side of Grosvenor Square. No wonder there is so much sickness and depravity in the Metropolis. People do not get proper exercise."

Her smile widened slightly, and Giles got the distinct impression that he had been insulted again.

"Depravity?" he repeated softly, determined to put this hoyden in her place. "I fail to see how depravity can result from lack of exercise, my lady. From my own experience, I can assure you that some forms of depravity make quite strenuous demands on one's constitution."

Lady Harriet's response to this quite shocking pronouncement was everything Giles could have wished. He saw her attractive hazel eyes widen in horror as the implications of his words sank in. She made a valiant effort to maintain a pretense of innocence, but the vivid flush that stained her cheeks gave her away. Her struggle with her temper was clearly reflected on her heart-shaped face, and Giles felt himself bracing for the scathing retort he saw building in her eyes.

"Well, if anyone would know, it must surely be you, my lord," she said icily, her eyes raking him disdainfully before she swung around and strode away, her back rigid with indignation.

Repressing a chuckle, Giles easily caught up with her, but all his attempts at resuming a civilized conversation were greeted with silence or reluctant monosyllables.

After several minutes of this uncomfortable silence, Giles began to wonder if perhaps his remark had not been a trifle strong for a chit born and raised in the country. It was not his custom to apologize to anyone, much less to a female as outspoken as this one, but it occurred to him that Lady Harriet might have been truly offended by his deliberately crude words. Traces of the rosy blush still lingered on her cheeks, proof that her sensibilities had indeed received a shock. And if he were not careful, Giles thought wryly, the chit might refuse him out of hand. For some odd reason he did not care to examine, the thought of being rejected by a diminutive spinster of no particular attraction for a man of his tastes made him suddenly all the more determined to have her.

"Lady Harriet," he said coaxingly, searching for the words to undo any harm he might have done. "Lady Harriet," he repeated when she paid not the slightest heed and continued to stride along the lane in what Giles privately considered a defiant, rather unladylike manner.

"I fear I have said something to offend you, my dear," he continued, addressing her profile.

"You fear?" she replied scathingly, raising her small nose a fraction. "Do not take me for a complete flat, my lord. You said it quite deliberately to put me out of countenance."

She still would not look at him, but Giles relaxed, confident that he could cajole the chit out of her peevishness. "Perhaps you are right, but in any case, I am sorry to have upset you," he said, surprised that the admission came so easily to his lips. He was about to add one of the many insincere flatteries he used so carelessly with his London flirts, when Lady Harriet stopped abruptly and turned to face him. One look into her hazel eyes and Giles was glad he had not attempted to flirt with her.

"Your apology is accepted, my lord," she said dryly. "But I must ask you to remember that you are not in London, and that I am not one of your London flirts. And furthermore . . ."

Giles never did learn what other startling remark Lady Harriet would have unleashed upon his head, for she stopped abruptly and turned her head back in the direction they had come, a curious smile tugging at her lips.

No sooner had Giles glanced over his shoulder than he saw the cause of her amusement. The pace of the white horse careening towards them might well be described by a fanciful imagination as *vent-à-terre*, and the fair-haired rider could be none other than Lady Harriet's Prince Charming. Giles felt his jaw clench angrily.

The horseman drew rein beside them with a practiced flourish, and Giles saw that Lady Harriet had not exaggerated. The tall youth who sprang lightly from the white horse's back was nothing short of magnificent. Giles found himself staring in reluctant admiration at the perfect, classical Greek features, a shapely mouth of almost feminine beauty, topped by a nose of such aristocratic proportions that Giles felt he might well be in

the presence of one of Praxiteles's sculptures. The golden hair
was styled à la Brutus, with not a single strand out of place in
spite of the violence of the gentleman's arrival. And his
eyes . . . Giles drew a deep breath and expelled it slowly, suddenly understanding Lady Harriet's languishing sigh when she
attempted to describe their color. Wild cornflowers were but a
pale comparison to the brilliant, deep sapphire blue of the
young man's eyes, which Giles grudgingly had to admit were
startlingly beautiful. Enough to turn any chit's head, he
thought cynically. Enough to eclipse even the Earl of Kimbalton, Giles acknowledged grimly.

For the first time in his life, Giles felt himself outclassed. It
was a humbling experience, which did nothing to cool his rising temper. He tore his gaze away from the blond Apollo, and
forced himself to look at Lady Harriet, quite prepared to find
the hopelessness of his own case reflected on her face.

But, inexplicably, she was looking at him.

Giles swallowed, conscious that his mouth was dry. And
then he noticed the glint of amusement in Lady Harriet's eyes,
and realized with some annoyance that the wretched chit must
have watched his awestruck examination of the newcomer. He
took refuge in anger, pulling his brows down into a glower, a
reflex which brought a grin to the lady's face.

"Lady Harriet," the young man exclaimed, his voice as
sweetly melodious as Pan's flute. Giles ground his teeth in
frustration as he watched the blond gallant bow gracefully
over Harriet's fingers, which he brought to his lips in a prolonged and unnecessarily warm salute.

"Sir James," Lady Harriet trilled, in what Giles privately
considered deliberately saccharine tones. "What a delightful
surprise. I trust dear lady Rathbone is well."

"Indeed she is, my lady. In fact I am the bearer of a personal
note from my mother begging you to honor us with your presence at a small musicale she is planning for next week."

"Next week?" Lady Harriet repeated, dimpling prettily. "I
may not be here, Sir James," she continued with what appeared to be genuine regret. "Lord Kimbalton," she said,
throwing a quizzical glance in the earl's direction, "allow me
to present a neighbor and particular friend of mine, Sir James
Rathbone."

*A particular friend,* indeed, Giles thought disgustedly,
bringing his brows down in a scowl calculated to depress this
pretentious young cockscomb. He found himself the object of

a steady blue gaze, which held no hint of welcome. Sir James's startlingly beautiful eyes, fringed with lashes the length of which Giles had rarely seen, even on the most beautiful female of his extensive acquaintance, reflected not only hostility, but also curiosity and apprehension. And a hint of jealousy, Giles noticed, the discovery restoring some of his comfortable cynicism. The puppy was truly infatuated with the little chit, he thought, at a loss to understand why such a paragon of masculine beauty—who would no doubt cut a devil of a dash among the fairer sex in London—would throw himself away on a female with neither beauty nor sweetness of temperament to recommend her. And furthermore, he thought, with a savage sense of perverse pleasure, the wench was an ape leader and a harridan into the bargain. Sir James was welcome to her.

"Your servant, my lord," Rathbone said stiffly, inclining his magnificent golden head a fraction less than was strictly polite.

Giles nodded even more curtly and turned back to find Lady Harriet's gaze upon him again, a gleam of devilment dancing in their hazel depths. The expression wrought an astonishing metamorphosis in her features, softening and animating them into an illusion of such delicate loveliness that Giles caught himself staring. Even as he watched, however, the light went out of her eyes, and her lips settled back into a fatuous smile. The devil take the wench, he thought, abruptly revising his decision to abandon the field to the blond baronet. The minx had deliberately misled him into thinking her a dowd.

"His lordship has just returned from Paris with my brother," he heard Lady Harriet explain politely, as though the flash of awareness that had passed between them had never happened. "Peter will be glad to see you again, Sir James," she continued. "I hope you may be persuaded to take tea with us."

The baronet's expression mellowed noticeably at this invitation, but a flicker of a frown still marred his perfect features. "With pleasure, my lady," he replied. "Am I to understand that you have succumbed to the temptations of London, Lady Harriet, and intend to abandon us for more sophisticated entertainment?"

Giles caught an undertone of anxiety in the younger man's voice, which—for reasons he did not bother to examine—he found vastly amusing. Lady Harriet cast him an enigmatic glance before she flashed a dazzling smile on the baronet.

"Surely you must know how I dislike the Metropolis, Sir James," she said with nauseating coyness, her tone suggesting that she shared innumerable other such familiarities with the baronet. "Not only is it noisy and full of filth, but if what I hear is true, there is an alarming increase in depravity in Town, which I cannot approve of."

Although Lady Harriet had not glanced in his direction, Giles knew instinctively that this diatribe was expressly for his benefit and smiled cynically. He would have to teach the lady not to make snide remarks about her future husband's choice of residence and lifestyle.

"That is just as it should be, my dear," he drawled provocatively. "You are much safer in the country, wouldn't you say so, Rathbone?" At the baronet's startled expression, Giles took exceptional delight in adding to the young man's discomfort.

"It is not London that has caught the lady's interest, I should add, but Kimbalton Abbey. Lady Harriet and her brother will be my guests there for a few days."

The baronet's expression of chagrin was everything Giles could have wished, and it also amused him that Lady Harriet appeared none too pleased at his suggestive choice of words.

Giles could not repress a thin smile. "Of course, if the Abbey meets with Lady Harriet's approval, she may wish to prolong her stay there," he added casually, watching the baronet's sculptured features mirror the uneasy thoughts which must be jostling his mind as the implications of the earl's words sank in. Giles was unprepared for the swift and cutting reaction from the lady, however, who greeted his deliberately provocative remark with derision.

"That is hardly likely, I imagine," she remarked coolly. "I have promised to be back at Lark Manor in time for Reverend Coulton's annual bazaar."

Sir James glanced from Lady Harriet to the earl, evidently nonplussed, but Giles merely smiled as they turned to continue along the lane, Sir James's white charger following meekly behind them.

"We shall see," he murmured gently. "We shall wait and see."

"With you and Peter to lend me countenance, Aunt, I cannot see anything improper in spending a day or two at Kimbalton

Abbey," Harriet protested for the fourth or fifth time since the Egerton traveling chaise had left Lark Manor that morning.

Aunt Sophronia snorted her disagreement. "I still think it odd that his lordship should invite us to visit when Lady Kimbalton is not in residence," she remarked huffily. "And in such a rag-mannered fashion, too. Hardly am I given time to get used to the idea before I am obliged to leap into my traveling gown and throw heaven-knows-what assortment of clothes into a valise, all in such a devil of a bang. I cannot like such casual disregard for the proprieties, love. In my day, no decent young lady would tolerate such disregard for her consequence, let me tell you."

"I am sure that Violet packed everything that you will need, Aunt," Harriet said soothingly. "So do not fly into a pelter, I beg of you. And Peter is with us, after all. What can be improper about that? Besides," she added with somewhat less that complete honesty, "I have always wanted to see the famous Abbey. It is featured in all the Guide Books, you know."

"I am well aware of that fact," Lady Sophronia answered curtly. "Unfortunately, I am also privy to the less than savory reputations of the Montagues. The present earl's brother, for example, was a rakehell and libertine of the first stare, you know. And if one can believe the gossip mongers, Kimbalton himself is wholly given over to debauchery."

Harriet stared at her aunt in surprise. "Where did you hear that, Aunt?" she demanded, her interest miraculously aroused.

"Ah, it is common knowledge that he has a London mistress in keeping, instead of getting himself leg-shackled and setting up his nursery as a decent gentleman should. And I could tell you stories about his father that would curl your hair, dear. The former Lord Kimbalton had the audacity to seek an alliance with the Egertons many, many years ago." Lady Sophronia sighed and her eyes glazed over with memories. "Of course, my father had no taste for such a union, and when it came out that the rogue had stolen a kiss behind the potted palms, Papa sent him to the rightabout."

"Stolen a kiss?" Harriet repeated in a bemused voice. "Never say that *you* let this hardened rake kiss you, Auntie?" she exclaimed, torn between horror and amusement.

"He was a handsome rogue, I have to say that for him," Lady Sophronia remarked, ignoring Harriet's question. "Not like this Friday-faced son of his, I can tell you. Too starched up for his own good is Giles Montague, my dear, especially when everyone knows he is as much a libertine as his brother."

"Well, I cannot see that keeping a London mistress is so terrible a crime," Harriet remarked casually. "After all, many single gentlemen have such arrangements, I understand. Do you know who she is, Aunt?" she added innocently.

Lady Sophronia seemed to become suddenly aware of the inappropriate nature of their conversation and glanced at Harriet sharply. "No, I do not, my girl," she snapped. "And furthermore, you are too much of an innocent to be discussing such things, Harriet. It is not at all proper."

"I am not *that* innocent, Aunt Sophy," Harriet protested, amused by her aunt's sudden prudery. "Peter must know who she is. I shall ask him."

"I forbid you to do anything of the sort, Harriet," her aunt exclaimed in shocked tones. "Such topics are not proper for young ladies' ears. It behooves us to ignore such masculine aberrations and hope that when these libertines do take wives, they will put debauchery behind them." She stopped abruptly, staring anxiously at her niece. "Why this sudden interest in Lord Kimbalton?" she demanded. "Has it anything to do with this wild notion of yours to visit the Abbey?"

Harriet's gaze wandered to the familiar Sussex hedgerows flashing past the window. The signs of autumn were evident in the bedraggled hawthorns and the denuded blackberry vines, the latter still clothed in a scattering of yellow leaves waiting for a random gust to carry them off in swirls of color. Although the late-September sun shone brightly, the birds appeared lethargic, she thought, sitting in puffed silhouettes on gates and stiles. The sight should have depressed her, but Harriet was conscious of a sense of exhilaration, a most unfamiliar rush of excitement that she suddenly felt the need to share with her aunt.

She turned back to meet Lady Sophronia's anxious stare and smiled, her excitement tempered by a sense of guilt at not having told her aunt about Lord Kimbalton's offer. "As a matter of fact, it has everything to do with it, Aunt." She paused, wondering at her own elation. "You see, Lord Kimbalton has made me an offer of marriage."

Harriet watched as the significance of this revelation sank into her aunt's consciousness. "What did you say, child?" Lady Sophronia gasped, her naturally ruddy complexion pale with shock, her blue eyes wide with disbelief. "What a naughty tease you are, Harriet," she said crossly. "How dare you give me such an unpleasant start, dear? Marriage, indeed? Why you hardly know the rogue. And anyway, he is not the type to let himself fall in parson's mousetrap."

Harriet merely smiled. "You are quite off the mark, love. The earl is most anxious to form a suitable alliance. I gather Lady Kimbalton is hounding the poor man to set up his nursery."

Her aunt stared at her, mouth at half-cock and eyes bulging. "Never say you are *serious,* child," she managed at last, her voice unsteady.

Wishing she had broached the subject earlier, Harriet smiled tentatively. "You dislike the idea so much, Aunt? Peter seems to think it would be a grand match."

"So Peter is involved in this, too, is he?" Lady Sophronia remarked acidly. "I might have known it was one of that boy's mad starts. And why was I not informed? When did this happen? The man has not been here two days yet, and you expect me to believe this farradiddle about making you an offer? *You,* of all people, Harriet. You are not Montague's style, girl. The notion is preposterous."

Lady Sophronia looked so upset that Harriet reached over to take her aunt's plump hand in hers. "I shall overlook the unflattering aspersions you are casting on my appearance, Aunt," she chided gently. "But preposterous or not, the offer was made."

Her aunt stared at her for several moments in stunned silence. Then she swallowed and fumbled in her reticule, pulling out a delicately embroidered lawn handkerchief. "Never say," she began, mopping her brow vigorously, "never say you have *accepted* him, child."

Harried grinned and patted her aunt's hand reassuringly. "Not exactly," she replied in a teasing voice. "His lordship seems to think I should be overjoyed at the prospect of becoming the Countess of Kimbalton. I disabused him of that notion soon enough, of course."

"Of course," her aunt repeated weakly. Then the significance of Harriet's words seemed to register, and she sat up abruptly. "Never say you have *refused* him, love?" she demanded in stronger tones.

Harriet let out a whoop of laughter, but before she could chide her aunt on this blatant inconsistency, the carriage made a sharp turn under an immense stone arch and entered the grounds of Kimbalton Abbey.

Whatever pleasant expectations Harriet might have harbored concerning the ancestral home of the earls of Kimbalton—and as yet she was unwilling to admit to any particular interest whatsoever—began to dissipate as the traveling chaise bowled up the mile-long drive, lined with carefully clipped rhododendrons, which brought them to the elaborate porte-cochère before the massive double oak doors to the Abbey.

Her first impression was one of oppressive control and unmitigated severity. Even before she descended from the carriage, Harriet's soul shrank at the austerity and grandeur she perceived all around her. Not a leaf was out of place in the massive hedge of rhododendrons, and for a fanciful moment, Harriet wondered wryly if the unfortunate bushes ever dared to break out of the cubelike form that had been imposed upon them. Did the living plants ever yearn for freedom? she wondered. Did they ever feel the urge to rebel against this unnatural shape and throw out shoots in wild abandon, reaching for the sky? Or had they become so cowed by that force which kept them implacably in this preordained form, that they no longer questioned their Fate?

Harriet shook off these romantical notions and extended her hand to the earl, who was waiting to hand her down from the carriage.

"Welcome to Kimbalton Abbey, Lady Harriet," he said with a stiff formality that seemed to echo the lifeless forms of the rhododendrons. The impression was so strong that Harriet glanced up for reassurance, only to find herself chilled anew by the expression in the earl's cool gray eyes.

She withdrew her hand quickly, repelled at the fleeting comparison that had intruded upon her consciousness. The earl was as chiseled and sculptured as his hedge, she thought, turning away abruptly to follow her aunt and brother up the deep granite steps to where the huge door now stood open, framing the rigid figure of a butler, who— to Harriet's heightened imagination—seemed to be equally carved in stone. Irrationally, Harriet longed for the familiar, much maligned presence of her grandmother's butler; even with all his crochety stubbornness, at least Harvey was human.

"Welcome to the Abbey, milord." The stonelike figure inclined his head in minimal recognition of his master, but Harriet noticed that the butler's eyes were focused on some point in the far distance where—given the sourness of his expression—something highly unpleasant was taking place.

Harriet had to fight the overwhelming urge to turn around and climb back into her carriage and flee home to the warmth and safety of Lark Manor. It was then that she realized that the butler had not welcomed his lord *home*, but merely to the Abbey, as if Lord Kimbalton had been a visitor to his own estate. Perhaps he was, she thought, following the earl as he led his guests across the cavernous entry into what could only be—if Harriet's perusal of the Guide Books was correct—the famous Great Hall.

"We had no warning of your arrival, milord," the butler said in faintly accusing tones as he ushered the party into the vast room, where a flustered scullery maid was busy laying a fire in a cold hearth, designed—again according to the Guide Books—to hold the trunks of seven whole trees.

"Monsieur Marceau will undoubtedly tender his resignation when he is informed of your arrival with several guests, milord," the butler murmured, with a complacency which Harriet found bordered on the impertinent.

Evidently Lord Kimbalton thought so, too, for his response was curt. "Then let us save him the trouble, Carruthers," he said coldly. "Tell him he will have refreshments up here in twenty minutes or pack his bag and leave immediately." He paused and glared around the room. "And where is Mrs. Holloway?"

"I shall send her up immediately, milord," the butler said promptly, slipping silently out of the room.

While her awe-stricken aunt settled herself gingerly on an ornately carved settee in a massive style popular—if the Guide Books could be trusted—over four centuries ago, whose rigid back must have discouraged innumerable callers more stalwart than Lady Sophronia, Harriet stood and stared around her in dismay. To the casual observer, the room must appear a monument to the most enduring of English traditions, she had to admit, but her eyes saw the vast formal chamber, its walls hung with every weapon wielded by countless generations of Montagues, in quite a different light. Aside from the lack of physical warmth, which should have emanated from a blazing fire in the huge hearth, the room

lacked that other kind of warmth that only accrues in the wear
and tear of living. This place showed no signs of having been
lived in recently. At the far end of the room, some of the furniture was still shrouded in holland covers, Harriet noted.
And in spite of the heroic efforts of the little maid, the slug-
gish fire showed unmistakable signs of smoking. Perhaps the
chimney needed cleaning, she thought, feeling the first stirrings of hysteria curling up inside her. If she were not careful,
she would create a quite reprehensible scene in the midst of
all this oppressive grandeur and disgrace herself in the eyes of
Lord Kimbalton.

Abruptly remembering the purpose of her presence at the
Abbey, Harriet glanced uneasily at her host. The earl's face
still showed traces of annoyance, but he smiled faintly at her
before stalking over to a gigantic sideboard where a veritable
army of crystal decanters stood in rigid formation, as if on parade, flanking the most atrociously ugly silver epergne that
Harriet had ever seen. The earl splashed generous portions of
brandy into two heavy glasses and handed one to Peter. Harriet
wondered what his reaction might be if she demanded a glass
for herself. She suddenly felt in dire need of the stimulation
the fiery liquor would provide.

Before she could pluck up her courage, however, the doors
were thrown open and two footmen appeared carrying an immense silver tray and tea service, which they carefully placed
on a low table beside the claw-footed settee, under the watch-
ful eye of the butler.

"It appears you are to do the honors, Aunt Sophy," Harriet
remarked, moving to a seat beside her aunt on the vast expanse
of settee. "I could use a hot cup of tea."

Her aunt eyed her speculatively. "Shouldn't you . . ." Lady
Sophronia began in an undertone, but Harriet shook her head
and tried to settle herself more comfortably, only to find that
the settee was as unyielding as it appeared. When she lifted the
delicate Limoges cup to her lips and discovered that the tea
was tepid, Harriet set her mind to devising excuses for cutting
her visit short.

Later, when the anxious Mrs. Holloway had shown the
ladies up to their rooms and sent up a sour-faced female—who
claimed to be Lady Kimbalton's abigail during her infrequent
visits to the Abbey—to unpack their valises and lay out their
dinner gowns, Harriet shared her feelings with her aunt.

"What possible excuse can we give for leaving tomorrow at

dawn?" she demanded, struggling with the heavy, dark purple
curtains that covered both windows of their shared sitting
room, and obscured what little sunlight remained of the autumn afternoon. "Perhaps you could develop a severe case of
measles, Aunt. Surely that would induce his lordship to hasten
our departure."

The curtains finally ceded to her tugging, releasing a cloud
of dust as they slid open, revealing a prospect of park and
woodland that seemed to stretch for miles in every direction.

"Don't be missish, Harriet," her aunt scolded cheerfully.
"Give the place a chance, girl. The Guide Books say the
Abbey has several hothouses with fruit trees and an orangery.
Besides an artificial lake and a gazebo designed by Inigo
Jones."

"Do the Guide Books say anything about the cold tea served
in the Great Hall?" Harriet interrupted rather acidly. "I trust
that the French cook has not packed his bags and left, for I am
perfectly ravenous, Aunt."

When the dinner gong sounded and the ladies descended to
the Great Hall, wrapped in woollen shawls against the cold,
they found that although a respectable fire was blazing in the
hearth and the holland covers had been removed from the rest
of the furniture, the room was as inhospitable as ever.

The dinner, served in a room equally as impressive, on a
table which might have accommodated half of General
Wellington's troops with ease—or so it seemed to a bemused
Harriet—was sparse yet elegantly prepared, very much in the
French style. Accustomed as she was to hearty English country fare, Harriet picked at her food dispiritedly. The French
cook would have to go, she mused absently, then paused, startled at the train of her thoughts. Whatever was she thinking of?
she wondered, glancing apprehensively at the earl, seated in all
his splendor at the head of the massive table.

He was staring at her again, as she had known he would be,
and Harriet dropped her eyes to the elegant fricasée of sole on
her plate, swimming in its congealing sauce. She put down her
fork and took a sip of wine instead. What did it matter if the
temperamental French cook stayed or left? That at least would
not be her concern. This whole madcap notion of Peter's had
been a terrible mistake. She could see that now. True, yesterday she had been tempted enough to agree to this hare-brained
escapade, but exactly what had tempted her, Harriet could not
for the life of her remember. Perhaps it had been the appear-

ance of Sir James at Lark Manor that had weakened her resolve. Seeing the two men together—no, it would be more accurate to say the man and the boy together—had opened her
eyes to a fundamental truth about herself she had never considered before. Harriet had never seriously considered accepting Sir James's offer, but his unswerving adoration had been a
comforting part of her life for the past two years. His attentions had made her feel attractive and desirable; it had erased
the memory of that painful London Season, when she had felt
gauche and inadequate in every sense. Sir James had eased
that pain and she was grateful to him. But could she marry
him?

She glanced again at Lord Kimbalton, as if the answer to
her dilemma might lie there. He was listening to one of Aunt
Sophy's interminable stories, she realized, a polite smile softening the harsh lines of his mouth. He smiled too seldom, she
thought, and when he did, he was really quite attractive. And
yes, she thought, conscious of a quickening of her pulses, perhaps the earl had—all unwittingly of course—solved her
dilemma. His unexpected appearance at Lark Manor had
shown her, as nothing else could, that any thought of marrying
Sir James Rathbone was out of the question. His lordship's unequivocally masculine presence had shown her just how much
of a boy Sir James really was, a wonderfully handsome, kind,
and loyal boy, but a boy nevertheless. And Harriet knew she
did not want a boy for a husband. She wanted . . . she hesitated, unwilling to admit such intimate longings even to herself.

Against her will, her eyes were drawn again to the head of
the table. Could it possibly be that she wanted Giles Montague, the Earl of Kimbalton? She rejected the notion instantly.
What a ninny she was to allow such a preposterous notion to
enter her head. The man was an inconsiderate, overbearing
brute. True, when he smiled as he was doing now, he could
make a female's heart do strange things. And when he looked
at her with those hooded gray eyes, quite as if he could read
her most intimate, immodest thoughts, as he was doing this
very instant . . . With a start, Harriet realized she had been
staring at her host. Abruptly she tore her eyes away and looked
down at the cold fish on her plate, feeling her cheeks grow
warm. She had let her imagination run away with her again,
she told herself crossly. The rogue would think that she was

flirting with him, when actually it must be the rich food that had made her feel quite queasy all of a sudden.

She took another sip of the excellent wine. Once she was safely back at Lark Manor, Harriet decided, she would ask Mrs. Porter for one of her herbal potions for indigestion. That would take care of this odd fluttering she was experiencing in her stomach.

And by then, Harriet told herself smugly, she would be free of Lord Kimbalton and his ridiculous proposal.

She could be comfortable again.

# CHAPTER FOUR

# Momentous Decision

The following morning, quite determined to shake the dust of Kimbalton Abbey from the soles of her half-boots without further delay, Lady Harriet rose early and donned her green merino traveling gown. Slipping into her aunt's bedchamber, she smiled affectionately at the sound of Lady Sophronia's gentle snores, and for a moment entertained the notion of allowing her aunt, who was not an early riser at the best of times, an extra hour between the sheets. Perhaps she should take a perfunctory tour of the grounds and the famous hothouses before she informed the earl of her decision to leave, Harriet thought. She stood for a moment, undecided, then slipped out again, closing the door softly behind her.

On the landing, Harriet came upon an ascetically gaunt valet reverently carrying her brother's freshly pressed hunting jacket in brown corduroy.

"Good morning, Finley," she said brightly. "Be so good as to tell my brother that I shall require his escort later this morning. We are going back to Sussex."

"Very well, milady." Harriet heard the valet's startled response echo behind her as she swept down the stairs, determined not to remain in this inhospitable mausoleum a moment longer than politeness dictated. In the cavernous front hall, Harriet commandeered a young footman—who stammeringly admitted, in answer to her queries, that his name was Tom and that his lordship had gone out riding an hour ago—to conduct her to the breakfast room. Expecting another bleak monstrosity, she was pleasantly surprised to find herself in a comfortable room whose solid oak refectory table was designed to seat no more than twenty guests. Harriet was relieved to see a friendly fire crackling in the hearth, although only one of the heavy curtains in the several bow windows had been drawn—almost grudgingly, she thought—to let in the pale morning sun.

"Draw the curtains for me, will you, Tom. We need more light in here," Harriet said impulsively, moving to stand at the one uncovered window, where she hoped to obtain a more informal view of the grounds. What she saw made her spirits sink. The breakfast room was evidently situated at the back of the house and overlooked the artificial lake the Guide Books had made so much of. Artificial was undoubtedly the only adequate word to describe it, Harriet acknowledged, gazing critically at the lifeless body of water, lying placid and unnaturally still in the early sunlight. No attempt had been made to soften the lake's austere shape with clumps of flowering shrubs, or break its monotonous lines with clusters of willow trees. No such heresy as a boathouse or landing dock marred its symmetrical shores, and nothing so informal as a friendly rowing boat beckoned past or present generations of children to explore its calm surface.

There was no sign of the swans touted by the Guide Books, and Harriet wondered irrelevantly if the regal birds were still slumbering.

The sound of the door opening and shutting behind her caused her to turn, expecting to confront the stone-faced Carruthers with a fresh pot of tea. "I trust the tea is not tepid this morning, Carruthers," she began, determined not to be subjected to further heresies at the breakfast table.

"Oh!" she exclaimed, gazing into a pair of amused gray eyes. "G-good morning, my lord. I thought . . . I was expecting . . ." She paused and tried again. "They told me you were out riding, my lord," she remarked, watching a cynical smile flicker on the earl's lips.

"I had some estate business to take care of, my dear, or I would have invited you to accompany me," Lord Kimbalton replied smoothly, tossing his gloves and whip onto a narrow table by the door. "I see you have been admiring the view. I have taken the liberty of ordering my curricle for ten o'clock. I thought to give you the grand tour in style."

"You should not have troubled yourself, my lord," Harriet replied stiffly, turning back to the window. "I have seen quite enough of the Abbey already, thank you." Too much of it, if truth be told, she added to herself. Now that the actual moment of rejection had arrived, Harriet felt a stab of uncertainty. It was one thing to reject a man's offer of marriage; she felt quite up to that, in fact she rather relished giving the odious, toplofty earl a magnificent set-down. But how does one tell a gentleman that his family seat—one that had harbored Montagues for centuries and figured prominently in every available Guide Book—was depressingly large, and cold, and uncomfortable, that his grounds were unnaturally austere and devoid of spontaneity, and that his staff—with the possible exception of Tom—was impertinent and incompetent?

"I see," he said softly, and Harriet jumped to find Lord Kimbalton at her elbow, gazing down at her enigmatically. "You do not like the lake?" he inquired. "It is attributed to Inigo Jones, you know. As is the summer-house and the Greek-styled Belvedere on the south side."

"Inigo Jones must have been in his cups to have conceived anything so unnatural," she replied, determined to be as honest as possible.

"Unnatural?" the earl repeated quizzically. "Of course it's unnatural. It is, after all, an artificial lake, my dear girl." He sounded put out, and Harriet's spirits rose. Perhaps if she made him angry enough, he would recognize the absurdity of an alliance between them.

"It is monotonous and unsightly," she remarked, gesturing towards the offensive creation. "And where are the swans?"

"Swans? What swans?"

"They are mentioned in the Guide Books," Harriet explained impatiently. "I was quite looking forward to seeing them," she added perversely.

Lord Kimbalton laughed. "So you have looked up the history of the Abbey, my lady? I am flattered."

"Actually, it is my Aunt Sophy who reads the Guide Books, my lord," Harriet felt compelled to clarify. "She was much taken with the swans."

"They died off several years ago, and my brother never replaced them," the earl explained. "His memories of them were not entirely happy ones, I am afraid." He paused, and Harriet could feel his eyes on her face. "I would be happy to replace them if that would give you pleasure, my dear."

"I doubt that a few swans would change my mind," she said ungraciously, feeling strangely affected at the earl's conciliatory tone.

"So you have already made up your mind, Lady Harriet?" he inquired quietly. "On such short acquaintance, too. Is that true?"

Harriet looked at him then, something in his voice drawing her gaze to his face. His eyes were unreadable, but there was no amusement in them, and for once his mouth was not curled into his cynical smile. It was a shapely, seductive mouth, she thought, and for an instant that seemed to last forever, she allowed herself to dwell on what it might be like to be the wife of a man like Giles Montague. A shiver ran through her, and Harriet pulled her traitorous thoughts back to the present. If she were not careful, she told herself crossly, she might find herself seduced and beguiled by this practiced flirt and libertine. That would be a disaster. To involve her heart and emotions in a decision that must necessarily be a practical, strictly sensible choice would be the height of folly.

She shook her head to clear her thoughts. "Only partially true, my lord," she found herself saying without clearly understanding her own hesitation. "In my own way, I am as prejudiced against marriage as you are." She looked up into his eyes again to make sure he followed her logic. "I meant it when I told you there is little to tempt me into an alliance with you."

Lord Kimbalton raised a black eyebrow. "You are certainly frank, my dear, if nothing else."

"I hate hypocrisy," Harriet said firmly. "I think I owe it to you, and I certainly owe it to myself, not to pretend . . ." Her voice tapered off and she fell silent, her gaze returning to the unruffled surface of the lake.

"Pretend?" he nodded.

Harriet smiled self-consciously. *Not to pretend that we are in love* was what she had been thinking, but of course one could not say such a mawkish thing to a man like Giles Montague, a man who had been on the Town for years and kept a beautiful mistress in London, to whom he must be all too anxious to return. She sighed and looked at him, surprised to find sympathy in his gray eyes.

"Pretend that any marriage between us would be anything but a convenience," she said in a rush before she lost her nerve. "A convenience for you because of all the reasons Peter has explained to me. And a convenience for me . . ." Her voice trailed off again and for the life of her Harriet could not think of a plausible reason to throw herself blindly into a union with a man who could not wait to leave her. "And there you have it, I suppose," she murmured disjointedly. "I cannot seem to convince myself that marriage to you would be any convenience for me."

Harriet knew what the earl's answer would be before he said it. The glint of amusement in his eyes told her so.

"A family of your own?" he suggested softly.

Harriet felt the heat rise instantly to her cheeks and turned away, chiding herself for her brazen frankness, which had practically invited his immodest response.

"Perhaps," she murmured, wondering how she came to be discussing such intimate things with a man she scarcely knew. "But any man would do for that, surely?" The words were out before she could stop them, and she saw the earl's eyes open in shocked surprise, before he let out a crack of delighted laughter.

"I beg your pardon, my lord. My wretched tongue ran away with me again. What I meant was—"

"I know exactly what you meant," the earl cut in smoothly, his voice warm with amusement. "But I am persuaded that any man would *not* do for Lady Harriet Egerton. At least, I intend to do my best to convince you of it. But come, my dear," he added, "I would not encourage anyone to make momentous decisions before breakfast. I suggest we ring for some hot tea—really hot tea this time." He grinned so engagingly that Harriet could not repress a smile. "And after breakfast, if you will allow me, I would like to drive you around the estate and you can tell me—quite frankly, of course—everything you would change about the Abbey if you were mistress here."

Harriet stared at Lord Kimbalton, wondering what trick the rogue had up his sleeve. His request sounded quite innocuous, she thought, and perhaps if she did indeed tell him frankly exactly why she could never be happy in a place like the Abbey, he would let her go home.

The idea of getting out of an uncomfortable situation so easily appealed to Harriet, and she smiled. "I would love a cup of hot tea, my lord," she confessed. "And it is a lovely day for a drive," she added, disregarding a nagging suspicion in the pit of her stomach that she had played into the earl's hands.

Lord Kimbalton glanced warily at the lady sitting beside him on the narrow seat of the curricle. Not for the first time since meeting Lady Harriet Egerton, Giles was struck by her quiet dignity. She had said nothing but the barest civilities since allowing herself to be lifted into the high seat of the sporting vehicle. This in itself had surprised him, for he had quite expected the intrepid Lady Harriet to swing herself up with her usual disregard for convention. But when he turned from giving the groom instructions about the horse he had ridden that morning, which seemed to have developed a slight limp, her ladyship had been standing demurely waiting for his assistance.

Giles stared at her for a second until she extended her gloved hand to him. This small, feminine gesture, a tacit acknowledgement of her need for his assistance, gave Giles an unexpected jolt of pleasure. In other females of his acquaintance, this same gesture would most certainly have been accompanied by flirtatious glances, girlish simpers, and fluttering eyelashes. Lady Harriet employed no such tricks to fix his attention. Her hazel eyes regarded him expectantly, the golden flecks beginning to dance with some secret amusement he could only guess at. Impulsively, Giles took her outstretched hand and brought it to his lips, holding it there while he watched astonishment, then confusion replace the laughter in her eyes. Had he expected her to flirt with him? he wondered, surprised at his own foolishness. Had he wanted her to?

Disgusted at this uncharacteristic mawkishness, Giles dropped the gloved hand and grasped Lady Harriet about the waist, lifting her easily into the curricle. She weighed almost nothing at all, but his hands, casually slipping down to the flare of her hips as he settled her on the leather squabs, told him that the wench was more shapely than he had imagined. The deuce take it, he thought as he swung up beside her and took the ribbons. If Giles Montague, fastidious to a fault about his women, had taken to mooning over this country chit with no charm to speak of, then it was high time for him to get back to London. To his lovely Ophelia. Giles allowed himself two full minutes, as his brother's team of Welsh-breds settled into their traces, to immerse himself in highly pleasurable recollections of his last night with Ophelia before leaving for Paris six months ago.

Abruptly, Giles pulled his mind back to the realities of the moment, reluctantly banishing all traces of Ophelia's luscious, compliant body to the darkest corner of his consciousness. The sooner he concluded the business at hand, he reminded himself grimly, the sooner he could lose himself in . . . But physical gratification must wait for now, he thought, heroically repressing the tightening of his groin. He must learn to keep his London life—his real life as he had always considered it—entirely separate from the make-believe life he needed to establish here at Kimbalton Abbey, with a make-believe wife, and a make-believe family. He grinned cynically at the thought of starting his own nursery. That would have to be taken seriously, he mused. There was nothing make-believe about breeding children, and he would have to come to terms with that sooner or later. Preferably later.

Giles glanced at the silent profile of the woman beside him, and it struck him rather forcefully that there was nothing make-believe about Lady Harriet either. For the first time since embarking on this campaign to find a suitable wife, Giles felt a tinge of apprehension. He knew precious little about dealing with females other than on strictly amatory levels. What would little Harriet's reaction be if he brought the full force of his charm to bear upon her? he wondered idly. He suspected she would slap his face for him and order her carriage for immediate return to Lark Manor. And that would be that, he thought wryly. The wench would bolt like a scared rabbit if he tried to seduce her as he had countless females before her. No, he corrected himself, remembering the chit's reaction to his recent caress, Lady Harriet would react like an outraged cat, all sharp claws and uninhibited hissing. His Harriet was no rabbit. She would be far easier to manage if she were, of course. But for some odd reason Giles was glad she was not like Ophelia. He shook himself out of this daydreaming. He would have to stop thinking of Ophelia if he hoped to have any success in wooing Harriet.

He glanced at her again and found Lady Harriet looking at him quizzically. "You have been wool-gathering, my lord," she said accusingly. "I asked what you intend to show me first."

"I do beg your pardon, my dear," he responded, glad that his thoughts were not transparent. "I had hoped to interest you in the tenants' cottages, the Home Farm, the mill on the river, the stables, and naturally the hot-houses. The Dower House is in pretty sad repair, I am afraid, since my grandmother died before my father married, but we might take a look at it if you like."

"Lady Kimbalton does not make her home at the Abbey, I take it?" Lady Harriet asked.

"No, she prefers London," he said rather shortly. "My mother finds the Abbey rather . . ." He stopped abruptly, realizing that he was about to give Lady Harriet quite the wrong impression of her future home.

"Quite depressing, I suppose you mean, my lord," the saucy minx completed his thought for him, her hazel eyes daring him to contradict her. "I fear I am tempted to agree with her ladyship. The place is quite hideously uncomfortable."

Giles felt his jaw muscles clench, but cut off the sharp remark that rose to his lips. "Surely you are exaggerating a little, my lady," he managed to say stiffly.

Lady Harriet let out a quite unladylike whoop of laughter. "You are ready to come to cuffs with me already, my lord," she pointed out. "And I have only made one disparaging remark about the Abbey. You did tell me to be frank, as I remember. I intend to take you at your word."

"You are determined to find fault with everything, I see," Giles muttered savagely, wondering what he would do if she did refuse him.

"Not at all, my lord," she replied with enervating cheerfulness. "I shall merely tell you my thoughts honestly, as we agreed that I should."

And the wench proceeded to do exactly as she promised. By the time he had been told, with fulminating frankness, that the tenants' cottages all needed new roofs, the sheep on the Home Farm showed disturbing signs of inbreeding, the machinery used at the estate mill was hopelessly outdated, the stables needed whitewashing, the hot-houses were understaffed, and the Dower House was a disgrace, quite unfit for his mother to call her home, Giles was reduced to a state of simmering fury.

"Aside from the faults you have mentioned, Lady Harriet," he forced himself to say through gritted teeth as he turned his horses' heads towards the highest point of the grounds, a treat he had been saving for last, "is there anything else you would like to see changed about the estate?" Although he tried to keep the sarcasm out of his voice, Lady Harriet's rueful smile told him that he had failed to conceal his growing displeasure.

"Oh, dear," she answered with deceptive meekness, "I am sure I could find a few more if I set my mind to it, my lord. But I see you are already most annoyed with me, so perhaps we should go back."

The earl pulled the team to a halt beside a gate and jumped down. "There is one other thing I want to show you," he replied, reaching up to grasp her small waist. He paused, deliberately settling his hands more securely around her. "That is if you are not too tired to walk up that hill, my lady." If he expected her to show embarrassment at the intimacy of his touch,

Giles was disappointed. Lady Harriet took one look at the Oriental gazebo nestled among the trees at the top of the grass-covered slope and shook her head.

"Oh, no. Of course not," she said, smiling down into his eyes with complete lack of self-consciousness. "I am a country girl, as you should know by now, my lord. Besides, hills have always intrigued me. I like the feeling of being so close to the sky."

After that, Giles could not stand there holding her any longer but had to swing her down and follow her as she started up the winding path to the top of the hill. *His* hill, he thought wryly. His refuge from his father's indifference and his mother's smothering attentions. And from Brian's thoughtless teasing. And, of course, from Richard, he though bitterly. As a rule Giles tried not to think of Richard, whose childhood ambition seemed to have been to emulate Giles in everything. He had been relieved when Brian—in one of his less bellicose moods—had purchased a commission for Richard in one of the less distinguished regiments. One in which the name of Richard Montague would not cause undue comment.

"Oh, this is wonderful," Lady Harriet was saying, gazing avidly out at the surrounding countryside. "It reminds me of home," she added softly, her voice nostalgic. She turned to stare at him, her hazel eyes full of understanding. "This is your special place, is it not?" she asked, gesturing towards the small gazebo.

"How did you know?"

She laughed delightedly, and Giles wondered how many other women he spent his time with would have seen the hill for what it was. "It *feels* like a special place," she explained. "I should know, for I have one myself."

"You do? Why did you need one?" He was surprised at his own interest; he really wanted to know.

"Everybody needs a secret place," Lady Harriet explained, her eyes for once serious. "Where one can be alone and think one's own thoughts without being told how nonsensical they are." She paused for a moment, then continued in a softer voice. "When my father married Anabella, I thought that my life would end. I resented her immensely, even though she was only a few years my senior. But when she had the boys, three of them one after the other, I realized that she envied me. Can you imagine?" she laughed. "Anabella envied me because I could cope with the boys when they were naughty—and they often are—and when they all came down with chicken pox. Bella was terrified that she would catch it, too, and lose her looks. She is very beautiful, of course."

"Of course?" he questioned.

"Oh, yes," Lady Harriet replied, her eyes suddenly full of amusement. "You cannot think that my father would have anything to do with a dowd, do you? He was a stickler for perfection, my father. I must have been a great disappointment to him. Thank goodness Peter does not take after him in the least."

A fleeting note of wistfulness caught his attention, and Giles wondered what sort of father the late viscount could have been to find fault with a lively child like Harriet. Before he could give voice to this oddly intimate thought, Lady Harriet turned towards the gazebo.

"Am I allowed to trespass in your secret place, my lord?" she inquired, pausing at the shallow steps leading up into the dim interior.

There was nothing flirtatious or arch about her expression as she gazed at him over her shoulder, and Giles was struck once more by the innocence and trust he saw reflected in Lady Harriet's hazel eyes. The wench was naive beyond belief, he thought, recalling other females he had brought to this same conveniently isolated hideaway for quite different reasons.

He smiled briefly. "You may go wherever you wish, my lady," he replied, wondering at the sudden quickening of his pulse as he followed the slight figure up the wooden steps and stood watching her unself-conscious examination of the dim interior. Perhaps now was the opportune moment to give little Harriet a taste of seduction, he thought cynically. If she were a normal kind of female, she must be more than ready—at the advanced age of twenty-five—for a man's amorous advances. The notion excited him, and he forced his feverish thoughts back to the beautiful and complacent Ophelia, waiting for him in London. It would not do to treat his future wife to an indecent display of passion, particularly when she was still teetering on the brink of rejecting him. He had felt it this morning in the breakfast room, and Lady Harriet's reluctance had hung between them during their drive over the estate.

But now Giles felt an unexpected softening in the lady's resistance, and his instinct told him to press his advantage. Perhaps if he kissed her? A chaste kiss, of course, although Giles suddenly felt anything but chaste. He felt like . . . A jolt of de-

sire made his mouth go dry as Lady Harriet trailed her fingers
innocently over the length of the rustic table in the center of
the gazebo. That table had been the site of many secret childhood feasts, filched from the Abbey's immense pantries or
wheedled out of their old cook, Mrs. McDonald. But a less innocent memory flashed unbidden into his mind. A memory of
a buxom lass—what was her name? he wondered. Jenny?
Jeanie? He could not remember, but he recalled her pliant
body all too clearly, and the summer afternoon they had spent
together in the gazebo putting that same table to unorthodox
but highly pleasurable use.

Lady Harriet moved over to an opening in the gazebo's trellised walls and leaned on the weathered railing. She had taken
off her green bonnet, and that prosaic item of female apparel,
lying innocently on that memorable table, helped to steady
Giles's riotous thoughts. This was his future countess, he reminded himself, not a local wench eager for an afternoon of
pleasure with one of the Montague boys, nor his sophisticated
London mistress, who had learned—in the four years she had
been in his keeping—just how to please him. This woman was
his chosen bride, and Giles felt a sudden need to overcome
Lady Harriet's reticence once and for all.

Resolutely, he moved towards the figure at the window.

No sooner had Harriet set foot inside the dim gazebo than
she realized her mistake. This enclosed, intimate area was no
place to be alone with any man, particularly not the stranger
who had taken it into his head to make her his countess. Although she could see the patchwork of blue sky through the
lattice of the walls and pagoda-shaped roof, Harriet was uncomfortably conscious of the presence of the man blocking the
doorway. Idly, she trailed her gloved fingers across the worn
planks of the rustic table, wondering how she could escape the
compromising situation which became even more threatening
as it dawned on her that she was indeed alone and at the mercy
of a man of dubious morality. Harriet glanced at the earl, only
to find him standing, booted feet apart, perfectly still, observing her with a predatory stare she had read about in romantical
novels—the kind her stepmother always left lying under pillows or on window seats behind drawn curtains—but which
Harriet had never expected to encounter in real life.

She turned towards an opening in the wall which boasted a
breathtaking view of the meandering river in the valley below,

and leaned against the rough railing, acutely aware of the uneven beating of her heart. She had behaved in a very foolish manner, she told herself severely. Only an innocent fresh out of the schoolroom would have unwittingly walked into a trap such as this. That is what came of being so independent, she thought wryly. Aunt Sophy had warned her many a time that her disregard for propriety would get her into trouble one of these days. And she had been right, of course. Lord Kimbalton must even now be thinking that she had come into the gazebo intentionally with dalliance in mind, offering him an open invitation to take liberties with her person. The notion alarmed her, and Harriet took a deep breath of country air to calm her nerves.

Almost as quickly as the notion of danger occurred to her, it dissipated, leaving her ashamed at her own missishness. Surely she had nothing to fear from a man whose only interest in her arose from convenience? If Peter had told her the truth—and there was no reason to doubt that he had—Lord Kimbalton would not dare risk her ire by forcing unwelcome attention upon her, would he? Harriet found the notion that the earl must surely be on his best behavior less comforting than she had expected. If she had not known better, Harriet would have said that she was disappointed, but naturally that was ridiculous, was it not? She was certainly no flirt, and had no intention of leading the earl to think she expected anything from him besides his name. Besides, she told herself firmly, what sort of woman would hanker after the amorous attentions of a heartless rogue who had shared himself with countless other females? And doubtless would again, she thought, remembering the shadowy presence of Lord Kimbalton's London mistress, who even now must be anxiously awaiting his return.

Harriet repressed a shudder, whether of revulsion or pity she could not tell.

"You are not frightened of me, are you, my dear?"

The voice was low and seductive, and came from so close beside her that Harriet jumped.

"Oh, no," she murmured, forcing herself to relax and look up at him. The predatory gaze that had discomposed her had disappeared, replaced by a lazy smile echoed in the earl's hooded grey eyes. "No, of course not, my lord," she repeated more firmly. "What a ridiculous notion." She smiled faintly.

Lord Kimbalton raised an eyebrow, and his lips twitched.

"You are so quiet, I am terrified at the prospect of receiving a crushing set-down and having to go back to London to face my mother unwed. It would be a cruel, heartless fate, I can assure you. Doubtless my esteemed mother already has a chit handpicked for me. She claims young girls are easier to mold into obedient wives and mothers than females who have been out for a year or two."

Harriet could not help smiling at the lugubrious expression the earl adopted during this speech. "Perhaps you should take her ladyship's advice, my lord," she ventured. "A young girl would doubtless hold you in far greater awe than I would, especially if you glowered at her."

"Do I glower at you, Harriet?" he said softly.

"Yes, indeed, my lord."

"And you do not hold me in awe? Not even a little?"

Harriet laughed. "Indeed not, my lord. I feel that most gentlemen already suffer from inflated opinions of themselves without us ladies giving them any encouragement by fawning on them."

"That is hardly flattering of you," he drawled in an amused tone.

"I never flatter, my lord," she answered frankly. "And we had agreed to be honest about this . . . this arrangement, had we not?"

The earl stepped closer and took one of her hands in his. "Am I to understand that you are accepting my offer, Harriet?" he said softly, although Harriet was startled to note the urgency in his voice. Before she could protest, he stripped off her glove and carried her hand to his lips and kissed it lingeringly, his eyes gazing down at her intently. Harriet felt her mouth go dry, and could not for the life of her dredge up an adequate response from her suddenly paralyzed brain.

Kimbalton turned her hand upwards and set his lips in the soft center of Harriet's palm, the unexpected heat sending shivers of ecstasy through her whole body. The warmth of his hot breath on her exposed wrist made her dizzy with longings she did not dare to examine too closely, and quite suddenly Harriet knew what it must be like to be seduced by a man as virile and knowledgeable as Giles Montague. She closed her eyes and let herself enjoy the flood of erotic delight that invaded her senses with every lingering kiss pressed into her palm. That was all it would take, she realized, half convinced already that she desired nothing else but to let herself sink into the overwhelming maelstrom of this man's sensuality.

"Harriet?"

An insistent finger under her chin brought her abruptly to her senses. The earl's hooded eyes held that predatory gleam again, and they were fixed on her lips. He held her open hand against his chest, and Harriet distinctly felt the hammering of his heart. What had she done to unleash this kind of passion in a man she hardly knew? Harriet wondered, bewildered at her own immodest yearnings. Or was this all a deliberately planned seduction to gain her acquiescence? The notion took hold in her fevered brain and extinguished her excitement like a dash of cold water. Mortification at being so easily taken in brought the color to her cheeks, and Harriet wished that she had not removed her bonnet. She had nowhere to hide from this villain who had brought her so close to disaster.

"Are you accepting me, Harriet?"

His voice was still seductively soft, but Harriet heard uncertainty in his tone, which surprised her. Was the man not aware that he had almost turned her into a mindless jelly? she wondered. Could it be that the rogue was not quite as confident about his own power as she had imagined?

"I need you, Harriet," he continued before she could think of a suitable reply. "I can think of no other woman whom I would rather have as my countess." He still held her hand imprisoned in his against his chest, and any doubts Harriet might have had regarding his sincerity evaporated. "You are everything Peter described and more," he added. "Sensible, practical, and your grasp of estate affairs quite cinched the matter."

If Harriet had needed to be reminded of the prosaic nature of their proposed arrangement, the earl's last words were direct enough to bring her to her senses with uncomfortable abruptness. He was not going to kiss her, she thought, trying in vain to repress the odd ache which had replaced the wild euphoria of a moment ago. No man could be expected to call a female sensible and practical and kiss her in the same breath. But then, of course, she had not really wanted to be kissed, had she?

Harriet refused to answer that question, even in her own mind. Instead she focused on the earl's actual admission that he needed her. It was nice to be needed, she told herself firmly. And he really wanted her for his countess. That surprised her until she remembered that the qualities he admired in her were limited to sensibility and practicality. What else had she expected? she asked herself reasonably. She knew herself to be no beauty. For that the Earl of Kimbalton, her future husband—for the first time Harriet allowed herself to savor the title—had his beautiful opera singer or actress or whatever she was, in London, awaiting his pleasure.

"Dare I take your silence for acceptance, Harriet?"

"I could never live without flowers about me," she blurted out, surprising herself at the tenor of her words, which smacked at capitulation.

The earl obviously felt that she was all but won, for he clasped both her hands in his and smiled down at her. "You may indulge each and every one of your rustic inclinations, my dear," he said magnanimously.

"I would want rose-trees—"

"As many as you want, Harriet. I shall give orders to the gardeners—"

"No," she interrupted, anxious to control the transformation of the Abbey landscape. "I shall deal with the gardeners myself. And do I get free rein in the house, my lord? The place is practically uninhabitable."

He looked slightly taken aback at this. "The Abbey is a famous national monument," he began, but Harriet cut him short.

"I can understand that, my lord, but if I must live in a monument, I insist that it be a comfortable one. I refuse to spend the rest of my days in a drafty mausoleum."

He was still for a long moment before answering. "You drive a hard bargain, my lady. But I have to admit I would not relish living here myself, and as you know, my mother will not come near the place. So refurbish all you want. I shall tell my steward to order anything you wish."

It was Harriet's turn to remain silent. There was so much she did not know about this man whose marriage proposal she was about to accept, but she dared not ask. "You will definitely spend all your time in London, my lord?" she finally inquired, wishing to make their relationship perfectly clear.

"Most of it," he replied shortly.

Perhaps that would not be so bad, after all, Harriet thought. She would be able to transform that monstrosity of a house, and make these severely tailored grounds into a semblance of a garden without a husband telling her what she might or might not do. The prospect of an absentee husband was beginning to look more attractive all the time.

"Good," she replied, deliberately repressing any hint of emotion. "And I would not be expected to preside over your London residence during the Season, my lord?"

The earl regarded her with hooded eyes, and Harriet knew he was thinking about his mistress. She did not know how, but she sensed it in her bones. She would have to accept the presence of that mysterious woman in her life, since it was obviously an important part of the arrangement the earl proposed. Harriet smiled wryly to herself. That should present no particular difficulty to a female as sensible and practical as Lady Harriet Egerton, she told herself firmly.

"I would certainly expect you to remain in the country, my lady," he said dryly. "That would be part of the arrangement, of course."

Of course, she repeated to herself. And that was that. She was about to commit herself to an arranged marriage with a wealthy, powerful, and harshly attractive nobleman who would probably be little more than a stranger to her for the rest of their lives. "Of course," she said aloud, and pulling free of him, Harriet walked out into the sunlight.

She no longer felt the least inclination to kiss Giles Montague.

# CHAPTER FIVE

# A Convenient Countess

Two days after that decisive encounter in the gazebo, the deed was done. Harriet always thought of her marriage to the Earl of Kimbalton as *the deed* in her own mind. It was hardly the kind of nuptials romantical young girls dream about, she told herself prosaically, as she stood beside the earl, listening to the hastily summoned vicar inform her in his dry, sententious voice that she must honor and obey a man who wanted little else from her. What had she expected? Harriet knew herself to be neither young nor romantical, and the Reverend Oliver Matthews was right to dwell, almost obsessively she noted, on the duties of her new station rather than on any joy she might derive therefrom. From this day forward, her duties as the Countess of Kimbalton would fill her days and define her life, Harriet realized, and whatever happiness she found in her new role would spring from her success in achieving the goals she set herself.

Happiness had not been part of the agreement, of course. Harriet was well aware that, in his arrogance, the earl assumed that what he offered her was enough. A very advantageous alliance by anyone's standards. Reverend Matthews obviously thought so, too, but as she listened with half an ear to the vicar's sonorous voice echo among the rafters of the Great Hall, Harriet wondered if Giles Montague had ever experienced true happiness. Was he happy with that mysterious woman who drew him back to London? Did he love her? The notion, intruding so insidiously into her consciousness in the middle of her own wedding ceremony, was oddly unsettling.

Harriet glanced surreptitiously up at her new husband and detected nothing but a faint annoyance on his dark face. He held her hand in his and was intent on keeping the makeshift wedding band from slipping off her finger. The ring was at least two sizes too large for her slim finger, a fact she had calmly pointed out to him the evening before, when he had made the selection from the vast collection of family heir-looms spread out on the enormous oak desk in the cavernous study. Harriet had been astounded at the size of the collection, although when the earl's steward opened the vault and began laying out a seemingly endless stream of glittering baubles for her perusal, she should have guessed that in this, as in everything else in the Abbey, size and tradition were of paramount importance. It was evident from the quantity and quality of the family jewels that the Montagues had treasured every significant piece, dating perhaps back to the ring placed by the first Baron Montague upon the finger of his long-dead lady.

None of the Montague rings fit Harriet's finger, a circumstance which had prompted her to make an unwise remark about ignoring the dictates of Fate. She had been treated to a particularly scathing look from her irate bridegroom, who had finally selected a plain gold band with delicate ivy leaves engraved on it. The ring had been his grandmother's, he informed her, and although it was certainly too large, it would have to do until he could order one for her in London.

Harriet wiggled her finger experimentally, and the ring slid down past her knuckle and only escaped falling off when the earl grasped it and pushed it, with more force than strictly necessary, back onto her finger. She heard him mutter something unintelligible and glanced up at him again, surprised that he could find no humor in the situation. His gray eyes were flat with annoyance, and her own smile faded. It was as she had feared, she thought resignedly, the earl had no sense of the ridiculous, and was provoked that she could show unseemly levity on such an occasion. Harriet turned her thoughts back to the Reverend Matthews, who was concluding the service in a voice that held a hint of reproof. Undoubtedly, he had witnessed the incident with the ring and, in a fit of perversity, Harriet had the irresistible urge to wiggle her finger again.

A sudden hush distracted her, however, and she raised her eyes to discover that the ceremony was over and her new husband was gazing down at her enigmatically. Harriet froze. She was strangely unprepared for the kiss he bestowed upon her, brief and impersonal though it was. And then she felt herself smothered in her tearful Aunt Sophy's comforting embrace. Much to her embarrassment, Harriet felt the tears spring to her own eyes, but she had no time for mawkishness for the entire staff of Kimbalton Abbey was gathered in the Hall for the occasion and waited to be presented to their new mistress.

The wedding breakfast was sparsely attended, partly as a result of the unexpectedness of what Aunt Sophy insisted upon
referring to as the *happy event,* which allowed no time for formal invitations and detailed preparations. But Harriet suspected that the primary cause for the unseemly haste with
which the affair was concluded could be attributed to the earl's
eagerness to return to London. He was far too well bred to
allow his impatience to show, of course, but Harriet had
sensed it in every glance, in every gesture. She had the strange
sensation that her new husband had already left her—in spirit
if no corporeally—and was, even as he made his terse response to Reverend Matthews' traditional question, already in
London disporting himself . . . Harriet quailed at the thought
of the exact nature of Lord Kimbalton's London pleasures.
Such matters were, after all, none of her concern, and in truth
she was a little dismayed at the frequency with which her wayward thoughts dwelt on the mystery female who held her new
husband so firmly in thrall.

So while Harriet certainly understood the earl's eagerness to
conclude their arrangement and return to his former bachelor
existence, some perverse corner of her mind was deeply ag-
grieved at his insensitivity to her own needs. After all, it was
her wedding, too, she had complained to Peter the evening before, when the earl casually informed her that she was to be
married by special license and not wait the required reading of
the banns. Harriet had a scathing set-down on the tip of her
tongue, but before she could inform his lordship that she
would not be a party to such a havey-cavey scheme, her
brother drew her aside.

"Hold on there, old girl," the viscount murmured soothingly. "There's nothing wrong with a special license, love.
Everything will be right and tight and perfectly legal. Do you
think I would sanction anything less for my little sister?" He
smiled his boyish, charming smile, but for once Harriet was
unimpressed.

"Legal or not, I do not like it, Peter. And where does his
lordship expect to obtain a special license?" she demanded, a
telltale note of peevishness in her voice. "Does he intend to
ride all the way into Brighton tomorrow morning, while I sit
kicking my heels in this mausoleum?"

Peter had laughed at this show of temper. "We already
thought of that, dearest." His infectious grin widened. "Giles is
not the kind of man to leave anything to chance you should

know. We stopped in Brighton on the way to Lark Manor. The bishop there is related to Giles by marriage, and the old blighter was only too happy to issue a special license. Quite delighted he was, in fact, that Giles had finally decided to get himself riveted. The whole family has been on his back for months to secure the succession. Ever since Brian complicated everything by riding that green horse in the local hunt and—"

"Just a minute," Harriet interrupted. "Do you mean to tell me that Kimbalton had a special license in his pocket when he came to Lark Manor?" She spoke softly, but Harriet could feel the anger tightening within her. Was there no limit to this man's presumption? she thought, watching her brother's beguiling grin falter.

"I confess that he did, Harriet," the viscount admitted, his sunny expression momentarily overshadowed by anxiety. "But don't fly into the boughs, love. It was a lucky coincidence when you come to think of it. Giles is as anxious as you are, my love, to see this match brought to a happy conclusion."

"I am not *anxious* at all," Harriet declared abruptly. "In point of fact, I am beginning to have second thoughts about this whole affair. And let me tell you, Peter, I find it highly unflattering to be taken so much for granted. What if I had refused Montague's offer? I came perilously close to doing so, you know."

"But you did nothing so hen-witted, my love," the viscount said coaxingly. "Which only goes to show that you are the best possible choice Giles could have made for his wife. You are sensible and—"

"Yes, I know," Harriet cut in scathingly. "Sensible and practical to a fault. Besides which his lordship was kind enough to inform me that my grasp of estate affairs quite convinced him that he need look no further for a bride. Very convenient for him, would you not agree, brother?" she added with unmistakable sarcasm.

Harriet was reminded of her grievance the following morning when she left her room and encountered her brother on his way down to breakfast, dressed with unusual punctiliousness at that early hour for his role in the approaching ceremony.

"Dashed early to be out of bed, if you ask me," he mumbled as they made their way towards the stairs.

"If I had been consulted about this rag-tag affair, which naturally I was not," Harriet responded acidly, "I would have done things with a modicum of decorum, you may be sure."

"Hush, dearest," Aunt Sophy exclaimed, bustling up in time to overhear the sarcasm in her niece's voice. "Do not get into one of your pets, Harriet, I beg of you. The vicar has just arrived, and dear Kimbalton has sent me to bring you down to the Great Hall."

"*Sent* you, Aunt?" Harriet repeated coolly. "You must not allow that odious bully to order you about, dear. I can assure you that I have no intention of doing so." She tilted her small nose as if to emphasize her words. "And since when is he your *dear* Kimbalton, Aunt? I declare that your wits have gone begging." She gazed anxiously at Lady Sophronia's flushed, excited face and forced herself to smile. "I trust his worship will not take exception to this gown, Aunt," she added, glancing down at the deep green muslin morning gown with its modern narrow skirt she had chosen from the modest selection at her disposal. "I suppose it never occurred to his lordship that I might have wished to be married in white. Had I known that this was to be such a ramshackle affair, I might have chosen to bring something more suitable."

"Nonsense, child," Lady Sophronia replied quickly. "You look charming as always. Come, Peter," she addressed the viscount. "Escort us down to the Great Hall, if you please. His lordship is waiting."

"Dash it all, Aunt," the viscount interjected. "We ain't had breakfast yet. And I cannot answer for my wits unless I get some sustenance first. What do you say, Harry?"

"I could not agree more, Peter," Harriet replied, making straight for the breakfast room and directing Carruthers to bring up a fresh pot of tea. "This is my wedding day as well, unless I have misunderstood his lordship's intentions, so you may inform him, Aunt, that I will present myself in the Hall when I am good and ready," she announced, giving in to a mutinous urge to thwart the overbearing lord she had misguidedly promised to wed.

So it was quite twenty minutes later and in a rebellious frame of mind that Lady Harriet finally entered the Great Hall on her brother's arm. She noticed immediately that her bridegroom's lips were drawn into a thin line, and his darkly chiseled face marred by a scowl. But Harriet was undismayed at the lack of warmth in his greeting. Indeed, she would have been disappointed had the earl not shown any displeasure at her deliberate flaunting of his summons. A small victory perhaps, she thought, bestowing a dazzling smile on the vicar, who was fidgeting nervously with his prayer book, but one which would have to sustain her through the ordeal ahead.

Harriet turned to face the earl. Yes, she thought, gazing up into gray eyes that were—if such a thing were possible— colder and more distant than ever and devoid of all expression.

"I am ready, my lord," she said calmly, returning his stare without flinching.

The earl gazed down at her for several seconds without speaking. Harriet could hear the vicar shuffling through his prayer book and clearing his throat discreetly. Her own heart seemed to still momentarily as the nonsensical notion struck her that perhaps the earl was also having second thoughts about this precipitous and irreversible step he was about to take. She wished fervently that she could ask him. He would disclaim any such notion, of course; things had gone too far for either of them to turn back without setting off an unthinkable scandal. And quite suddenly Harriet knew in her own mind that she would not turn back even if she were given the unlikely choice of doing so. She wanted this marriage. The realization took her by surprise, for only yesterday morning she had told the earl that there was little to tempt her into accepting his offer. But by the time he had brought her back from their drive, she had done so, when only a few hours earlier she had informed her brother that she wished to return home.

But he had needed her, he said.

Harriet recalled her decision to humor Lord Kimbalton by allowing him to conduct her on a tour of the estate. She had intended to be polite, a conciliatory gesture before announcing her desire to return to Lark Manor unbetrothed. She had deliberately been more critical of the estate than was strictly called for in order to prepare him for rejection. She knew her uninhibited remarks had angered him; by all accounts the earl should have been more than happy to see the last of her.

But he had told her she was *needed* at the Abbey. *He* needed her.

Harriet remembered how her resolve had wavered at this startling revelation. The prospect of spending the rest of her life as the Countess of Kimbalton had suddenly become a challenge rather than an imposition. And then she had found herself discussing *conditions*. And the earl had agreed to each and every one without a qualm. Well, perhaps not without a qualm, she recalled, but he had certainly given her full rein in restoring and renovating the house and grounds. The prospect of being mistress of such an establishment—without interference from Lord Kimbalton—had seduced her as perhaps nothing else could. And at least he had not lied to her. She *was* needed here. The house cried out for light, and air, and color, and for the warmth that only comes from being lived in. And as for the grounds . . . Harriet felt her fingers itch to begin the transformation of these austere grounds into a garden of delight.

Yes, she thought contentedly, she was needed here, and this man who was glowering at her could make it happen.

Harriet relaxed and smiled up at her soon-to-be husband. She was startled to see an answering glimmer in his gray eyes, and it suddenly dawned on her that the poor man was almost as nervous as the vicar. She was distracted by a slight cough from her brother, who stood by her side ready to do the honors. Harriet could not suppress a grin. All these big loobies were as nervous as cats, she realized; the earl, her brother, and the lanky vicar. While all she could think of was how soon a shipment of rose-trees could be brought in from Brighton.

But first there was a marriage to celebrate.

"Shall we proceed, my lord?" she suggested mildly.

Later that afternoon, when silence had fallen once more on the Great Hall, the domestics having returned to their posts, and the vicar's gig disappeared down the driveway, the new Countess of Kimbalton stood at the window of the Yellow Saloon gazing pensively out at the severely tailored grounds. She was alone. The earl had been closeted in his study with his steward, Mr. Mulligan, for the past two hours; Peter had gone out riding, and Aunt Sophy had retired to her room for a much-needed rest. Harriet was thankful for the solitude.

The aftermath of her marriage seemed oddly anticlimactic, Harriet thought ruefully, and was made even more so when Carruthers tapped discreetly at the door to inquire if her ladyship wished to order tea served in the Great Hall.

"No, Carruthers," she answered, determined to commence without delay the changes she wished to introduce as mistress of the Abbey. "We will take tea in here this afternoon."

The butler pursed his thin lips and drew himself up majestically. "Her ladyship always preferred to maintain the tradition of serving tea in the Great Hall, my lady," he enunciated in chilling tones, staring at Harriet down an extraordinary expanse of nose, held at an angle calculated to tell the world what he thought of changing by so much as a hair's-breadth the way things should be done.

"Lady Kimbalton is in London," Harriet responded dryly. "So we will have tea in here. And, Carruthers," she added firmly, "when we take tea *en famille*, I do not wish to see that silver monstrosity, nor do I wish to drink cold tea. Tell Mrs. Holloway to use the Wedgwood set, if you please."

After the butler had made a silent exit, Harriet relaxed and moved over to stand before the crackling fire. Although they had been at the Abbey for over two days now, and the earl had ordered fires lit in every room, Harriet still felt a lingering chill in the air. She rubbed her hands briskly to warm them, wondering how her new husband would react to this first break in his precious tradition.

The earl was the first to join her, and Harriet turned to find him standing in the threshold, a frown on his face.

"Carruthers tells me you have ordered tea in here, my dear," he drawled in a bored voice. "I assured him that he must have misunderstood you. We always have tea in the Hall."

Harriet's heart sank at the implacability she saw in his eyes, but she drew herself up as tall as her slight frame would allow and returned his stare boldly. So this was to be their first tug-of-war, she thought. Even on her wedding day he was not going to allow her to exercise her right as mistress of this house. Worse yet, he was about to break one of the promises he had made to her in the gazebo. How many more would he disregard entirely, she wondered wryly, now that he had got what he wanted? That stiff-necked Carruthers must have gone straight to his master to confirm her orders. The notion enraged Harriet, but she forced herself to smile. Something told her that if she allowed her autocratic husband to get away with this petty foolishness, she would never have the freedom she had anticipated in this marriage.

"Naturally, you may drink your tea wherever you wish, my lord," she said sweetly. "I shall have mine in here as I informed Carruthers." She watched in fascination as Lord Kimbalton's jaw muscles clenched visibly. "I had hoped you would join me," she added, "because there are several matters we should discuss. But if you prefer, I shall ask Carruthers to bring up two trays." She moved towards the bellpull.

"It is a tradition at the Abbey to serve tea in the Great Hall." His voice was expressionless but Harriet easily recognized the

note of authority in it. An authority that would take all her resolution to stand up to, she realized.

"So Carruthers has already informed me, my lord." She
paused and turned to face him, carefully keeping her voice
neutral. "But it is so much cozier in here, do you not agree?"

The earl glared at her for several moments, but Harriet refused to be cowed. Finally, he strolled over to stand beside
her, one elbow on the pale marble mantel. "You are determined to defy me already, I see."

"Oh, no, my lord," Harriet responded calmly, her eyes on
the fire. "I merely believed the promises you made to me regarding my role in this house." Once the words were out, Harriet could not believe she had actually said them, and held her
breath, waiting for the wrath of Jove to fall on her head. When
nothing happened, she glanced at the earl expectantly. "You
do intend to keep them, I trust, my lord?"

How she ever found the courage to ask such a thing, Harriet
did not stop to ponder, but she knew instinctively that if she
quailed before her new husband now, she would never become
the true mistress of Kimbalton Abbey. So she held his gaze
and watched his gray eyes darken menacingly.

Then, quite unexpectedly, he smiled, and Harriet released
the breath she only now realized she had been holding.

"I seemed to have been beguiled into making rash promises,
my lady," he said mildly. "And naturally I intend to keep
them."

"I cannot imagine anyone beguiling you into doing anything
you did not wish, my lord," Harriet replied lightly, glad that
the tension had eased between them. And then she remembered the mystery lady in London, and blushed. Undoubtedly,
the earl would be putty in her hands, she thought. Especially if
she were as beautiful as Peter had—rather improperly, to be
sure—described her.

"Which brings us to another question, my lord," Harriet hur-
ried on, anxious to cover up her gaffe. But before she could
voice her curiosity regarding the earl's intended return to London, the door opened to reveal the stony-faced butler.

"Tea is served, my lady," he announced with prim satisfaction, and Harriet knew that he had disregarded her orders and
served it in the Great Hall. She felt a surge of anger at the servant's impertinence before recalling that the man was only
doing what his master had ordered. She turned furiously to the
earl, only to find his amused gaze on her.

"We will have our tea in here, Carruthers," he drawled pleasantly. "As her ladyship wishes."

Harriet was so surprised at this unexpected capitulation that it took her a moment to gather her wits together. "Thank you, my lord," she murmured as soon as the butler had closed the door behind him.

"Now tell me what matters you wish to discuss with me, my dear?" he said.

Harriet felt a tremor of alarm. Suddenly this did not seem quite the right moment to ask her new husband when he intended to leave her. "Oh, it can wait until after tea, my lord," she replied nervously, avoiding his eyes by settling herself on the yellow brocade settee before the hearth.

"Tell me now," he insisted, with such a devilish gleam in his eyes that Harriet was certain he had guessed what she wanted to say.

"There is so much to attend to here at the Abbey, my lord," she began, anxious to appear nonchalant about the delicate question she must ask. "I merely wished to know how soon you intend to return to London.

There was an awkward pause. "I see," the earl said finally, his voice once more cool and remote. "I am de trop, I gather? Is that it, Harriet?"

"Oh, no," she answered quickly, and then hesitated. "Well, actually I doubt you would enjoy staying here with everything turned topsy-turvy, my lord. And I intend to dismiss the French cook, so meals will be irregular until I can find a replacement. I thought I should warn you, that is all."

"So I *am* in the way." Harriet did not raise her eyes, but the tone of his voice told her that the dark frown had returned to his brow, and he was annoyed with her again.

"Very well, my dear," he said finally, his voice full of cynical amusement. "I shall remove to London at first light tomorrow. Will that suit you, my lady?"

Quite suddenly, Harriet was not sure the removal of her new husband to London suited her at all. But it was part of the agreement they had made, she reminded herself grimly. An agreement that bound Harriet quite as firmly as it did Lord Kimbalton. It was what she had agreed to live with.

"Thank you, my lord." She looked up into her husband's cool gray eyes and smiled. "That will suit me very well indeed."

\* \* \*

His wife's words resounded in Giles's ears all the way up to
London the following morning.

On sudden impulse, he had suggested to the viscount over
the breakfast table that they leave the carriage and trunks to
their valets and ride the rest of the way. They would make
considerably better time, he had argued. Peter had grinned and
responded with a lewd wink, obviously under the impression
that his friend was impatient to get back to his love nest on
Curzon Street. And this was indeed the case, Giles told himself as he allowed Carruthers to heap another serving of York
ham and coddled eggs on his plate. But at the moment his
thoughts were on Harriet.

His wife.

Giles savored the taste of the word on his tongue. He had a
wife. He was free again. The incongruity of this notion
amused him; most men in his set would have thought exactly
the opposite. He knew that it was only partially true, of course.
Harriet had set him free from his mother, free from the Marriage Mart rounds the dowager was undoubtedly planning for
him, and most welcome of all, she had relieved him of that
nagging sense of duty unfulfilled that had marred his pleasure
in life almost from the moment he received news of Brian's
accident and his own accession to the title. Now everything
was as it should be, he thought, except that, for some odd reason, he could not stop thinking of Harriet.

The wench had made him mad as fire yesterday morning, of
course. Deliberately so, he had no doubt. He had been forced
to wait all of twenty minutes, kicking his heels and listening to
the vicar natter on about the needs of the parish before Lady
Harriet had appeared in the Hall, cool and regal despite her
small stature, to take her place at his side. When he had seen
the amused defiance in her hazel eyes, he had suddenly been
assailed by doubts. Who was this female he was taking so casually to wife? he had wondered. Was she the dutiful, obedient, sensible creature Peter had made her out to be? Giles had
certainly believed so, but might he not have been deceived by
her diminutive size and meekness? Of course, she had been
neither meek nor mild during their encounter on Oak Hill, he
recalled wryly, but he had put that down to maidenly skittish-
ness. When he had cornered her in his own gazebo and given
her a taste of the famous Montague charm, he had been well
pleased with her sensible response and ultimate acceptance of
his offer.

But during the marriage ceremony she had revealed a deplorable lack of seriousness and no awareness at all of the great honor he was bestowing upon her. It had troubled him that none of the family jewels fit her small finger. Neither the traditional betrothal ring all Montague brides had worn for generations, nor any of the gold wedding bands he had planned to use. He would be obliged to purchase a special ring for her in London, a circumstance he would much rather have avoided. He had not reckoned on carrying thoughts of Harriet to London with him at all, but if he must make this purchase for her, she would naturally intrude upon his time. And upon his thoughts, he told himself wryly, recalling the delightful smile she had given him in the Yellow Saloon yesterday afternoon at tea-time.

His amusement faded when he remembered the reason for his wife's smile. She had exhibited a deplorable eagerness to see him leave for London. If he had not known better, he might have suspected that she would have preferred him to set out immediately the knot was tied. Could she have been nervous about the wedding night? he wondered. Come to think of it, he had not actually indicated that he had no intention of exercising his marital rights last night. Not that the thought had been entirely absent from his mind, of course, but he had been in no mood for virgins. Furthermore, Harriet was not particularly his type, although sooner or later he would be expected to start his nursery. Harriet would expect it, too, since she had confessed to a desire for a family. The thought intrigued him, and he wondered if perhaps he should have done the deed last night after all.

"The horses are ready, milord." Carruthers's dry voice interrupted Giles's train of thought. He got to his feet and eyed the butler thoughtfully.

"I shall be in London for some time, Carruthers," he said casually. "I am depending on you to see that Lady Kimbalton gets no resistance from the staff in her plans for the Abbey. She has my full permission to make all the changes she sees fit. I depend upon you to assist her."

The butler's face remained impassive. "As you wish, milord."

"Come on, Peter," Giles turned to the viscount, suddenly anxious to be gone. "It is high time we were on the road."

"What's the big rush, old man?" Peter replied lazily, getting to his feet and following his host out into the vast hall. "Besides the obvious, of course." He grinned. "Anyone who does not know you would think you are hen-pecked already."

Giles returned the grin as he pulled on his gloves and allowed Carruthers to assist him into his greatcoat.

"Could be they are right." He laughed at the irony. The notion that his new wife could have any influence at all on his life in London amused him. Their agreement clearly stated that she would make her home in the country as mistress of the Abbey. He could wash his hands of her until he decided to start his nursery, couldn't he?

He walked out of the Abbey and mounted his restive horse, determined to put the past four or five days behind him. But as Giles cantered down the long driveway, Harriet's reaction to his announced departure came back to him.

*That will suit me very well indeed,* she had said.

Well, it suited him very well, too, he thought cynically, although long before he had reached London, he had begun to wonder if he would find his new wife as convenient as he had supposed.

# CHAPTER SIX

# Christmas Crisis

"But what about the succession?" Aunt Sophy had demanded in bewilderment when it became evident to her that her niece's new husband had bolted at dawn the day after their wedding.

Harriet felt her color rise at her aunt's indiscretion and waited until they had passed into the breakfast room, out of earshot of Tom, the footman, whose eyes had fairly leaped from their sockets at her ladyship's plain speaking.

"I declare, Aunt, you must wish to see me die of mortification to mention such things before the servants," Harriet protested as the door closed reluctantly behind them.

The two ladies had descended to the breakfast room together that morning, at an hour which Harriet's aunt had considered indecently early for a young bride to be up and about.

"What will his lordship think?" Lady Sophronia protested. "The dear man is probably still abed himself, as is half the staff no doubt. There is absolutely no need to take your new duties so seriously, my love."

It was then that Harriet—rather unwisely she later discovered—informed her aunt that Lord Kimbalton had already removed to London.

"London?" her aunt repeated in astonishment. "Whyever would he do anything so nonsensical as that, pray?"

"Because I suggested that he do so," Harriet replied, exasperated at having to explain a situation which should have been obvious to her aunt. But Aunt Sophy had refused to believe that her niece's marriage had been a mere convenience for the earl. Harriet hoped that the early desertion of the new bridegroom—a piece of information she had received from her abigail together with her morning chocolate—would convince her aunt that although Harriet was certainly the undisputed mistress of Kimbalton Abbey, she was not Lord Kimbalton's mistress, but merely his wife.

In truth, Harriet was more than a little put out that the earl

had gone off without so much as a by-you-leave. By week's
end, however, she had convinced herself that she was well rid
of the disagreeable man, and proceeded to throw herself into
the restoration and refurbishing of the Abbey with a
vengeance. In this task she soon discovered that she could
count on the unexpected support of Carruthers. Perhaps it was
her decision to fire the irascible Monsieur Marceau that ame-
liorated the stony-faced butler's disapproval of her, she
thought, or perhaps it was her willingness to seek his advice
regarding a local replacement for the intractable Frenchman.
In any case, Harriet was delighted that the transition was made
with a minimum of fuss, and by the end of the first week, Mrs.
Jones's hearty English dishes began to appear regularly on the
dinner table.

By the end of the second week, the new Countess of Kimbalton had managed to set the whole place on its ears. Aunt
Sophy had taken on the not inconsiderable task of sending off
to London for samples of fabric to replace curtains and refurbish the upholstery in a number of rooms. Harriet herself decided to concentrate on making what changes she could in the
grounds before the cold weather set in.

Mr. Mulligan received her civilly when Harriet sought him
out in the estate office above the coachhouse one morning. But
when the steward saw the extensive list of bushes, bulbs, rose-
trees, seeds, tools, and other gardening paraphernalia her ladyship deemed essential to carry out her plans for the grounds,
he blenched.

"Does your ladyship not consider that perhaps the labor involved in such an undertaking might not be too much for the
four estate gardeners?" he inquired diplomatically.

Harriet met this resistance with a practical solution. "Not at
all, Mr. Mulligan," she replied blithely. "I intend to hire at
least six lads from the village to help us. Crofts and Brown
both have sons of an age for this kind of work, and I am sure
there will be no shortage of other lads willing to earn wages
before the holidays." She smiled at the steward expectantly,
and Mr. Mulligan gave in without a murmur.

"I shall take care of it, milady," he assured her. "But I warn
your ladyship that it will take more than a sennight to cart
these supplies over from Brighton."

Harriet was not perturbed. She set the gardeners and their
new helpers to digging rose-beds, although when the men discovered that they would be required to destroy considerable

portions of the earl's pristine parkland, they showed some reluctance to desecrate the thick sod that, according to the elderly Tom Brown—who had gardened for the grandfather of the present earl, he told her proudly—was reported to be over four hundred years old.

"Four hundred years, indeed?" Harriet repeated, unimpressed. "Then it is high time we dig some of it up and plant flowers instead." And by the time the cartloads of bulbs, rosetrees, and other flowering plants began to arrive at the Abbey, Harriet had so won over the men with her enthusiasm and good humor that they would gladly have dug up all ten acres of the famous Home Park had her ladyship so directed.

By mid-November the earl's park had taken on a decidedly rakish air with large clumps of rose-trees clustered in apparently haphazard groups behind the house in waves of newly turned earth and bare-branched ranks beyond the back terrace.

Harriet was ecstatic. She worked from dawn to dusk directing the lads in planting the hundreds of daffodils, snowdrops, crocuses, and wood hyacinths in casual drifts beneath the austere oaks and sycamores growing at meticulously spaced intervals across the Park. She also insisted upon setting a number of them around the earl's gazebo. Harriet always thought of this trysting place as his, for when she went there, as she did whenever she had a free moment, his presence was palpable and somehow reassuring.

There came a moment, however, when the weather drove her indoors, and she had to send the gardeners home and take refuge among the dozens of samples Aunt Sophy had accumulated and the army of seamstresses who had been hired to cut and sew the new curtains as soon as the fabrics began to arrive from London.

By mid-December, Harriet's initial spurt of energy had exhausted itself and she began to look forward to her first Christmas at Kimbalton Abbey.

"Will his lordship come to the Abbey for the holidays?" Aunt Sophy asked her one morning at breakfast.

Harriet took one look at the driving sleet beating against the windows and shrugged. "How should I know, Aunt," she responded, reluctant to admit that her thoughts had been running in much the same direction. "I have not heard from him, as you well know."

"The man is a heartless rogue to ignore you in this manner, Harriet," her aunt remarked. Ever since Lady Sophronia had come to accept that Lord Kimbalton had indeed left his new bride to go gallivanting up to London with no intention of returning within the near future, Aunt Sophy had severely revised her opinion of the earl.

"It would serve him right if you were to return to Lark Manor for Christmas, dearest. I must admit that I find the prospect of decorating this barn rather daunting."

Harriet could not argue with her aunt's reluctance to attempt the monstrous job of preparing the Great Hall for Christmas celebrations. The Abbey as a whole did not inspire her with holiday spirits. In spite of the whirl of activity during the past weeks, Harriet had experienced a strange sense of loneliness during her rare moments of solitude. Attributing her low spirits to idleness, she had pushed herself to take on further duties. The village of Petersfield, lying as it did on Montague lands, was nominally part of her responsibility, particularly the orphanage which housed a dozen or more homeless children, and Harriet arranged for baskets of food and clothes to be delivered there on Christmas Eve.

Although both ladies had received several holiday invitations from neighboring families, Harriet was not in the mood to entertain on a grand scale at the Abbey, which she would be expected to do if she remained in Hampshire. Her aunt's idle suggestion opened a host of more interesting possibilities.

"Do you think we could, Aunt?" she murmured wistfully.

"Do what, dear?"

"Spend Christmas at Lark Manor, of course."

Her aunt stared at her for several moments, a glimmer of compassion in her blue eyes. Then her round face broke into a conspiratorial smile. "Not only do I think we could, my dear Harriet; I am convinced that we *should*. That would teach that reprobate of a husband of yours to treat you so shabbily."

"Then let us go upstairs and start packing," Harriet exclaimed, her spirits miraculously revived. "Mulligan assures me that the weather will clear during the night. We could be in Lark Manor by tea-time tomorrow."

And Giles Montague could stay in London until he died of old age for all she cared, Harriet thought rebelliously.

"We could have our Christmas ball," Aunt Sophy suggested excitedly. "And go sleighing with Sir James and the Biddletons."

Harriet laughed delightedly, her moodiness forgotten. "And

put up our kissing bough again this year. Remember how popular it was with the younger crowd last Christmas, Aunt?"

"And with Sir James as well, dear, if I remember correctly," her aunt teased.

Harriet blushed at the memory of Sir James's chaste kiss. "Perhaps this time Squire Russell will be more successful in stealing a kiss from you, Aunt," Harriet countered.

"What nonsense you do talk, Harriet," her aunt scolded. "You should not forget that you are a countess now, dear, and must act accordingly."

"Pooh!" Harriet exclaimed, dismissing that honor with a wave of her hand. The real attraction of returning to Lark Manor, she realized suddenly, was that she could forget all about being a countess. But could she forget the earl as well? she wondered. Christmas had always been a time of celebration in her family. Even after her father had died, Peter had always made it a point to return to Lark Manor or to Egerton Hall—wherever the family had agreed to gather that year. Where would Peter go this year? she wondered. Where would her husband go?

She pushed the thought aside, angry at herself for caring where and with whom Lord Kimbalton spent his Christmas.

The snow began to fall in sporadic flurries shortly after the earl's crested traveling coach left the Blue Swan Inn at Guilford. By the time it passed through Petersfield and turned into the stone gates of Kimbalton Abbey, the flurries had thickened to a steady white curtain that blanketed the rhododendrons lining the driveway.

Giles grimaced at the two men who rode in the carriage with him. "One day later and we might have had to rack up in Guilford," he remarked to no one in particular.

"I can think of a dozen worse fates, my lad," drawled the broad-shouldered buck in a fashionably long, fur-trimmed greatcoat. "I know at least two actresses living comfortable, retired lives in Guilford on the proceeds of their labors."

"Not all of it on the boards, I'll wager," the Viscount Bridgeport responded with an amused leer. "Trust you to know all the available females in every hamlet in the realm, Robert. How the devil do you do it?"

"Lots of hard work, lad," the Marquess of Monroyal drawled laconically. "Lots of hard work—take it from one who knows."

"I wouldn't doubt it for a moment, you old lecher," the viscount countered, a hint of envy in his voice. "Tell me, Robert, do you remember all the wenches you have ever bedded?"

The marquess glanced at the younger man and grinned. "I suppose you do, Peter? But what am I thinking of? Of course you do, or you would not be asking such damned fool questions."

The viscount bridled at the implied criticism. "I see nothing wrong in counting one's conquests, as it were," he said curtly.

The marquess let out a crack of laughter. "Listen to the puppy, Giles. If that don't beat the Dutch." He fumbled at his elegant velvet waistcoat and drew out a jeweled quizzing glass, which he raised nonchalantly to his right eye to examine his fellow traveler. "Gad, you are an innocent cub, Egerton. Conquests indeed. My God, man, if you have time to count 'em, I always say, you are wasting precious time, lad. Take it from—"

"A man who knows," the viscount interrupted caustically. "Yes, I know that, Robert. Perhaps that is why you are looking rather jaded of late," he added slyly. "Too much of a good thing, don't you know. By the time you do decide to set up your nursery, old man, methinks you won't have an ounce of energy left to do your duty." He grinned at the dark frown that settled on the older man's face.

"Insolent whelp," the marquess drawled with studied indifference, but Giles sensed that the noted rake was angry at the aspersions cast upon his prowess. "I ain't like Montague here," the marquess continued coolly, waving an elegantly gloved hand at the earl. "Nobody is about to corner me into parson's mousetrap. Don't hold with virgins. Never touched one in my life and don't intend to. Luckily, I have three brothers who will doubtless do the honors for me when the time comes to secure the Stilton line."

"Unless they all take after you, Robert." The viscount grinned to take the bite out of his words, and the atmosphere in the coach relaxed noticeably.

But the marquess's facetious remarks about virgins and Giles's own recent marriage had brought his own virgin bride vividly to mind. Harriet, he thought, conscious of a sudden eagerness to see her diminutive form again. He carried a tiny—to his mind at least it was ridiculously tiny—gold wedding band, expressly ordered to fit her finger, so unlike those of other, long-gone Montague brides. For some inexplicable reason,

Giles was suddenly anxious to place it firmly on his wife's finger.

He leapt down from the carriage without waiting for the footmen to let down the steps and took the stairs two at a time. Only when he reached the open door and turned to usher in his two cronies did Giles realize that his eagerness had amused them.

Monroyal ascended the steps at a leisurely pace, a devilish grin on his handsome face. "Steady, old man," he murmured with a knowing wink as he brushed past Giles into the cavernous hall. "Don't let the wench see you in such a state, Giles, or she will demand your soul as well as your body. Believe me——"

"I am not in any *state*—as you call it," Giles interrupted brusquely. "And my wife is not a wench, Stilton. I'll thank you to remember it in the future." He was surprised at the menacing tone of his voice.

The marquess made him a deep, ironic bow. "My deepest apologies, old man. Never meant to suggest anything of the sort."

Monroyal was laughing at him, and Giles could hardly blame him. It was simply not done to display such eagerness to see one's wife. Giles turned to Carruthers and allowed the butler to remove his greatcoat.

"Inform her ladyship that I am here, Carruthers," he said shortly. "And we could all use some hot tea, I am sure."

The butler cleared his throat. "Lady Kimbalton is not presently in residence, milord," he announced tonelessly, his gaze fixed on a portrait of an unknown lady with two small children and numerous dogs clustered about her that had graced the wall of the Hall ever since Giles could remember.

Giles froze, arrested in midgesture. It was several seconds— which seemed like hours—later that he realized the marquess was chuckling audibly at his elbow. Giles completed the task of pulling off his leather gloves before he trusted himself to speak.

"And just where did her ladyship go, Carruthers?" He spoke softly, but the butler heard—as Giles had intended him to—the steel in his voice.

"Her ladyship removed to Sussex, milord. Hardly more than a sennight ago. To Lark Manor to be more precise, milord."

"The dove has flown, I gather," the marquess drawled

softly. "How unfortunate. I was looking forward to meeting this paragon."

"Lark Manor?" the viscount repeated uneasily. "Now I wonder why Harriet would do something so hen-witted."

"I imagine her ladyship found the prospect of spending Christmas in this barn rather daunting, although I must say it appears less chilly than usual, Giles. I trust you are not planning to drag us all across Sussex in this weather, old man," he added plaintively.

Giles ignored him. "Send up some tea, if you will, Carruthers," he said stiffly.

"In the Great Hall, milord?" The butler still did not meet his eyes.

"Is there a fire there?"

"There are fires in all the rooms, milord. Her ladyship expressly requested it."

"Then we will take tea in the Yellow Saloon," Giles found himself saying without consciously thinking about it. It was in that room that he had last taken tea with his countess, he remembered. She had defied him there, and he had humored her. It was there also that she had suggested he leave the Abbey. He pushed the memory aside.

"We will stay here tonight, Carruthers," he said abruptly. "Tomorrow we will go on to Lark Manor."

"Tomorrow is Christmas Eve, Giles," the marquess protested as the earl led the way to the Yellow Saloon, which was indeed far cozier than the Great Hall, just as Harriet had claimed, he remembered. "Do you really intend to drag us all over the countryside on Christmas Eve?"

"We could stay here and get drunk," the viscount offered. "A bloody sight more comfortable."

"We should have stayed in Guilford," the marquess murmured with a heartfelt sigh. "I should have insisted upon it."

"We are going to Lark Manor," Giles said firmly, "but a drink does sound good, Peter," he added, strolling to the sideboard to pour three glasses of French brandy.

"Here's to poor old Giles and parson's mousetrap." The marquess's dark gray eyes clashed mockingly with Giles's over the raised glasses. "May he never live to regret it."

Giles smiled faintly and raised his own glass. "And may it snap shut on your rascally neck, Robert, when you least expect it.

\* \* \*

December the twenty-fourth dawned cold and crisp. The snowfall had ceased during the night and the pale winter sun tempted Harriet to steal an hour from her morning tasks for a brisk trudge through the woods looking for fresh mistletoe for the kissing bough. She was looking forward to the dinner and ball that evening with delight, and in celebration of the progress the two ladies had made in restoring the Abbey, Harriet had been persuaded by her aunt to order a new gown for the occasion. In honor of the season, she had chosen a rich red velvet trimmed with green braid sprinkled with dozens of tiny seed pearls. She would add her mother's pearl parure, she thought, stamping the snow from her half-boots and entering the warm hall under the disapproving eye of old Harvey.

The butler never failed to complain about the commotion created in his domain by the bustle of seasonal activities, but even Harvey's sour face could not dampen Harriet's spirits today. If it were not for the fact that he reminded her somewhat of the crusty old Carruthers at the Abbey, she would have liked it better, but she refused to allow memories of that other life to intrude upon her present happiness.

That evening began very auspiciously with the arrival of the jovial Sir John Biddleton and his family, long-standing friends and neighbors. Sir James arrived shortly after, his astonishing masculine beauty as glittering as ever, which set both Biddleton girls twittering with nervous admiration. It never ceased to amaze Harriet that such a truly beautiful specimen as Sir James could be so unconscious of the havoc he invariably caused among feminine hearts. Her own excepted, of course. She smiled fondly at the golden head bent so elegantly over her hand. Never a hair out of place, she mused; never a crease in his form-fitting pantaloons, never a wrinkle in his pale blue coat, never a cross word, an impatient gesture, an improper glance. Sir James was truly a paragon. It was unfortunate that she could not return his regard. He still harbored a *tendre* for her, that much was evident from the soulful glances she intercepted from his cornflower blue eyes.

The Biddleton girls were wildly jealous of Sir James's preference for her, in spite of her recent marriage—a state of affairs Harriet did everything in her power to counteract. At fifteen, Sarah was too young for such things—at least Lady Biddleton always claimed so—but seventeen-year-old Jane, a gentle, auburn-haired beauty with eyes as green as pale jade, gazed longingly at the young baronet whenever he was present, a circumstance of which Sir James seemed to be supremely unaware. Harriet had thought to be kind in placing Jane next to Sir James at table, but she soon saw that the girl had been struck dumb by the proximity of her god, and seemed to have lost her appetite into the bargain.

The level of festivities picked up noticeably as soon as the dinner guests moved upstairs and were joined by those invited to the ball. Harriet was deluged with congratulations on her newly acquired status, but was obliged to fend off several oblique inquiries about her absent husband. This was the only flaw she could find to the evening, which cast a momentary pall on her spirits. But by the time the orchestra had swung into its fourth set of country dances, Harriet had deliberately pushed all thought of Lord Kimbalton to the back of her mind and was about to join one of the several sets on the dance floor on the arm of Sir John Biddleton, when an agitated Harvey coughed nervously at her elbow.

"What is it, Harvey?" she demanded, wondering if they were indeed running low on the hot cider punch, as Aunt Sophy had warned her they might, hot cider being a favorite among the younger set.

"The Viscount Bridgeport is downstairs, milady," the butler murmured. "Anxious to see you, his lordship is."

"Peter is here?" she exclaimed delightedly. "Send him up, Harvey. What are you thinking of? Bring him up immediately." She made her excuses to Sir John and moved eagerly towards the stairs.

Harvey coughed again and cleared his throat. "Excuse me, milady. There are two other gentlemen with his lordship. A Lord Kimbalton, I believe, and a Lord Monroyal. Shall I send them all upstairs, milady?"

Harriet stopped abruptly and turned to gaze at the impassive butler. "Kimbalton is here, too?" She felt all her gaiety drain out of her. If her husband was here, he must be furious with her. She could not doubt that he had already called at the Abbey and discovered her absence. Perhaps if she directed Harvey to bring him up to the ballroom, the earl would not make a scene in front of all these people, she reasoned. On the other hand, he must be travel-stained and weary; anxious for a chance to make himself presentable. She had better go down to welcome them and ask Mrs. Collins to get their rooms ready.

"I will go down, Harvey," she said shortly, turning again towards the stairs. Rooms, she thought apprehensively. What room could she put the earl in? She and her aunt had always occupied the twin bedrooms in the master suite, and Lady Sophronia had quite naturally returned to the chamber she considered her own upon their arrival from the Abbey. Would her husband expect to be installed there, as was his right? Harriet quailed at the thought. She could not, *would* not evict Aunt Sophy at this time of night. He could not expect that of her. Could he?

She arrived at the head of the stairway and paused to gather her courage. At least Peter would be there to support her, she thought gratefully. She had missed her brother, and the thought of seeing him again lifted her spirits so that her step was light as she made her way down the curving stair. And there they were, three tall, elegant men standing together, three pairs of eyes fixed upon her as she came down. Harriet looked straight at her brother, and he smiled at her, his infectious grin warming her chilled heart and causing her to forget her fear. She smiled at him, her most brilliant, spontaneous, thankful smile, and held out both arms, rushing a little unceremoniously down the last steps to find comfort and support in his familiar embrace.

"Peter!" she exclaimed, alarmed at the slight tremor in her voice. "What a wonderful surprise, love. I did not expect to see you."

She withdrew her arms from around the viscount's neck and found that he was grinning down at her, blatant admiration in his blue eyes. It also struck her rather forcibly that the warm greeting she had given her brother might well have been—perhaps *should* have been—directed at her husband.

"Gad, Harriet, my sweet," the viscount exclaimed loudly, "you are a sight for sore eyes." He held her away from him and ogled her shamelessly. "I declare, lass, I have never seen you looking so well. Giles here is struck dumb with admiration, and no wonder, love, you are quite ravishing."

At the mention of her husband's name, Harriet's smile faltered. "Must you always exaggerate, Peter?" she chided, patting his cheek affectionately. "You never learn, do you?"

And then, unable to ignore his presence any longer, Harriet turned to the earl, a polite smile glued to her lips. "Greetings, my lord," she said, offering her hand. For a dreadful moment, she feared he would ignore it, so when he did take it with both his, Harriet felt her fear give way to relief. The relief was short-lived, however, for after carrying her fingers to his lips, the earl did not release her hand, but stood gazing down at her with hooded eyes. "My lady," he replied with cold formality. "I trust I find you well."

The greeting was so innocuous and so far removed from what Harriet had expected from her lord that she was momentarily disconcerted. Then she noticed that the gray of his eyes had turned to dark slate, a sure sign of anger. Fear tightened her stomach again. So, he was biding his time, she thought, and not yet ready to vent that anger on her. Her smile became a shade less cool. If the wretch thought to intimidate her, she would not give him the satisfaction of knowing he had succeeded, Harriet decided, turning towards the third gentleman with a much warmer smile.

Harriet's smile paled somewhat when she looked into the Marquess of Monroyal's dark gray eyes. In that brief glimpse before he veiled them, Harriet saw a world of depravity mirrored there, and worse yet, a quite lecherous thought concerning her own person. But his smile when he raised her hand to his lips was utterly charming, and Harriet convinced herself that her mind was playing tricks on her.

"Robert Stilton at your service, my lady," the marquess said in a softly seductive voice that belied the formality of his words.

"You are welcome, my lord," Harriet replied coolly and withdrew her hand abruptly. "Harvey"—she turned to the hovering butler—"see that their lordships are made comfortable. In the West Wing," she added pointedly. "And then I hope you will join the festivities, my lords. Supper will be served in about an hour." She linked her arm through Peter's and steered him up the stairs. "You can show them, dear, since you know the way already." She was glad when the viscount took the hint and shepherded the gentlemen up to the third floor, casting a wicked wink at her over his shoulder as he followed them.

The addition of three handsome London gentlemen to the gathering—two of them eminently eligible—caused no little stir when the Viscount Bridgeport ushered them into the ballroom twenty minutes later. Harriet felt obliged to accompany the newly arrived guests around the room, making them known to her friends and neighbors. As they approached Sir James Rathbone, Harriet vastly enjoyed seeing the three Town Tulips momentarily awed out of their careless banter.

"Good God!" she distinctly heard the marquess mutter under his breath.

"I know," the viscount muttered back. "Disgusting, ain't it?"

"I can't believe this," the marquess whispered in Harriet's ear. "If you had wished to put us all in the shade, my lady, you might have done so less painfully. What can I do to compete with such perfection?"

"Nothing at all, I should say," Harriet replied prosaically, deriving no little amusement from the marquess's pained expression. "Sir James, you have already met Lord Kimbalton and my brother, I believe. Let me make Sir James Rathbone known to you, my lord," she murmured, addressing the marquess. "Sir James is a particular friend of ours."

Sir James inclined his glorious head at just the correct angle to acknowledge the marquess and then turned to his hostess. "The next dance is mine, I believe, Lady Harriet," he said gently, the warmth of his gaze betraying his feelings and causing Harriet to blush.

"The supper dance is promised to me," she heard her husband say brusquely, in a flat voice that brooked no argument. Harriet knew better than to make an issue out of it. She smiled warmly at the baronet.

"Perhaps the after-supper dance, then, my lady?" Sir James inquired, impervious to the earl's blatant attempt to cut him.

"That is promised to me, unless I am mistaken," the marquess put in with a malicious smile.

Harriet bristled. She might be willing to take orders from her husband, but she refused to be bullied by some lecherous stranger.

"I am afraid you are, my lord—mistaken, that is," she added sweetly. "I would be delighted to grant you the dance, Sir James." She smiled encouragingly at the bewildered young man.

"Touché, my dear," the marquess murmured as the baronet drifted off to join the Biddletons. "I like females who are not mealy-mouthed widgeons, afraid to say boo to the cat," he added, his gray eyes surveying her with lazy insolence.

Harriet took instant umbrage. "I am not your *dear,* sir," she said in a tightly controlled voice. "And your taste in females is of supreme indifference to me. But I will not permit my friends to be mocked by someone like *you.*" Harriet injected as much scorn as she could into these words, and was gratified to

see the marquess's face suddenly devoid of its habitual cynicism. "No doubt you find it amusing to come jaunting down
here from London and make fun of the locals, sir, but I find
nothing at all amusing in such execrable manners, and I do not
hesitate to tell you so."

"Harriet," the earl said sharply. "You are making a scene."

Harriet turned on him, her fury overriding caution. "And
that goes for you, too, my lord," she snapped. "You were indescribably rude to poor Sir James. I *had* promised him the supper dance. If you had really wanted it, you could have said so
in a civilized manner."

"Harriet, love—"

"But of course you did not," Harriet continued, as though
her brother had not spoken. "You merely wished to embarrass
poor Sir James. As though it were his fault that he is more
handsome than the three of you oafs put together."

"Harriet, listen to me—"

"And you," Harriet turned on her brother, her fury unabated.
"All you can do is stand around with a silly grin on your face?
I suppose you think this whole disgusting episode amusing . . ." Harriet paused to catch her breath and became aware
that she had indeed begun to attract the interested glances of
some of her guests. She also saw that the marquess was
strangely silent, and that her husband's face had turned to
granite, his eyes to gray ice.

She had disgraced herself utterly and forever. The devil fly
away with her tongue, she thought as the enormity of her unladylike outburst began to rise up to suffocate her. Not only had
she insulted her husband, but also his friend—a marquess no
less—and her own brother. She looked at Peter, a mute appeal
in her eyes.

He responded as she knew he would. "Come with me,
love," he said coaxingly, taking her by the elbow and leading
her away towards the refreshment room. "It seems to me that
after all that blather, you must need to wet your whistle, sweetheart. I never heard such a great to-do about nothing."

"It was *not* nothing, Peter," Harriet protested. "You all behaved like beasts to poor James."

"Perhaps," the viscount agreed. "But in case you had not
noticed, love, your poor Sir James came out with flying colors.
And furthermore, he gets to dance with you after supper.
Which is more than you can say for any of us."

"I shall not dance with that wretch," Harriet declared vehemently.

"I presume you mean Giles. Very well, sweet, I shall take you in to supper. How's that?"

"Thank you, Peter," Harriet murmured, thankful for her understanding brother. "I didn't mean what I said about you, you know."

"Oh, yes, you did, Harriet. And you were right, too."

"He will never forgive me."

"Giles? Of course he will. A hundred years from now, I'll wager he will not remember a thing you said, love."

Harriet gave a watery giggle. "I love you, Peter, but what am I to do in the meantime?"

The viscount grinned at her. "You'll muddle through, love. Never fear."

Harriet hoped that, for once, her brother might be right.

# CHAPTER SEVEN

# A Second Chance

Harriet never could recall how she got through the rest of the evening. Peter took her in to supper, but her husband and the marquess did not join them. Indeed, the earl paid no attention to her whatsoever, although Harriet sensed his eyes upon her, particularly when she granted Sir James his promised dance after supper. The baronet waltzed as he did everything else, to perfection, and as she glided round the room in his arms, Harriet was able to relax and forget the cloud hanging over her head. She was an accomplished dancer herself, and knew they made an attractive couple.

Lord Monroyal made no attempt to dance with her, for which Harriet was deeply grateful. Perhaps the man was not entirely lacking in sense after all, she thought, allowing herself to be led off the floor by the ever attentive Sir James. She scanned the room for a glimpse of her husband and discovered him listening with apparent fascination to the bright chatter of young Lady Rothingham. Harriet smiled faintly at the perversity of men. The lady in question was undoubtedly the kind of female who would appeal to any red-blooded man who was not past his dotage. Old Sir Henry Rothingham had been almost at that point in his life two years previously, when he had met the amply endowed, brazenly beautiful widow of a wealthy Brighton tradesman. Their marriage followed as a matter of course. Few had doubted that Sir Henry stood a lame dog's chance against the fulsome charms of the ambitious widow, and those who foolishly wagered to the contrary lost their money.

Harriet was roused from her reminiscences when the earl—who had refrained from dancing at all thus far—drew Lady Rothingham onto the dance floor to join a set forming for the country dance. For some inexplicable reason, the sight of her husband's dark head inclined to catch some witticism from the dashing blonde widow in her low-cut pink gown, which revealed far more than it covered, made Harriet's heart contract painfully. Lady Rothingham's tinkling laughter floated across the room, and Harriet flinched at the flirtatious note she heard in it.

"Anger suits you, my lady," a seductive voice drawled close to her ear, making Harriet jump. "It makes your lovely eyes sparkle, and brings a delicious color to those cheeks." The marquess gestured at the dance floor, where the earl had just come together with Lady Rothingham, the latter presenting a delightful demonstration of fluttering lashes and heaving bosom. "I would tremble to be in Montague's shoes tonight," he remarked. Then, apparently startled at what he had said, the marquess glanced at Harriet and grinned wryly. "What bouncers I do tell, my dear," he murmured sotto voce.

Harriet snorted in disgust and looked away, all too conscious of her flushed cheeks.

"I would not worry your lovely head about Montague," he said after a pause. "Buxom, simpering females are not his style at all."

"Lady Rothingham is very beautiful," Harriet heard herself say before she could stop.

The marquess laughed. "Oh, yes, if you like fulsome, fluttering females," he drawled. "Give the wench five more years and she will be a hag. Take my word for it. Whereas you, my dear Lady Harriet—"

"And *you,* my lord, have a knack for improper conversations," Harriet interrupted frostily. "Now if you will excuse me."

Harriet refrained from seeking out her husband for what remained of that dreadful evening, but at long last the moment she had dreaded arrived as the first guests began to take their leave. Thirty minutes later, Harriet's Christmas ball was definitely over and the doors of Lark Manor closed firmly behind the last stragglers. Harriet was infinitely grateful when her brother took the other two gentlemen into the library for a final drink, and she was able to escape upstairs with Aunt Sophy.

After Lucy had prepared her mistress for bed, Harriet sank down gratefully before the dresser to have her hair brushed. The events of the evening had left her tense, and her pulse raced with anxiety every time the image of her husband's icy gray eyes intruded upon her memory. What steps would the earl take to punish his wayward wife? she wondered, wishing for the umpteenth time that she had guarded her tongue more carefully. Harriet never doubted that he would demand retribution for her hoydenish display of ill manners. Most likely he would drag her back to the Abbey in disgrace. Perhaps even tomorrow morning. Christmas Day. No doubt he would enjoy cutting short her brief escape from his bleak ancestral residence, depriving her of the outdoor activities she had planned for the young sons and daughters of her neighbors who had missed the ball. Whatever it was, Harriet promised herself that she would accept her husband's demands without protest. Perhaps she could, in some small way, show him that she could be the dutiful wife he had expected her to be.

The abigail's practiced strokes lulled Harriet's battered nerves, and as the tension gradually slipped away, she began to feel that perhaps she might be able to sleep after all. Her eyes closed and the muscles in her neck and shoulders slowly relaxed, leaving her with a sensation of drowsiness. When the healing strokes stopped abruptly, Harriet protested.

"Don't stop yet, Lucy," she murmured sleepily.

"Milady." Something in the abigail's voice warned her, and Harriet's eyes flew open to find Lucy staring at the open door, the hairbrush suspended in midair.

Harriet did not need to turn her head to know who was standing there. She felt a rush of anxiety, and knew that the abigail's labors had been in vain. She was as nervous as a cat again.

"You may go, Lucy," she said with a calmness that surprised her. She took the brush from the abigail's fingers and watched the girl scurry from the room, her face pink with embarrassment.

Only then did Harriet raise her eyes to Lord Kimbalton's face.

So he was not going to wait until tomorrow, she thought, her mind racing with a strange mixture of fright and exhilaration at finding herself alone with a man in her bedchamber. She was to have a peel rung over her head now, in the middle of the night, without any warning, just when she was at her most vulnerable, burnt to a socket by the evening's fiasco. She might have guessed that the earl would not resist the opportunity to give her a monumental set-down for addressing him in terms that no self-respecting, dutiful wife would dream of using to her lord and master. It was all her own stupid fault, she told herself, and the sooner he said whatever it was he intended to say, the sooner this quite dreadful scene would be over, and she could go to bed.

"You wished to speak to me, my lord?" Harriet was mortified at the faint tremor she heard in her voice.

He said nothing, but Harriet was appalled at the cynical little smile that played briefly over his lips. This was going to be far worse than she had anticipated. Her husband was not going to let her off with a severe trimming; he would probably wish to punish her most horribly for defying him. Harriet gritted her teeth. Whatever happened, Harriet vowed stubbornly, she would behave like a lady; she would be the sensible, practical, dutiful wife she had promised to be. Nothing the earl could say or do would provoke her into an immodest display of temper ever again.

Harriet was beginning to feel she just might brush through the approaching scene with her dignity intact, when she noticed that her husband's eyes had turned dark again, and glittered with an odd intensity which threatened to shatter her fragile self-control. Was he angry enough to beat her? she wondered, her mouth suddenly dry with fear.

"Are you going to beat me, my lord?" Harriet had intended to sound contemptuous and unafraid, but the quaver in her voice gave her away.

A swift look of astonishment crossed the earl's face, and then he laughed harshly. "It had not occurred to me to do so," he drawled. "But perhaps I should. No doubt I would find it immensely pleasurable, my dear."

The hint of wickedness in his voice alarmed her anew. "Then what *are* you here for, my lord?" Harriet's words had scarcely left her mouth when a terrible thought fluttered at the back of her mind. It was then that she noticed the earl's state of undress, and she froze. How she had failed to see that her husband was in his shirtsleeves and had cast off his elegantly knotted cravat, Harriet could not imagine. She shivered and turned to gaze into the beveled glass over the dresser. Of course, she thought dully. What better way of putting a rebellious wife in her place than to subject her to that ultimately humiliating ordeal of the marriage bed.

Harriet had known, of course, that sooner or later it was bound to happen. She was not a complete flat, but although she had a pretty fair notion of the basic contortions involved in coupling, the exact details of the intimate marital ritual had never been exactly clear to her. On the day before her marriage to the earl, Lady Sophronia had taken it upon herself—in the lamentable absence of Harriet's mother, who would normally have instructed her daughter on what to expect on her wedding night—to acquaint her niece with the mysteries of conjugal bliss. Since she had never entered the married state herself, Aunt Sophy's account had depended largely on hearsay and on her own vivid imagination.

Accordingly, Harriet's notions of correct wifely behavior in bed consisted of a curious mixture of resignation, revulsion, and regal indifference. She should offer no resistance whatsoever, her aunt had insisted stringently. Gentlemen reportedly did not take kindly to being thwarted while in the throes of their animalistic impulses. Aunt Sophy had never explained—although Harriet had repeatedly requested further clarification—exactly what such impulses were, and what gentlemen did while in the throes of them. When pressed for details, the severely embarrassed lady had thrown up her hands and advised Harriet not to dwell overmuch on the inevitable, but to close her eyes and fix her mind on something pleasant. Such as roses, she suggested. Think of roses and leave the details to the gentleman, who would doubtless know how to take care of things.

"Cannot you guess what brings me, Harriet?" she heard her husband murmur as he strolled across the room to stand behind her, his amused gaze meeting hers in the mirror. Harriet could not suppress a shudder, and instantly the earl's hands were on her shoulders, gripping them gently.

Harriet watched in morbid fascination as her husband's fingers massaged her shoulders. It was not unpleasant, she realized, but what was this sudden touching a prelude to?

"You are tense, my dear," he murmured softly. "You are not frightened of me, are you, Harriet?"

She smiled faintly. "You have said you are not here to beat me, my lord," she replied coolly. "So why should I be afraid?"

"You are, nevertheless," he replied. "But you have no need to be, my dear. I am not a monster. And I have brought you this from London." He placed a small jeweler's box on the dresser in front of her.

Aunt Sophy had warned her that men bearing gifts were the most dangerous. Invariably they wanted something in return, more often than not something highly immoral. She stared down at the box as though it contained a nest of adders.

The earl flicked open the box to reveal a small, beautifully engraved wedding band. He picked it up and reached for her left hand. "I noticed you are not wearing a wedding ring, Harriet," he remarked, slipping the gold band on her third finger.

"Your grandmother's ring kept slipping off," Harriet explained, intrigued at the warmth of his fingers. "I was afraid to lose it, so I left it at the Abbey."

"Does this one please you better?"

"Oh, yes," she whispered. "It is beautiful, my lord."

"My name is Giles."

Harriet glanced up at his image in the mirror. "Giles," she repeated hesitantly. "Thank you for remembering."

Suddenly Harriet felt his hand in her hair, lifting the heavy curls and letting them slither through his fingers. She closed her eyes and sat perfectly still, wondering how she could put a stop to this intrusion without appearing to repulse him. Before she could act, she felt the warm touch of his fingers on her chin, her face was lifted and a light kiss feathered on her lips. "You are welcome, my dear," he whispered against her mouth, and then his hand cupped her face and he kissed her again, more deeply this time, and Harriet felt the first tremor of fear curl up inside her. And then he opened his mouth over hers, and Harriet was shocked at the hot wetness of his tongue against her closed lips.

*Offer no resistance whatsoever.* Her aunt's words rang in her head as the earl's tongue traced the crevice of her lips, apparently seeking entry. The notion was so foreign to her that Harriet could not suppress a murmur of protest, which caused the earl's fingers to twine more firmly into her hair and his other hand to slip down her neck to the lace frill of her robe. Before she could divine his intention, his hand had gently captured her breast. Harriet jumped in shock, wondering how she was supposed to remain passive under the onslaught of emotions that the earl's kiss and touch had unleased in her.

"Easy, lass," the earl murmured softly, but Harriet scarcely heard him. Her entire attention was focused on the enveloping warmth of his hand on her breast. She held her breath as the pressure shifted into a massaging motion, gently circling her nipple in a slow, infinitely disturbing caress. The resulting sensation was like nothing she had ever experienced before, both wickedly sinful and delightfully relaxing at the same time. It seemed to Harriet, in her heightened state of awareness, that the earl's hand was actually touching her bare skin. The double layer of fragile silk that covered her seemed to conserve the heat of her husband's touch, and Harriet unexpectedly found her whole body glowing with excitement and an odd sense of anticipation.

Suddenly the warmth decreased, and Harriet felt the earl fumbling at the closing of her robe. He slipped his hand inside and cupped her breast again. The renewed contact made her shudder and she gasped. Instantly her mouth was invaded in the most intimate way, and Harriet went rigid. The earl's tongue was actually inside her mouth she realized, distraught at the indignity of such unseemly behavior. She could feel it quite distinctly running over her tightly clenched teeth. The faint taste of brandy was unmistakable.

Both hands came up instinctively to push him away, and Harriet twisted her head to escape his questing tongue. But his fingers in her hair held her firmly in place, while she felt him become more insistent in his attempt to breach the barrier of her teeth. Harriet moaned softly in alarm, hoping that her husband would sense her distress and release her, but the sound appeared to trigger quite the opposite reaction. Harriet felt herself pulled to her feet, the earl's hands grasping her firmly by the shoulders, his mouth still in possession of hers. Before she realized what he was about, Harriet felt her robe pushed from her shoulders and slither to the floor. Then his fingers were groping at the tiny buttons on her night-rail, and Harriet froze. What was he doing? she wondered, too terrified to accept the answer that rose immediately to mind. He could not really mean to strip her of all her clothes, could he? The notion appalled her. She grasped the momentary distraction of his hands to pull away from him, her fingers flying protectively to the half-open neck of her gown.

"What are you doing?" she whispered, her heart beating uncomfortably. Her husband's eyes were dark gray again, the darkest Harriet had ever seen them. So it was not just anger that affected their color, she thought irrationally. Passion evidently did so, too. Could it be that her husband was in the throes of one of those animalistic impulses Aunt Sophy had mentioned? Harriet hoped desperately that she was mistaken, but the earl's eyes were glittering strangely, and his breathing was uneven. He stood perfectly still, staring at her as if he were giving considerable thought to her question.

Then he laughed and the sound, though neither loud nor harsh, grated on Harriet's already exacerbated nerves and chilled her to the bone.

"I would think that must be pretty obvious, my dear wife," he drawled, that cynical smile Harriet disliked so much flitting across his mouth. "I was about to remove your clothes."

His booted feet were set slightly apart on the pale green Axminster carpet, and as Harriet watched, a knot of apprehension twisting her stomach, he rocked on his heels and laughed again. Harriet thought she had never encountered a more terrifying sight. His face hardened into that familiar frown she knew so well, and his whole face was set and hard as if carved from granite.

"You cannot be serious, my lord," she heard herself say in a tremulous voice quite unlike her own.

The earl smiled, but Harriet saw no humor in his hooded eyes. "Have you never heard of a husband's conjugal rights, Harriet?"

Harriet flinched at the crudeness of the scene and dropped her gaze. "Of course, my lord," she murmured primly, furious that such a simple answer could draw the telltale color to her cheeks.

"Very well, then. I assume you are also aware of what goes on in the marriage bed. Am I right?" he insisted, when Harriet could find no words to answer such a mortifying question.

She struggled to swallow the lump that had suddenly formed in her throat. "No, my lord," she confessed truthfully. But when she saw the frown settle firmly on his brow, she hastened to add, "I mean yes. Aunt Sophy explained it all to me." This was nowhere near the truth, of course, but by that time Harriet merely wished to avoid the earl's wrath at any cost.

He looked at her oddly for a moment, and then held out his right hand imperiously. "Then come over here," he said in a gentler voice. "You have nothing to fear from me."

That was certainly a bouncer if ever she had heard one, Harriet thought, clutching her open gown with fingers that she willed not to tremble. He was about to inflict unspeakable humiliation upon her, and she was not supposed to care? It was only on the rarest occasions that Harriet had seen herself unclothed, modesty precluding such indecorous actions as examining her naked form in the pier glass. As a child she had indeed done so, fascinated by the budding growth on her chest, but Aunt Sophy had come upon her one afternoon and inflicted a punishment so severe that Harriet had learned her lesson. Ladies did not, and never should take the least interest in

their bodies. If she persisted in such low-bred behavior, her
aunt warned her, she would grow warts on her nose.

"You cannot mean to . . . to do so," she stammered, unable
to name the deed he had threatened.

"Indeed I do," he said, his voice sounding implacable to her
tortured senses. Harriet stared at the earl, her panic rising.
What dignity would she have left, she wondered, if she allowed herself to be treated to this unspeakable horror? Whom
did the wretch think he was talking to? A slut from the streets?
One of his scarlet women? His London mistress, perhaps?

The memory of her husband's mystery woman gave Harriet
pause for thought. What nameless indignities did that unfortunate female have to endure from the man who paid all her
bills, and no doubt showered her with expensive baubles and
geegaws? Harriet wondered, glancing down at the wedding
ring he had so recently placed on her finger. As his wife, she
had imagined herself entitled to a certain amount of consideration, but what if this were not so? In truth, Harriet did not
know. She had assumed that as mistress of Kimbalton Abbey
her position carried with it certain guarantees of respect. But
what if she were mistaken? What if the earl intended to use
her, as she imagined he used his mistress, to pacify his animalistic impulses?

She would not put up with such depravity, Harriet decided
quite suddenly, lifting her small chin defiantly. Surely she had
the right to refuse to behave like Haymarket ware, she told
herself, not entirely sure what the term meant, but certain that
it referred to women of ill-repute.

"No, my lord," she said, gazing at him steadily, although
her heart was beating painfully.

"No?" he repeated curiously. "No what, my dear?"

"No, I will not be party to a vulgar display, my lord," Harriet explained, wondering where she could have found the
courage to defy him. To avoid seeing the inevitable displeasure reflected on his face, Harriet picked up her robe and
slipped into it, pulling the sash tightly about her as if the frail
garment provided a small degree of protection.

"I see," she heard him say with a hint of cynical amusement
in his voice. "You are defying me, I gather?" The voice was
silky, but Harriet detected the underlying ruthlessness of steel.

"Oh, no, my lord," she answered quickly, terrified at her
own temerity. "I meant no such thing. I merely wish to remind

you that I am your wife, not some poor creature you may insult when it pleases you."

"I have insulted you, Harriet?" He sounded surprised, but Harriet was not to be so taken in.

"Yes, my lord. You propose to treat me like a whore." Harriet blushed at her audacity in using a word she had never in her life thought to utter, but she continued defiantly. "And that I cannot permit, my lord. Surely I deserve better than that from you?"

He stared at her for so long that Harriet grew nervous. His gaze lingered on her lips, and then traveled down her form until she was made to feel as uncovered as though he had indeed removed her clothing. Had she convinced him? she wondered. Or would he merely think her conduct contentious and unseemly for a wife?

Finally, he seemed to come to a decision. "Perhaps you are right, my lady," he said rather formally. "We will continue this discussion at Kimbalton Abbey. Be prepared to leave tomorrow morning."

"Tomorrow, my lord?" she was startled into repeating. "But that is Christmas Day."

"Yes," he said abruptly. "And I want no argument on this, Harriet. We leave tomorrow." Without another word, he turned and left the room, closing the door sharply behind him.

When Giles got back to his bedchamber, he went straight to bed, but sleep eluded him. It had all seemed so simple when he had made that sudden decision to visit his wife's bed. He was pleasantly relaxed after drinking a glass of brandy in the library with Monroyal and Egerton, and the sharp edge of his anger at Harriet's hoydenish behavior had softened considerably by the time his valet had removed his evening coat and laid out his night raiment. In truth, Giles remembered wryly, he had felt unusually mellow, although the necessity of occupying a guest chamber instead of the master suite still rankled.

And then, out of nowhere, had come the brilliant notion that tonight would be an excellent time to visit his wife's bed. At least it had appeared brilliant at the time. He would have to do his duty by her sooner or later, he told himself firmly. And tonight Harriet had looked quite lovely in her festive red gown, with that honey gold hair curling seductively against the delicate column of her neck. But it was the fashionably low décolletage that had drawn his eyes to the exposed mounds of her breasts, and quite suddenly his hands had itched to touch them.

But he had not touched his wife all evening, Giles remembered. She had made him quite furiously angry with her outspoken criticism of him and his friends. So he had refused even to dance with Harriet, and had endured with outward indifference the sight of her in the arms of that puppy Rathbone, who obviously still harbored tender thoughts for her. But she was his, he thought with considerable satisfaction, and it was high time he reminded her of that fact.

After dismissing his valet and pulling off his cravat, Giles had gone in search of his wife's room. Harriet had been having her hair brushed when he opened the door, and the sight of that mass of honey-colored curls had delighted him. When he finally did touch her, Giles had been charmed at the way her breast fit into the palm of his hand. The firm fullness of her stirred his blood, and he was suddenly confident that the seduction of his virgin bride would prove to be less troublesome than he had feared.

He was wrong, of course.

Although Harriet submitted relatively tamely to his kiss, she had taken instant exception to the removal of her night-rail. In fact, she actually accused him of treating her like a whore. The notion that this might be even partially true appalled Giles, who had always prided himself on his breeding and self-control. Perhaps he had been rather too eager to claim what was his, he thought wryly, turning over and settling himself in a more comfortable position. But what disturbed him the most was that Harriet's accusation—unfounded as it naturally was—had deprived him of any desire to pursue the seduction. Quite simply, he had lost the impetus which had brought him to his wife's chamber in the first place.

The sudden and quite unexpected fizzling of his desire had disturbed him more than he cared to admit. To cover his embarrassment, he had struck back automatically, confident that once back at Kimbalton Abbey, his prowess would reassert itself.

With this comforting thought, Giles had finally fallen asleep. But he awakened the next morning with the nagging realization that he had acted too harshly in demanding that Harriet accompany him home to the Abbey immediately. After all, he could hardly blame her for his own incompetence, could he? Giles cringed at the word. It was not a matter of incompetence or inability, he told himself firmly. He had been perfectly able to bed his wife, but had been momentarily disconcerted by Harriet's demand for his respect. Well, Giles thought as he submitted to his valet's razor, he certainly did respect her. There was no question about that. He would tell her so this morning, he decided, and temporarily cancel his plans to return to the Abbey.

Filled with these good intentions, Giles sauntered down to the breakfast room. He had barely finished a healthy serving of York ham with bacon and coddled eggs, when the old butler shuffled in and cleared his throat.

"What is it, Harvey?" the earl inquired.

"Begging your pardon, milord, but her ladyship is wishful of having speech with your lordship after breakfast, if convenient, naturally. Her ladyship is in the library, milord." Without waiting for a reply, the cantankerous old retainer turned and shuffled out of the room.

When Giles entered the library several minutes later, he found Harriet standing by the window, nervously tapping her riding crop against the skirt of her deep green riding habit. She turned at the sound of his entrance, and Giles noticed that her cheeks were flushed a delightful shade of pink.

"What may I do for you, my dear?" he inquired pleasantly.

"I would like to entreat you, my lord," she began in a faintly agitated voice.

Giles held up a restraining hand. "There is no need to entreat me to do anything, my dear," he assured her. "I am only too happy to delay our departure until a time more suitable for you. I cannot imagine what inspired me to think of traveling on Christmas Day."

"You were angry, my lord," she pointed out quietly.

"I was?" Giles would much rather allow last night's embarrassing episode to fade into the past, but his wife seemed to have a tiresome penchant for speaking her mind. "Now why would I be angry?" he drawled in a bored voice, hoping that his wife would take the hint and let the subject die.

Harriet slanted her eyes at him. "I cannot believe that you have forgotten what you did last night, my lord."

No, he had not forgotten, he thought wryly. How could he forget—not so much what he did, but what he was unable to do? For the first time in his life, Giles Montague had walked away from a lady's bedchamber unfulfilled.

His silence must have made her uneasy, for Harriet continued in her alarmingly forthright fashion.

"You had every right to be furious with me. I behaved abominably, my lord, as you must know. I wish to beg your forgiveness, and to assure you that, in spite of what you may think, I am very mindful of my duty."

Giles began to relax. Perhaps Lady Harriet would turn out to be precisely the wife he needed after all, he thought. Sensible, practical, and above all dutiful. He was charmed by the fresh wave of color that mantled her cheeks, and was about to tell her so, when she continued in a rush.

"I promise faithfully never to be so missish again, my lord. Aunt Sophy warned me how it would be, but my wretched tongue ran away with me." She paused, and Giles had the uncomfortable impression that Harriet believed herself to be responsible for his own flawed performance of the evening before.

"If I swear to behave more decorously in future, my lord, would you forgive me for last night?"

Giles groaned inwardly. It was as he had feared. The chit blamed herself for their truncated encounter. What would be her reaction, he wondered idly, if he were to confess . . . but that was impossible. He refused to admit it. Perhaps he had been in his cups, and that was why he couldn't . . .

She was regarding him with anxious hazel eyes, and Giles dragged his thoughts away from the notion that had plagued him since last night.

He smiled, "Of course you are forgiven, my dear Harriet. Do not give it another thought."

Harriet smiled tentatively, but she was not finished yet, he saw with a feeling of dread.

"Thank you, my lord. Does that mean you will give me a second chance?"

The implications of that innocent question rocked Giles back on his heels. Was the chit actually suggesting . . . ? No, that could not be. No delicately raised female would dare suggest anything so blatantly inviting. Would she? Of course, Harriet was like no other decent female he had ever met, so perhaps . . .

"Are you inviting me to your bed tonight, my dear?" he murmured softly, conscious of the stirrings of desire.

His wife's face reflected a riot of emotions. She paled noticeably. "I see you are determined to humiliate me, my lord," she replied in a cool, tight voice. "Very well, there is nothing more to say. I shall go upstairs to pack." She turned and almost ran towards the door, but Giles was there before her, his arm barring her escape.

The impetus of her flight threw Harriet against Giles's chest, but before he could react, she had pushed herself away and stood glaring at him, her eyes shining with unshed tears. Giles was strangely touched.

"Forgive me, Harriet," he murmured, instantly contrite. "That was crude of me. And of course, you may have as many second chances as you wish." He smiled faintly into her gold-flecked eyes, which he suddenly noticed were quite beautiful. "If that makes any sense," he added wryly.

When she made no response, Giles swung open the door and watched her hurry away, leaving the faint scent of summer roses behind her.

# CHAPTER EIGHT

# The Black Sheep

Harriet went straight up to her aunt's room after her interview with the earl. She sought—as she had so many times in her childhood—the comfort and serenity of Aunt Sophy's understanding heart. Lady Sophronia took one look at her distraught niece and dismissed her abigail.

"Whatever has happened to send you into high fidgets, love?" she inquired mildly, patting the place beside her on the settee. "Do not tell me that Lord Kimbalton has refused your request to remain at Lark Manor until tomorrow?"

Harriet sank down gratefully, accepting the lace handkerchief her aunt put into her hands and blowing her nose soundly. "He is a heartless rogue," she exclaimed as soon as she had controlled her rage. "Oh, I hate him!"

"There, there, my love." Aunt Sophy put a comforting arm around her niece's trembling shoulders. "Do not fly into one of your rages, dear. I gather his lordship is determined to leave today for the Abbey?"

"No, he is *not*," Harriet replied wrathfully. "He has changed his mind. Oh, Auntie," she wailed, fighting the urge to throw a tantrum. "He is truly odious."

"What have you done to arouse his ire, Harriet?" her aunt demanded, with what Harriet considered a deplorable lack of feeling. "I warned you to watch your tongue, dear. Men do not like females to defy them."

"I did not defy him," Harriet burst out. "Well, perhaps a little. But he behaved abominably, Aunt. Am I expected to keep a rein on my tongue when the wretch insults me?"

"Insult you, dear? Are you sure you did not misunderstand his lordship's intentions, Harriet? You are so prone to jump to conclusions, you know. I wouldn't wonder if you had misjudged him."

Harriet snorted in disgust. "I did not misunderstand anything, Aunt," she replied between gritted teeth. "He came to my chamber last night," she added after a moment's hesitation, "and we had a terrible set-to. But it was not my fault. He was simply too odious to bear."

Her aunt was silent for several minutes. Then she cleared her throat and squeezed Harriet's clenched hands in hers. "I warned you that men can be very unfeeling at times, dear. A wife's duty is to make the best of it, child." She sighed gustily. "I know it must be hard for you to accept. It was hard for me, too, I must admit. That is why I never married. The whole business of the marriage bed is enough to send a decent female into a fit of the vapors."

Harriet was distracted by her aunt's unusual candor. "You never felt the desire for a family of your own, Aunt?"

"Naturally, I dreamed of having children of my own, love. But the process a female has to endure to become a mother is altogether too humiliating to consider."

"You have no regrets at all?" Harriet wanted to know. "You never fell in love with any of your suitors, Aunt?"

Her aunt smiled fondly at her. "I rather fancied the Marquess of Portland at one time, my dear. But I was painfully shy as a girl, and all he wanted was to get me alone in the shrubbery. Believe me, child, the one time he succeeded cured me of ever wanting to marry anyone. The man turned into an octopus."

Harriet giggled. Her aunt's account of her aborted relationship with the Marquess of Portland reminded her forcefully of the heated kiss her husband had stolen from her the night before. She had been shocked by the intensity of the embrace, it was true, never having experienced passion before, but Harriet had not found the kiss unpleasant enough to swear off kissing forever. In fact, now that she had had time to reflect upon the incident, she felt a faintly morbid curiosity about the culmination of such intimacies. What might have happened had she not pulled away? she wondered. What if she had allowed her husband to remove her night-rail? The very thought sent alarming shock waves through her body, and Harriet pushed the indecent notion out of her mind. Since she would never permit herself to be subjected to such vulgarities, it was pointless to dwell on it, she told herself firmly.

But much to her chagrin, dwell on it she did. And when it came time to accompany her aunt down to the dining room for nuncheon, Harriet was uncomfortably aware that the amorous interlude with her husband had altered her perception of gentlemen in drastic ways.

The three gentlemen were already assembled when Harriet entered the dining room with Lady Sophronia, and it took all of her fortitude to remain calm in the presence of so much latent masculinity. She steadfastly refused to look at the earl, but could not—in all politeness—ignore the remarks addressed to her by the marquess and her brother.

She thought, listening with half an ear as the viscount recounted a witty tale from his recent sojourn in Paris, could it be possible that Peter, her handsome, whimsical, amusing brother, behaved as lasciviously with unknown females as Lord Kimbalton had with her? She had difficultly believing that of him, at least it had never occurred to her to imagine what Peter did with other females. Now, as Harriet observed his blue eyes dancing with merriment, and his well-shaped mouth stretched into a thoroughly engaging smile, she suddenly saw her brother through wiser eyes. Women must surely find him attractive, she thought. Yes, undoubtedly they would. How many of them had fallen in love with his careless good looks? she wondered. How many had allowed him the kind of liberties Giles had taken with her last night?

At that moment the marquess asked her a question about the further changes she planned to make in her new home, and for the first time, Harriet actually looked at him. Yes, he was indeed a handsome rogue, she had to admit, surprised that she had failed to notice the fact sooner. His eyes were a deep slate gray, very like her husband's, but unlike the earl's, Lord Monroyal's were full of promises of sensual delights that he did nothing to hide. If her husband had ever looked at her as the marquess was doing this very instant, Harriet thought, feeling her cheeks glow, she would have refused his offer. It was extremely unsettling to be the object of a gentlemen's examination, particularly a gentleman as worldly-wise as the marquess. And although she knew she should not be doing so, Harriet was beguiled into speculations about what it might be like to be kissed by such a man.

The thought brought a deeper blush to her cheeks, and she was mortified to see the marquess's smile broaden, as if he had read her immodest thoughts.

Resolutely, she turned away only to encounter another pair of gray eyes regarding her intently. The echo of her husband's words from that morning came flooding back, causing her to lower her gaze in confusion. Would he come to her again that night? she wondered. Had he actually believed that she was inviting his return? Upon reflection, Harriet admitted that her question about the second chance had been ambiguous, but she had certainly not intended to suggest . . .

Or had she? No, that was impossible, she tried to tell herself, but the nagging doubt remained. Had she wished—deep in her secret heart—to repeat that intimate scene with her husband?

As it happened, Harriet's anxiety about the earl's intentions was resolved early that afternoon, when a groom arrived on a lathered horse from Kimbalton Abbey with an urgent message for his lordship.

"I regret leaving on such short notice, Harriet," the earl explained when he sought her out in the small conservatory adjoining the house. "But my presence is required immediately, and I would like to take Greybeard, if you have no objection. He will get me to the Abbey in good time." He was already wearing his greatcoat and riding gloves, and Harriet saw that he was impatient to be gone.

"Of course, you may take Greybeard, my lord," Harriet replied instantly. "I trust that nothing is seriously amiss at the Abbey." She paused for a moment, then added uncertainly, "Would you prefer me to go with you?"

She saw him hesitate before he spoke, and when he did so, his voice was cool and remote. "Nothing is amiss at the Abbey. I am called to London."

When he did not elaborate, Harriet's heart sank. He was going to see *her*, she thought resentfully. Perhaps that London whore merely wished to show the power she could exert over another woman's husband.

"I see," Harriet replied with equal coolness. She turned her back on him and continued to snip dead leaves for an ailing aspidistra, although she scarcely realized what she was doing. The vicious motion of the secateurs felt very satisfying, and Harriet wished she might deal with the earl as summarily.

"I wish you a safe journey, my lord," she added dismissively.

Harriet snipped a perfectly healthy leaf from the aspidistra and hoped that her husband would understand that she cared not a fig whether he stayed or left. In fact, given her present agitated state, she would prefer that he go and leave her alone. Obviously, he considered the summons from his London mis-

tress—for who else could it be?—far more important than
spending Christmas with his wife. So the devil might fly away
with him for all she cared.

She felt his silent presence behind her, but refused to relent.
After a few moments, his footsteps retreated and the door to
the conservatory closed behind him. Harriet heaved a sigh of
relief and gazed ruefully at the mutilated plant.

"I do beg your pardon," she said to the aspidistra, placing it
in a more convenient location where it would benefit from the
weak winter sunlight.

She felt an odd affinity for the straggly plant. Harriet knew
precisely how it felt to have an outside force exercise such
wanton destruction on her self-esteem and dignity. To be
routed by a London fancy woman had a very dampening effect
upon her spirits, she admitted morosely. But then, why should
she care if her husband found her so plain and unattractive that
he could not wait to get back to London? She had known
about the mistress when she accepted the arrangement Lord
Kimbalton had offered, had she not? She would just have to
channel her energies into keeping her end of the bargain, in
becoming the practical, sensible, dutiful wife she had
promised to be. She would show that ungrateful wretch just
how much he needed her to run her precious Abbey.

Feeling considerably revived, Harriet went into her private
sitting room and sat down at the spindle-legged escritoire. She
would write out an exhaustive list of the plants, bushes, and
seeds she would need for spring planting at the Abbey. The
thought of tearing up further portions of her lord's revered
park and planting more rose-trees gave Harriet a great deal of
perverse satisfaction.

Two weeks later, the Countess of Kimbalton and her aunt
were reinstalled in the Abbey, but not before Harriet had
learned a disturbing truth about her absent husband.

"You must not be so hard on Giles, love," the viscount had
told her as the two descended to the drawing room on the
evening of the earl's sudden departure.

"And why on earth not?" Harriet responded angrily. She
had made some caustic remark about the brevity of her husband's visit and the perversity of men in general, when Peter
had unexpectedly come to the defense of his friend.

"I can accept that his lordship finds the company in London
more stimulating than here in the country," Harriet continued

with deliberate sarcasm, "but I do think he might have shown a little consideration for me and his guests. And I cannot say that I appreciate having to play second fiddle to his fancy piece on Christmas Day."

She spoke with such vehemence that the viscount glanced at her curiously. "Is that what you believe, Harriet? That Giles has gone waltzing off to London on a whim, because he is bored here?"

"What else am I to believe?" Harriet snapped, cross beyond reason that her brother did not seem to sympathize with her plight. "He did not explain anything to me, merely announcing, in that autocratic way of his, that he had been called to London. Called to London, indeed," she spat contemptuously. "What kind of a flat does he take me for, pray?"

"Well, you are wrong on all counts, my pet," the viscount replied seriously. "Giles does not take you for a flat at all. On the contrary, he is delighted that you are not some simpering halfwit forever hanging on his sleeve. And as for the other"—he paused and glanced at her wryly—"you do not know Giles at all if you believe him capable of such rudeness. The truth is that he feels a deep responsibility for all those dependent on him, and it so happens that his . . . his fancy piece, as you call her, has not been well for some time now. That is why he was so late getting down to the Abbey for Christmas. He usually comes down by the middle of December, but he was reluctant to leave Town because he wanted to be sure that . . . that she got the best care. Apparently, she had a relapse, and the physician sent for him. So you wrong him if you imagine Giles left because he was bored, my pet."

Harriet was only partially mollified by this explanation. There were so many imponderables concerning the mystery lady in London that, for some reason she could not understand, Harriet was beset by the desire to know more about her.

"Is she very beautiful?" she asked as they entered the drawing room together. Her brother glanced at her uneasily.

"Yes," he said shortly.

"What does she look like?" Harriet insisted.

"Giles would have my liver if he knew I so much as mentioned her to you, Harry. So do not plague me with questions, there's a love."

"You know her then?" Harriet insisted.

"Of course, I know her, you twit. I introduced them four years ago."

"What is her name?"

"Oh, no you don't, lass," the viscount replied with a laugh. "I shall say no more, except that she is not what you think, and she . . ." He paused abruptly. "No, I'll say no more, Harry, so do not pester me."

If her brother had thought to ease her mind about Lord Kimbalton's absence, he failed miserably, Harriet thought wryly two weeks after that frustrating conversation. She had accepted the viscount's escort back to the Abbey, where he stayed only long enough to change his horses before continuing on to London. The Marquess of Monroyal had taken his leave a week earlier, pleading the obligation to spend the New Year with his parents in Devon. Harriet did not believe a word of this glib excuse, but was glad to see the last of a gentleman she distrusted so intensely.

Thinking she was well rid of intrusive gentlemen for several months, Harriet began to relax and gradually came to enjoy her new role as chatelaine of the Montague ancestral pile. In spite of her initial reaction, she soon discovered any number of truly charming aspects of the Abbey. As the weeks went by and the efforts of the two ladies to turn a national monument into a home became more noticeable, Harriet developed a sense of pride in the history of the house to which she now belonged. Not that she approved of all the weaponry and battle trophies displayed so arrogantly on the immense walls of the Great Hall, naturally. She was too peace-loving to bask in the reflected glory of those symbols of pain and death. But after she had ordered them all removed to be washed and polished—a monumental undertaking that required the hiring of extra help from the village—and the stone walls whitewashed to eliminate centuries of grime, she took to receiving the more noteworthy of her visitors there in regal state.

One afternoon in early April, Harriet returned from an invigorating gallop on Greybeard—who had carried his lordship to the Abbey over three months ago—to be informed by a taciturn Carruthers that a gentleman awaited her in the Great Hall.

"The Great Hall?" she repeated curiously. "You should have put him in the Yellow Saloon, Carruthers."

"The gentleman insisted on the Great Hall, milady," the butler replied through thin lips, an indication, as Harriet had discovered early in their acquaintance, of intense disapproval.

For a disturbing moment, Harriet imagined that her husband had come back home again, but then she realized that Lord

Kimbalton was master here and would hardly be kicking his heels in the Great Hall waiting for his wife.

"Bring up some refreshments, if you please, Carruthers," she said absently, too taken aback to her own sudden desire to see her husband again to think coherently. "And some hot tea for me."

After surrendering her saucy green beaver and gloves to the butler, Harriet made her way to the Great Hall. The sight of the man standing with his back towards her, idly kicking the fire with his gleaming Hessians, made her heart leap into her throat. It was only when he turned at the sound of her approach, that Harriet saw that it was not Giles at all, but a younger, slenderer, more handsome version of her husband.

She paused, momentarily surprised at the likeness. Then she advanced, her hand outstretched in welcome.

"You cannot be anyone but a Montague, sir," she said pleasantly, a smile of welcome on her lips. "Giles has yet to introduce me to all his family. But you are certainly welcome."

The stranger took her hand and raised it politely, but Harriet had the distinct impression that he did so reluctantly.

"Captain Richard Montague at your service, milady," he said stiffly, stepping back as though he wanted no further contact with her.

It was then that Harriet realized that the captain still wore his regimentals, somewhat the worse for wear, and that his left arm hung in a sling.

She smiled encouragingly and motioned him to be seated, an invitation he blatantly ignored in favor of a position before the fire. His eyes were more blue than gray, Harriet noticed, but the coldness was the same she had seen in her husband's. She imagined that they might well appear gray when the captain was angry, and if one could judge by the thin line of his lips, Captain Montague was in a fair way to becoming angry.

Harriet decided to ignore her visitor's rudeness.

"Lord Kimbalton did not mention that he had a relative in the military, Captain," she remarked, hoping to draw the visitor out.

"That does not surprise me," Captain Montague drawled in a voice perilously close to a sneer. "And it's Lord Kimbalton now, of course, ever since that fool Brian stuck his spoon in the wall. I can well imagine that old Giles is taking himself as seriously as ever, self-righteous blighter that he is."

Unable to determine whether the captain's remark was intended as a statement or a question, Harriet opted for the latter. "His lordship seems to be very attached to his home," she said noncommittally.

The captain gave a snort of disgust which put Harriet's back up. "He always did think more of his famous family tradition than he did of his family." He paused, as if struck by Harriet's presence. "And who are you?" he demanded rudely. "Some poor cousin or other he has brought in to take care of the place while he cavorts in London with that high-priced ladybird of his?"

Harriet gasped. She was accustomed to plain speaking but this was the outside of enough. She rose majestically to her full five feet four inches, conscious that she was pale with fury. "I am the Countess of Kimbalton, mistress of this house," she said icily. "And if you cannot keep a civil tongue in your head, I will ask you to leave."

The captain had the grace to blush. He looked at her with a mixture of chagrin and reluctant admiration. "That was unpardonably rude and uncouth of me, my lady," he said in a chastened voice. "I do hope you can forgive a rough soldier recently returned from the Spanish wars." He glanced anxiously at her, but Harriet was not to be cajoled so easily.

"I had no idea old Giles had found himself a wife," he continued when she made no reply. "Given the way things are between us, I naturally did not look him up in London to inquire as to his health. He probably would have thrown me out on my ear in any case." He grinned with sudden charm, and Harriet was struck once again by the resemblance to her husband.

"Am I forgiven, my lady? I do not relish having to sleep in the stables tonight."

"Perhaps if you told me exactly what relationship you have with my husband, I might consider it," she replied tentatively. "Are you perchance one of those poor cousins his lordship makes use of when it suits him?" she could not resist adding, just to show this outspoken young man that she was not to be intimidated by his blunt speaking.

"Touché, my lady." He had a charming laugh, and Harriet wondered why her husband never laughed in just that way. The captain was a handsome man, his skin bronzed by the Spanish sun, his blue-gray eyes filled with amusement. And his mouth . . . Harriet could not help noticing that the captain's mouth was identical to the earl's.

"I deserved that. And no, I am no cousin of his. I wish I were, it might have made life considerably easier for all of us."

Harriet gazed at him intently. "Then you must be his brother," she guessed. "The resemblance is obvious."

The captain's smile disappeared instantly. "Giles would not thank you for saying so, my lady." He paused, and then added in a harsh voice, "Yes, I am his brother. At least, a brother of sorts. Brian never minded so much, but Giles always acted as though I had desecrated the holiness of the Montague line." He turned his back and kicked at a smoldering log viciously.

Harriet sat very still, digesting the shocking information that her husband had a bastard brother. Watching the captain's rigid back, Harriet had a pretty good idea of why Giles had told her nothing about this brother who was not quite good enough to carry the Montague name. Given his stiff-necked pride in his family traditions, the earl must have hated the disgrace of having any relative of his born on the wrong side of the blanket. And if the captain was right, the relationship between the two men was anything but cordial. But that was not right, Harriet thought. They were brothers, whether they liked it or not, and one could not blame the captain for the misdeeds of the former earl. Or could one? she wondered. Evidently Giles must do so, for the captain had sounded quite terribly bitter about his treatment at the earl's hands. Well, Harriet decided impulsively, she would not be a party to such cruelty.

"I do not care a fig for what Giles thinks, Captain. You are very welcome at the Abbey while I have anything to say in the matter. And you had better call me Harriet."

The captain swung round, a reluctant grin on his face. "I cannot believe my ears, Harriet. Did you actually say that you have a say in what goes on at the Abbey?"

"I most certainly did," she acknowledged with a smile. She was beginning to like Captain Montague; she hoped he would not turn out to be as complicated and prickly as his brother. "Why does that surprise you?"

The captain raised an eyebrow. "I am bowled over to hear that Giles is actually allowing anyone to do anything without his approval and supervision, that's all. Marriage must have mellowed him."

Harriet had a sudden desire to confide in this young man who was so like her husband, yet not really like him at all.

"Giles approves of me," she murmured.

Harriet felt herself subjected to a brief but thorough

scrutiny. "I can see why," the captain drawled with a glint of admiration in his eyes. "How did he tear himself away from London long enough to meet you, Harriet?"

Telling herself that this careless reference to her husband's London amusements was not intentionally unkind, Harriet fought the sense of desolation which threatened to overcome her. "My brother, Peter Egerton, introduced us last year," she said calmly.

"So you are Bridgeport's sister? I ran into him a couple of times in Paris last spring. Still attached to the Foreign Office is he?"

"Yes. Peter and Giles were at Oxford together, and have remained good friends. In fact, Giles was with him in Paris last year."

"Lucky I wasn't there at the time," the captain muttered. He shot her a curious glance. "Where is he now, by the way?"

"Giles?" Harriet stalled, hating the necessity of revealing the earl's presence in London. "He is in London."

There was a brief silence before the captain said in a softer voice, "I'm sorry I asked."

Mortified at the thought of becoming an object of the captain's pity, Harriet rallied her best smile. "Oh, there is nothing odd about that. After all, that was part of our agreement," she said before realizing that she had revealed more than she intended about her marriage to the earl. She was glad when Carruthers chose that moment to usher in the footmen with the tea-tray and a decanter of brandy.

"I did not know if you would prefer tea or something stronger, Captain," she murmured, hiding her confusion by busying herself with directing the placement of the tea things.

"To tell you the truth, I would prefer tea if it is hot." The captain laughed, and Harriet felt the tension ease. "It always used to be so deuced cold that I took to drinking spirits instead."

"That has all changed, now," Harriet said, feeling on safer ground. "We now drink our tea hot, even in the Great Hall. And we do not sit in drafts either, thanks to the new curtains."

As soon as the door closed behind the servants, the captain's amusement faded. He accepted the steaming cup Harriet handed him and sank down in a leather armchair.

"Giles is a bloody fool to waste his time in London when he has a wife who can order hot tea in this mausoleum and actually get it." He smiled, as if to soften his words. "But I'm dashed glad he married you, Harriet. And that's the truth. You make the old place feel like home again."

Harriet blushed with pleasure. Nothing the captain might have said could have pleased her better, and she returned his smile. "I am happy you are home again to enjoy it, Richard," she said and meant it.

Now if only her husband could be so easily pleased, she thought wistfully, her life at the Abbey would be complete. At least it would be complete if only the earl could be brought to fulfill his commitment to start his nursery.

The notion of the role she was destined to play in securing the Montague line gave Harriet a comforting sense of purpose that she kept locked safely in her heart. It would not do to weave some romantical fantasy into this marriage. There was no place at the Abbey for such nonsensical, schoolgirl dreams. She was committed to be a sensible wife to a man who needed an heir, and Harriet was determined—after failing so miserably to please her husband on Christmas Eve—to curb her natural aversion to the inevitable intimacies of marriage. The next time the earl came to her room, she would be a submissive, dutiful wife to him, and in return, God willing, he would give her a child.

It was, she told herself practically, all she had to look forward to.

Lord Kimbalton was enjoying a quiet dinner at his club when the letter from his steward arrived, sent round from Montague House on Grosvenor Square. He received regular reports from Mulligan on the running of the estate, so he thought nothing of it, stuffing it in the pocket of his coat to attend to later.

It was considerably later, after he had visited Ophelia at the house he maintained for her on Curzon Street, and taken tea with her in the Chinese drawing room, that Giles finally opened Mulligan's letter. He had found Ophelia still too pale and drawn for his peace of mind. She had sworn to him that she was much recovered, but Giles did not believe her. The pale skin of her cheeks had become almost translucent, and her delicate neck appeared barely able to support the weight of her small head.

"I think I shall ask Dr. McIntyre to come around in the morning," he told her as she handed him the delicate Wedg-

wood cup and sat back in her chair as though the action had
exhausted her.

"Oh, my lord, there is no need," she protested in her soft,
musical voice. "I am so much better than I was at Christmas-
time, I assure you. And when the warm weather returns, I
know I will be as well as ever again. Please do not coddle me,
I shall become quite impossibly spoiled."

"I like to coddle you," Giles replied bluntly. And it was
true, he thought, watching his mistress's delicate hands lift the
heavy tea-pot. Had those blue veins always been so pronounced? he wondered. The uneasy feeling he had experienced several times in the past three months tightened his
stomach. "And you would tell me if you felt any worse, would
you not, my dear?"

"Of course, I would, Giles," she replied, a sweet smile hovering on her lovely lips. "But you must not worry about me.
Dr. McIntyre assured me that I am on the mend only yesterday."

Then the doctor was a charlatan, Giles thought angrily,
glimpsing the flash of pain in Ophelia's wide violet eyes before she lowered her lashes. He would have to find someone
else to come to Curzon Street to examine her.

He took his leave earlier than usual, depriving himself once
again of the pleasure of bedding her. He would be an absolute
brute not to see that his lovely Ophelia needed rest far more
than she needed demonstrations of his passion. He had come
to Curzon Street that evening with the express purpose of taking advantage of Ophelia's repeated assurances that she was
quite well enough to resume her duties.

That was exactly the way she had phrased it, he remembered wryly, and in the past the expression would not have
bothered him at all. In fact, he had always considered Ophelia
Brooks, impoverished widow of an officer in Wellington's
Army, an ideal mistress. She was unassuming, charming, well-
bred, and indescribably lovely, her pale gold hair a halo
around her heart-shaped face, and her violet eyes wide and
guileless. He had wanted her the moment he laid eyes on her,
and by a stroke of luck had been able to meet her through
Peter Egerton, who had served with her husband in the 7th
Hussars during the early campaigns in Portugal.

As his carriage deposited him on the steps of Montague
House, Giles was suddenly struck by an amusing thought. By
some odd coincidence he had acquired both his mistress, four

years ago now, and more recently his wife, through the offices of his good friend Viscount Bridgeport. Peter had solved two of the most pressing problems in his life, he thought, surrendering his tall beaver and gloves to the butler as he entered his London residence. He might have gone on to White's for a game of cards with friends, since the night was still young, but for some reason Giles felt restless.

The thought of Harriet, intruding so unexpectedly into his thoughts, brought back the uncomfortable memory of their last encounter on Christmas Day. She had come to ask his forgiveness for something that was not entirely her fault, and like an idiot he had said something crude to her. In some ways, his wife was such an innocent, he thought, remembering her shock when he had touched her breast. Thinking of Harriet's breast was a mistake, he found out, for once the memory of it came to him, he could not seem to think of anything else. The unexpected fullness of it had surprised and pleased him, and her mouth had been warm and sweet. There had been a promise of sensuality about her that he had been unprepared for and in his eagerness, he had made the mistake of rushing his fences. Monroyal was right, he thought, virgins were tricky, one never could be sure how they would react.

To distract his heated thoughts, Giles pulled out Mulligan's letter and opened it. When he got to the end of the missive, he swore under his breath and crumpled the letter into a ball. So that damned black sheep had returned, had he? And gone straight to the Abbey, of course. Dick had always liked to call the Abbey home, Giles remembered. Even when he had been a little tyke running around after his two big brothers, as he called them, making a nuisance of himself.

Richard Montague, whom Giles only grudgingly acknowledged as a brother, knew as much about the history of the Abbey as did Giles himself, and certainly a good deal more than Brian, who preferred more contemporary pursuits. Their father, damn his randy hide, had taken a perverse pleasure in raising the boy at the Abbey, giving him all the benefits he gave his legitimate sons, in spite of their mother's protests. But fortunately the old earl had died before he could settle one of his smaller estates on Richard, as he was fond of reminding the family he intended to do. And Brian had been reluctant to relinquish so much as a groat of his extensive income. In the end, Dick had cajoled his eldest brother into purchasing a commission in a reputable regiment, and they had seen little of him since then.

But now Richard was back from the war—wounded and decorated for bravery, according to Mulligan's report—and staying at the Abbey. For some reason the thought of harboring his father's bastard in the same house with Harriet did not sit well with Giles. He had never liked the boy, perhaps because his father's overt preference for the lively child, so like the old man in looks and temperament, had made Giles feel deprived of his father's affection. Whatever the cause, the two had always been at daggers drawn, while Brian had ignored both of them in his privileged position as the future earl. He wondered how Harriet had reacted to the news that she was related to a bastard. The thought disturbed him. Knowing Harriet, Giles would wager she had probably taken Richard in as though he were a legitimate Montague, which of course he was not. It had always irked Giles that his father had acknowledged Richard as his son, giving him the family name. There was something faintly shameful about a bastard any way you looked at it, Giles had always thought.

He would have to make a decision regarding Richard's future, he realized testily. Thanks to his father, they were all stuck with acknowledging Richard as part of the family, but Giles did not have to like it, he told himself, nor did he have to tolerate the presence of the black sheep at the Abbey, now that he was master there. And Harriet, he thought. He could not subject Harriet to the company of such a man, could he?

The devil fly away with the old earl, Giles swore under his breath, jerking the bell rope viciously. He would have to go down to Hampshire and settle the matter himself. Unless Richard had changed radically as a result of his stint in the army, Giles knew that his half brother would accept orders from no one else.

# CHAPTER NINE

# The Dutiful Wife

In many ways Captain Richard Montague reminded Harriet of her brother, and it was not long before she was on excellent terms with her husband's half brother. Lady Sophronia was immediately taken with the handsome young man and fussed over his wounded arm even more than Harriet did. Neither of the ladies would rest until a doctor had been summoned to examine the captain's left arm and renew the dressing. After the wound was pronounced to be mending nicely, Harriet took it upon herself to change the dressing every afternoon before they gathered in the Yellow Saloon for tea.

These informal gatherings became the highlight of Harriet's days. When they had visitors, as they frequently did at that hour in the afternoon, she was amused at the varying reactions of their callers to the presence of the old lord's by-blow in their midst. Some of them, like old Lady Hawthorn and her three spinsterish daughters, dithered visibly between outrage at having to take tea with a person of such dubious parentage, and indulgent condescension at the captain's unabashed and quite outrageous flattery, to which her ladyship was not at all immune. Other local gentry, like Sir William Cook and his good-natured lady, seemed to take Richard's presence for granted and conversed animatedly with him about local affairs on which topic Richard seemed to be intimately knowledgeable.

The captain himself settled quickly into the routine Harriet and her aunt had established at the Abbey. In the mornings he would ride with Harriet all over the estate, greeting the tenants as though he really were a true son of the house. On the occasional evening when they were invited to dinner or other gatherings at neighboring houses, Richard was their willing escort, and Harriet soon discovered that he was also a universal favorite with the local ladies.

One afternoon shortly after his arrival, Harriet was changing the captain's bandage in the small morning room at the back of the house when the door, which had been decorously ajar, was slammed open by an irate hand.

"A pretty sight indeed, my lady," a familiar voice drawled harshly from the doorway. "Just what do you think you are doing here alone with a half-naked man?"

Harriet jumped and spun around. The jolt of pleasure that had coursed through her at the sound of her husband's voice faded at the sight of his black scowl. Richard had come to his feet and now stood, glaring at the earl, the left arm of his shirt hanging around his waist, displaying a fair amount of bronzed torso. He made no move to replace it, defiance oozing from every pore of his body.

Harriet recognized the signs of an incipient brawl of major proportions. "Welcome home, my lord," she said calmly, ignoring the quaking of her knees. "I imagine you must be ready for a cup of tea. Let me finish fixing Richard's bandage, and we can all repair to the Great Hall." She turned and took hold of the dangling shirt, pulling it over the captain's broad shoulder. She paused, abruptly conscious of the intimate picture they must present to an infuriated husband.

"Oh, dear," she whispered, tugging ineffectually at the captain's sleeve.

Richard looked down at her, his gray-blue eyes glittering with devilish amusement, and smiled his most charming, intimate smile. "I fear his lordship is in one of his black moods, my pet. I think I can manage, if you will hold up my coat for me."

The earl's reaction was immediate and violent. "You will bloody well hold your own damned coat," he snapped, his brows drawn into a dangerous line. "And while you are at it, perhaps you can tell me what the hell you are doing with my wife."

Richard's mouth drew into a sneer. "I resent the implications of that remark, old man," he said with deceptive softness. "And I suggest you watch your blasted tongue unless you want me to darken your daylights for you."

The earl took a step forward, his fists clenched and his face mottled with rage. Harriet did not hesitate; she pushed between the two men, and faced her husband.

"Listen to me for a moment, my lord," she began, but the earl did not so much as glance down at her.

"Stay out of this, Harriet," he growled low in his throat, his gray eyes, dark with anger, fixed on the captain's face.

Harriet placed one palm tentatively against the earl's blue coat. "Giles, this is absurd. Richard has done nothing to incur your anger. I swear it."

From behind her, Harriet heard Richard's deep, cynical crack of laughter. "I am alive, my dear Harriet," he drawled. "That makes twenty-six years of anger my dear brother has been carrying about with him. I would hardly call that nothing, would you? Giles cannot wait for any excuse to throw me out of his house, even if it entails believing that you have seduced me, my dear." He laughed again, and Harriet sensed the bitterness in his voice.

"You bloody bastard," the earl growled. "You are the sod I do not trust, not my wife. No doubt it's the sort of rotten trick you would find amusing."

Harriet heard the captain's intake of breath. "Things do not change much, do they, brother?" he sneered. "Except that now you are the bloody lord of the manor and can throw me out of my home whenever the urge takes you."

"This is not your home," Lord Kimbalton snarled, and Harriet quailed at the venom in his voice. "And the sooner you get out, the better I shall like it."

Harriet lost her temper at all this male stupidity. "No, he will not," she declared forcefully. "The devil fly away with both of you. You are brothers, damn you. And this is the most ridiculous argument I have ever had to listen to. Stop it at once!"

The earl looked down at her, his eyes registering shock. The captain laughed delightedly.

"You will not swear like a navvy, Harriet," the earl said between clenched teeth. "And you will stay out of my business."

"If you think for one moment that I will stand here and let you make a cake of yourself, Giles, you are all about in the head. Besides, Richard is *my* brother now, too. And I refuse to let you bully him." Harriet sounded far more confident than she felt, but she forced herself to return her husband's stare without flinching.

"Bravo, little one," Richard murmured admiringly.

Harriet swung round on him, her fury unabated. "And you will cease provoking your brother with stupid remarks, if you please. Get your shirt on and stop smirking, or you will get no damson tart with your tea," she snapped, glowering at the culprit. Harriet never knew what inspired her to talk to these two grown men as though they were children, but it appeared to deprive them both of speech, which was all to the good.

In the ensuing lull, Harriet glared first at her husband and then back at the captain. She drew herself up to her full height and turned towards the door. "I shall await you in the Great Hall," she said regally. "And I trust you will both be on your best behavior."

There was no response from either of the startled gentlemen as Harriet stalked out of the room.

If it had not been for Aunt Sophy, Harriet doubted she could have endured the hostility that simmered between Lord Kimbalton and his half brother during the tea hour. Amazingly, her aunt appeared oblivious to the undercurrents of animosity that seemed to fill every pause in the stilted conversation like an unseen, evil presence. The two men studiously avoided addressing one another, and every effort Harriet made to draw them onto common ground failed miserably.

The time-honored ritual of drinking tea and making polite conversation gave Harriet ample time to examine the brothers at her leisure. The startling resemblance she had first noted was still present, but as she listened to Richard's light banter and basked in his pleasant smile, she could not help wishing that her husband possessed half his brother's charm. They were unmistakably brothers, she thought, observing the earl's tall frame lounging against the massive mantelpiece. Giles was an inch or two taller and certainly broader across the shoulders than Richard, but the latter was blessed with a lithe grace and elegance that made him a favorite with the younger ladies of the neighborhood.

Although the earl spoke little, Harriet was aware that her husband's gray eyes were often upon her. She steadfastly refused to meet his gaze, and it was not until she came down to the Great Hall before dinner and found him there before her that they had a chance for private conversation.

"I trust you approve of the changes Aunt Sophy and I have made in the Hall, my lord," she remarked, settling herself on the enormous oak settee, now embellished and made considerably more comfortable by plump horsehair cushions.

If truth were told, Harriet had been somewhat apprehensive about the earl's reaction to the drastic spring cleaning her aunt had insisted upon. But she also felt confident that the improved appearance and increased comfort could not fail to please him. She was less sure about the extensive changes she had made in the grounds, but so far the earl appeared not to have noticed the havoc she had wrecked on his four-hundred-year-old park.

The earl regarded her from beneath hooded lids. "I find it much improved," he said formally.

And there the conversation bogged down until Aunt Sophy appeared, accompanied by the captain, who was entertaining her with a yarn in which Spanish goats, army mules, and a loud-mouthed lass of gigantic proportions who spoke no English played prominent parts.

Dinner passed in relative harmony, which was threatened briefly when Richard inquired when the earl intended to replace the flock of rag-tag sheep in the Lower Pasture with more productive breeds.

The earl glared at his half brother stonily. "I will thank you to leave the running of the estate in my hands, Richard," he replied with such cool civility that Harriet felt the temperature of the huge dining room drop several degrees.

Luckily Aunt Sophy, sublimely unaware of the icy atmosphere, chose that moment to inquire whether his lordship had chanced to encounter her sister, Lady Cuthbert, at any of the London soirées. Upon receiving a rather curt negative from the earl, Lady Sophronia replied calmly that she was not in the least surprised to hear it, since her dear sister had been in poor health of late and may well be confined to her bed. This information was greeted with stony silence that persisted until Harriet, exasperated at having her dinner ruined by this deliberate surliness on the part of her husband, demanded to know if he had any news from her brother Peter, who had returned to Paris several weeks earlier.

Lord Kimbalton again answered shortly in the negative.

This carried them over until it was time for the ladies to retire, which Harriet was loath to do, since she did not trust the two gentlemen not to start another brawl. She shot an anxious glance at Richard, who grinned at her.

"Do not look so terrified, my dear Harriet. Short of wishing me in Jericho—which you can be sure he does—there is little danger of Giles committing violence in these ancestral halls. He has too much respect for them to sully the floors with my blood."

Harriet was not amused at this flippancy. "I thought I told

you not to be provoking, Richard. Much more of that sort of childish prattle, and I shall shoot you myself." She glared at him before sweeping out of the room.

Harriet was relieved to see that the brothers were still on polite, if not amicable, terms when they joined the ladies a short time later. She lost no time in requesting Carruthers to bring up the tea-tray, since—as she pointedly informed her aunt—she had endured more than enough contretemps for one day and wished to retire early.

When she finally escaped to her bedchamber, Harriet's relief was short-lived. No sooner had the door closed behind her, than she was beset by a very different kind of anxiety. Could her husband have seen her early retiring as an invitation? she wondered. Had that been a smile or a smirk on his face when she had said her good nights? Harriet collapsed on her tapestry stool and stared at herself in the beveled glass as Lucy attacked her hair vigorously with the brush.

She closed her eyes, trying to relax, but then she remembered that her husband had granted her that second chance, which in a moment of thoughtlessness she had begged him to. Was tonight to be that second chance? she wondered, half hoping that it might be, so that she could rid herself, once and for all, of the curse of her virginity.

It was the uncertainty of it all that was stretching her nerves to breaking point, Harriet told herself. Her aunt's terrifying accounts of conjugal intimacies had destroyed her common sense and turned her into a sniveling chit with more hair than wit. How bad could it be, when all was said and done? she wondered. There were thousands of married women in the world—why, her own mother must have endured it, or she herself would not be here.

Harriet shivered.

"Are you cold, milady?" the abigail inquired solicitously, but Harriet imagined she detected a sly undertone to Lucy's words. Were the naughty wench's thoughts running along the same lines as her own? she wondered.

She sat up straighter. "No," she answered rather shortly. "And that will be enough for tonight, Lucy. My head is hurting with all that pulling."

After Lucy had left, Harriet took up the brush and pulled it idly through her hair. Honey-colored, Anabella had always called it, doubtless to make it sound more attractive than it was. Her stepmother had tried very hard to marry her off, Harriet remembered, but even her considerable fortune had not seemed to help attract a suitable *parti*. She had been beset by a horde of charming yet thoroughly ineligible rogues, all of them with pockets to let and no real interest in her at all. She had quickly learned to recognize a fortune hunter, sometimes by the desperate glint in his eye, if he happened to be deeply in debt; or by the glib flattery he showered upon her, so ridiculously insincere that she had been tempted to laugh in his face.

And then Peter had brought the Earl of Kimbalton to Lark Manor, and she had—in a foolish, weak moment of inexplicable longing for that family she had all but despaired of having—accepted his offer. She had only herself to blame for that decision, Harriet told herself firmly, and she was honorbound to do her duty when Giles came to her again. And come he certainly would, she thought, trying to regain some of her natural sang-froid. That was the whole purpose of this marriage: to get heirs for the Montague line. And what if it did hurt? She had been hurt before, hadn't she? Like the time she fell of Greybeard when he was a colt new to the saddle. She had twisted her leg so badly Aunt Sophy had feared it was broken. But it wasn't. It had hurt like the very devil, but she had survived. Surely nothing Giles could do to her would hurt quite that much, would it?

Harriet smiled encouragingly at her reflection. She would not be a peagoose, that was for simpering females with no backbone. Lady Harriet Egerton was made of sterner stuff.

And then the door opened behind her, and Harriet's anxieties rushed back to knot her stomach. She could see him clearly in the mirror, in shirtsleeves and the tightly molded black breeches he had worn at dinner.

He closed the door softly, and Harriet drew a deep breath and stood up to face him. He did look rather splendid, she had to admit, every inch of his tall body radiating masculine power and lust. At least, Harriet imagined the strange glitter in his gray eyes must be lust, for Aunt Sophy had warned her that men were lustful creatures, each and every one of them, camouflaging their animal instincts beneath a thin veneer of civility. The notion that she was about to discover that baser side of her husband's character excited her, even as it terrified her.

Harriet reminded herself that this was the test of her female fortitude, and that if she faltered now, she would never be able to hold up her head again. She knew exactly what she must do, and she must do it without quailing. But first she must be absolutely sure of his intentions.

"You wished to speak to me, my lord?" she inquired, conscious of a sense of *déjà vu,* but proud of the calm serenity of her voice.

The earl's lips twitched into a faint smile, and his eyes dropped to her mouth, where they lingered—interminably, Harriet thought—until they slid down to the swell of her bosom.

And then Harriet knew. Before he opened his mouth to say it, Harriet knew.

"We have some unfinished business to attend to, Harriet," he drawled in an oddly husky voice.

But Harriet knew what he meant, and she did not hesitate. With fingers that trembled only slightly, she loosened the sash of her robe and let it slip from her shoulders to the floor.

She undid the top button of her night-rail.

Then she undid the second button.

On the third button she paused briefly, but *only* briefly before she undid that one, too. The fourth one came undone almost by itself. Her eyes were lowered, fixed on the progress of her fingers, which were now trembling visibly. The fifth button was stubborn, caught in a buttonhole too small for it. Harriet persisted, and the button gave way suddenly, causing the neck of her night-rail to gape revealingly. The sixth button was level with her breasts, and Harriet hesitated again, but overcame this momentary panic with renewed determination.

Her fingers moved down to the seventh button. Only three more to go, she realized, and then she would have to take it off. And this time, she must not fail.

"What the devil do you think you are doing?" His voice startled her, and Harriet glanced up uncertainly. Why was he angry at her again? she wondered. Was she not doing what he wanted?

"I am taking off my clothes," she said in a small voice.

"What the devil for?" he demanded.

"I thought that was what you wanted, my lord," she whispered, her fingers frozen on the seventh button.

In two strides he covered the distance between them and caught her roughly in his arms, crushing her against his chest so fiercely that Harriet thought her ribs would break. He buried his face in her hair, and Harriet could feel his warm breath against her neck. He said nothing at all, and a sick feeling of uncertainty crowded in upon her.

Her face was pressed into the earl's chest, and Harriet was disconcerted at the scent of him. He smelled like nothing she had ever experienced before. An intriguing musky smell of male body, shaving water, brandy, and other tangy scents she could not identify. It intoxicated her senses, and made her suddenly light-headed.

"Have I done something wrong again?" she whispered against the enveloping warmth of him, in a voice she did not recognize.

His arms crushed her tighter. "No, you have done nothing wrong at all, Harriet. Nothing at all."

"Then you do not wish me to remove my clothes?" Harriet could not believe that she was to be spared that ordeal.

"No," he replied sharply. "No, I do not."

But instead of the relief she had expected, Harriet felt perplexed. How was she to know what he wanted if he changed his mind all the time? she thought querulously, at a loss to understand the odd sense of disappointment that gnawed at her. Had she failed again? she wondered.

To her dismay, her husband suddenly released her and started buttoning her night-rail. His fingers were unsteady, she noted, through a haze of unshed tears.

Yes, she told herself dully, she *had* failed. His lordship no longer desired her. He was not going to bed her after all. Why else would he be dressing her instead of undressing her? She felt a wave of self-pity threaten to engulf her. Evidently she could not hope to compete with that mysterious mistress her husband kept in London, whom Peter had confessed was indeed a Beauty. Even now, as he fastened the buttons of his wife's night-rail, Giles must be thinking of *her*, wishing he were there with *her*, getting into *her* bed.

Harriet took a deep breath and pulled herself together. She must stop feeling sorry for herself this very instant, she told herself sternly. If she allowed herself to sink into a maudlin quagmire of sentimental blather, all would indeed be lost. Where was that famous common sense upon which she had always prided herself? Where was it written down that she had to compete with any other woman? She was the earl's *wife*, wasn't she? And it certainly was written down—Harriet was sure of it—that a wife was entitled to bear her husband an heir. Nay, it was her sworn duty to do so.

Harriet glanced up at her husband, who was struggling with that fifth button in its small buttonhole. A dark lock of hair hung down over his forehead, making him appear younger than his thirty-two years. Harriet's heart gave an odd lurch. His eyes were lowered, intent on the buttons, and for the first time Harriet noticed that his eyelashes, fanned out against his bronzed cheeks, were as long as any woman's. Her gaze dropped unconsciously to his mouth. Accustomed as she was to see his lips set in thin, disapproving lines, Harriet was startled to note that they could also be full and sensuous. She gazed at them in wonder, conscious of a sudden desire to touch them, to kiss them, to feel their heat on her body as she had at Christmas.

By rights, Harriet should be appalled at the quite wanton thoughts that chased through her mind, but strangely she felt neither shame nor embarrassment as she admired her husband's mouth with a new awareness. The lethargic sensation that was insidiously invading her body and mind alarmed her at first, but then the earl's fingers brushed against her breast, and Harriet knew, with a shock of recognition, that she was ready—even anxious—to be bedded by this man who was, quite incongruously, intent on securing the barrier of clothes between them.

Instinctively, Harriet's fingers closed around her husband's, stilling their progress with the buttons. She could not allow this to happen, she thought. This was her second chance, and she refused to make a mull of it. After all, if it was a wife's duty to produce an heir, surely it was a husband's duty to do his part in the process? And here was her husband quite obviously trying to shirk his duty. She would not permit it, Harriet decided, relieved that her practical instincts had reasserted themselves. If she had to take the initiative, she would do so without compunction.

Gently she drew the earl's hands away from the remaining buttons. "There is no need to fasten them all," she said, amazed at the steadiness of her voice. "I rarely do on a warm night."

Realizing that she still held his unresisting hands pressed against her body, Harriet released them reluctantly, smiling faintly up into his startled eyes.

With calm determination, she turned away towards the bed. "I do not know about you, my lord," she murmured, wishing she had the nerve to extend a more blatant invitation, "but I am going to bed."

She climbed into the four-poster, acutely conscious of her husband's enigmatic gaze following her every move. She settled herself against the pillows and regarded him innocently. He seemed undecided, and Harriet had an odd premonition that he was poised for flight. That would never do, she decided. There must be something she could do to entice him into her bed, but short of taking off her clothes, which he did not seem to wish her to do. Harriet was supremely ignorant of what a female might do to trigger that animalistic impulse Aunt Sophy had talked about in such hushed tones.

"Do you wear a night-shirt, my lord?" she asked anxiously, finding the prospect of a totally naked man getting into her bed suddenly rather daunting.

For the first time since coming to her room, the earl seemed amused. "Would you prefer me to wear one, Harriet?" he asked softly, a wry smile curling one corner of his mouth.

Harriet's heart gave a wild lurch. "I prefer that you please yourself, my lord," she whispered breathlessly. "It is all the same to me. Except that . . ." She stopped, horrified at the shameless thought she had been about to utter.

"Except what, Harriet?" The earl took two steps towards the bed, and Harriet's heart nearly stopped. Was he about to join her? she wondered, suddenly nervous. Or was he still undecided? She must think of something quite outrageous to prod him into action.

She smiled as a thoroughly shocking notion struck her. "I confess to a morbid curiosity to see how well you compare with Richard, my lord," she murmured innocently, slanting her eyes at him.

If Harriet doubted for a moment that she had found the precise challenge to incite her husband into action, she saw at once that perhaps she had overdone herself. The earl went quite rigid, his lips in their familiar taut line, and the muscles of his jaw bunched in anger. Harriet took one look at his thunderous scowl and feared for a moment that he would drag her out of bed and beat her.

Harriet closed her eyes and tensed for the angry words she knew were sure to be hurled at her. When the silence lengthened unbearably, and nothing happened, she dared to peek.

Lord Kimbalton was standing by her bedside, arms akimbo.

Harriet gasped, and her eyes flew wide open. There was a grim look on his face, but he no longer seemed apoplectic. His gray eyes glittered dangerously, and Harriet knew she had touched on a sore subject indeed.

She attempted a smile, which she knew was woefully unsuccessful. "I was only teasing, my lord," she began.

The earl smiled grimly. "I doubt that very much, my lady," he said in a harsh voice that made Harriet's heart sink. "How much of my brother have you seen, may I ask?"

Surprised at the implications of that angry question, Harriet sat up in bed, her cheeks flushed hotly, and glared back at him. "I do not deserve that, my lord," she said with forced calm. "I have seen no more than you did yourself this afternoon. Nor do I wish to see more, as you must know," she added sharply, feeling her indignation rise. "It is unkind of you to suggest otherwise."

He held her angry gaze for several minutes, but Harriet refused to back down. At last he seemed to relax, and she breathed again.

"Then I must certainly satisfy your morbid curiosity, must I not?" he said sarcastically, and before Harriet had time to react, her husband had tugged his shirt out of his breeches, pulled it roughly over his head, and thrown it down on the bed.

"There, Harriet, my sweet," he challenged her. "What do you say to that?"

Harriet took one startled look and closed her eyes tightly. She took several deep breaths to calm her racing heart. The unexpected sight of her husband's bare torso had caused unexplained tremors to course through her body. He was truly magnificent, she thought, broad, sloping shoulders rippling with muscles, chest covered by a black pelt of curly hair that tapered off into the narrow waistband of his breeches. Giles was a good deal hairier than his brother, and Harriet distinctly felt an aura of animal magnetism reaching out to envelope her. She felt quite dizzy at the thought.

"Well?" the earl drawled, a faint air of masculine complacency in his tone.

Harriet opened her eyes. No, she had not dreamed it. And now she was expected to say something. She knew that she should lower her gaze from this magnificent spectacle, but all modesty seemed to have deserted her. She examined him with unabashed pleasure, a tiny smile playing at the corner of her mouth. She could sit here looking at him for hours, she thought, but then she caught the uncertainty in his gray eyes and realized that he was unsure of himself. The notion surprised her into an unself-conscious response.

"You are truly splendid, my lord," she murmured warmly, her smile echoing her approval.

Her eager response seemed to take her husband by surprise, and Harriet could have sworn that he actually blushed. Perhaps she had tipped the scales in her favor after all.

The earl grinned suddenly, a devilish grin which caused Harriet's heart to leap into her throat again. "Perhaps it is time for you to see the rest of me, Harriet," he drawled, hands resting suggestively on the opening of his breeches.

Harriet froze and closed her eyes. This was definitely one of the major hurdles she must cross if she wished to seduce her husband, she thought, petrified at what she must do, yet even more anxious of what might happen if she made a mull of things. No doubt he would leave in the morning, on his way back to London and that mystery female who must have all the right answers to situations such as this. What would a successful mistress do at a time like this? she wondered. Surely nothing very different from what a dutiful wife should do?

"Well, Harriet? What shall it be?"

Harriet opened her eyes and looked at him, dazzled anew at the vast expanse of male flesh. "That might be interesting indeed, my lord," she heard herself say in a prim little voice that made him laugh.

And then he was removing his boots and breeches, and Harriet closed her eyes again, tightly, swearing not to open them even if the sky fell. She heard the boots drop to the floor and then the rustle of clothing.

"You may look now, Harriet," she heard him say in a strangely husky voice.

Harriet simply could not bring herself to do so. This was simply too much, she argued. He could not expect it of her. She turned on her side away from him and heard him chuckle softly. Then she felt the bed dip and he was suddenly there beside her, one hand resting lightly on her hip. After a moment, Harriet felt his grip tighten and he pulled her gently over onto her back. She steeled herself for the inevitable, but nothing happened.

"You may open your eyes now, Harriet," he drawled. "I am covered up."

When Harriet did so, she saw that this was not strictly true. His magnificent chest was still in full view, and the effect of its proximity on her heart rate was immediate. His head was propped up on one elbow, and he was looking down at her, eyes glittering in the candlelight. Even to Harriet's inexperienced and befuddled glance, the earl did not appear to be caught in the throes of any impulse, animalistic or otherwise. Her immediate thought was that she had made some unthinkable, gauche mistake again. She had succeeded in getting him into bed with her, and in her ignorance, had imagined that whatever had to follow would do so as a matter of course.

The hand that had held her hip moved up casually to her breast, but there was no urgency in the caress as there had been last Christmas. No desire, she thought bleakly. She had been right after all. Her husband no longer desired her. From that thought another sprang unbidden: had he ever desired her? Or was he merely here to do his duty?

Harriet was appalled at the notion. Appalled and humiliated. But before she could begin to feel the insidious pull of self-pity, her sense of honesty asserted itself. Had she really expected this cold, autocratic, self-possessed man to play the lover for her benefit, when she had specifically demanded that there be no pretense between them? Harriet remembered quite clearly how arrogantly she had laid down that condition that afternoon on Oak Hill, an afternoon that seemed to belong to another age entirely. How naive she had been to imagine that life with Lord Kimbalton would be that simple.

The hand on her breast stilled, and Harriet glanced up at the man beside her. His eyes were fixed on the dancing flames of the small fire that burned in the grate, and Harriet knew, with sudden painful insight, that he was no longer there beside her at all. Harriet could have wept with frustration, but she had learned long ago that tears served no useful purpose except to make her eyes red, so she turned her mind into more practical channels. She had obviously failed to arouse a sense of duty in her husband for he showed no signs of those animalistic urges she had been prepared to endure stoically. But was it entirely her fault? she wondered, watching the firelight glint on the earl's black hair.

Perhaps there *was* a competition going on here after all, Harriet thought with a sinking feeling. A contest between her and that mysterious female who seemed to exert such a strong influence on this man that he could not keep his mind on the unfinished business he had mentioned earlier. The notion of competing with a Beauty of the first stare dampened Harriet's spirits considerably, but her common sense whispered that as a wife she had a definite advantage. Or did she? Technically, of course, she was the Countess of Kimbalton. Nothing could change that. But she did not feel like a wife, nor did she know how to act like one, and only her husband could change that. Unfortunately, the earl showed no signs of wishing to change anything. The warm hand on her breast was lax and lifeless.

It occurred to Harriet that if anything, she was at a distinct disadvantage. How could she hope to compete with that infamous Lady of London until she learned the rules of the game, a game her husband seemed disinclined to teach her? The comparison amused her. She had often heard love referred to as a game, but what was it called when there was no love? Or if there was, the Beauty certainly held the trump card, for if the earl loved anyone, it had to be his mistress. Harriet was quite sure it was not his wife. For a fleeting moment, as the firelight drew her gaze to her husband's sensuous mouth, relaxed and oddly vulnerable, Harriet wished that bothersome female in Jericho. Perhaps if the Beauty did not exist in her husband's life . . . But she did, Harriet told herself sharply, and the only way to deal with this obstacle was to challenge the earl directly. That had always been her way, Harriet thought, and she should have done it sooner.

"Your thoughts are not really here at all, are they, my lord?" she murmured gently, throwing herself into action before she lost her nerve.

He looked down at her, his eyes blank and distant before he masked them. "What a ridiculous notion, Harriet," he said rather shortly. "You can see for yourself that I am definitely here." The smile on his sensuous lips, slight as it was, made Harriet's pulses do strange things.

"Oh, I can see that very well, my lord," she replied reasonably. "But I was talking about your thoughts, not your . . . your body," she finished in a rush, all too well aware, from the warmth radiating through her cotton night-rail, that his body was very definitely there beside her. "They are in London, are they not?"

He frowned and Harriet held her breath. "What nonsense is this?" he growled.

"I can feel it," she said simply. "You are worried about something . . . something in London?"

When he did not reply, his eyes returning to the fire, Harriet took her courage in both hands. "Is she still sick?" she asked softly. "Is that what worries you?"

He turned back to her, a thunderous scowl on his face. "Who told you this?" he said harshly.

Harriet was relieved that he had not pretended to misunderstand her question. "Peter told me last Christmas. He said that was why you had to leave in such a bang."

"Your brother had no right to discuss my business with you, Harriet," the earl snapped. "And you have no business mentioning such things to me. It is hardly proper."

Exasperated at this masculine obtuseness, Harriet forgot she was lying in bed with a naked man. "That is absurd, Giles, you must see that it is," she exploded angrily. "We all know about your . . . your arrangement in London, so why pretend that it is not my concern? You mentioned it yourself before we were wed. It was one of the conditions you placed on our getting married at all, in case you have forgotten. Peter also explained it to me in detail before I accepted your offer. So let us not pretend that—"

"In detail?" the earl interrupted in a startled voice. "What details are you talking about, Harriet?" He sounded quite monstrously put out.

Harriet clicked her tongue impatiently. "Peter would not tell me her name, if that is what perturbs you, my lord," she said. "He was most discreet. But he did say she is a real Beauty, and that he introduced you to her four years ago."

The earl stared at her so fiercely that Harriet wondered if perhaps she should have been less outspoken. But that was not her nature, and the sooner he came to accept that, the better they could rub along together.

After a long silence during which Harriet realized that her husband intended to ignore her initial question entirely, she repeated it. "So? She is still sick, I take it. Is that why you are worried?"

Still he would not answer her, but flopped down abruptly on his back and stared at the ceiling, his hands clasped behind his head.

Harriet raised herself on her elbow and gazed down at him. The covers were down near his waist, and Harriet stared in renewed wonder at the muscled expanse of chest.

"Well?" Harriet insisted, tearing her eyes away from the disturbing sight. "Answer me, Giles. Is she sick?"

"You are a deuced termagant, you know that, Harriet," he burst out, glowering at her.

"Yes, I know," Harriet responded prosaically. "But you have not answered my question."

"Yes," he said, his anger abruptly deflated. "Yes, she is very ill, and the damned quacks cannot seen to find a remedy."

A sliver of pain pierced Harriet's heart at her husband's words. So it was true, she thought dully, he had been thinking of *her* while he was in bed with his wife. Harriet could no longer doubt that the Lady in London had won this round, and if she wished to maintain a shred of dignity, Harriet knew that she would have to concede defeat. And do so gracefully, naturally. There was no other way.

"Then what the devil are you doing here in Hampshire, when you should be in London?" she demanded with asperity. "What a complete numskull you are to be sure. Just why *did* you come anyway?" she could not resist asking.

"You will not talk to me in that fashion, Harriet," he threw back at her, his frown menacing. "And I thought I told you not to use stable language. If you must know, I came because I learned that Richard was here."

Harriet stared at him for a moment before she grasped the implications of his words. "Aha!" she exclaimed. "And you came *vent-à-terre* to save my virtue from your brother, I suppose?" she inquired with heavy sarcasm. "You have windmills in your head, my lord. Cannot you see that poor Richard is in no condition to seduce anyone? His arm hurts more than he lets on, you know. And he was so gaunt when he arrived, it nearly broke my heart." She gazed at her husband speculatively, wondering how he would take what she wanted so badly to tell him.

"Your brother needs your help," she said softly. "And I think it is only right that—"

"Do not tell me how to run my life, Harriet," the earl cut her off harshly. "Richard can take care of himself."

"You are wrong about that," Harriet replied firmly. "But Richard can wait. There is someone in London who needs you, too, and you should not have left her to the mercy of quacks. I suggest you leave tomorrow at dawn," she added, wondering what kind of ninnyhammer she was to be sending her husband off to his mistress before he bedded his wife. It was not what Harriet had intended to say at all, but after it was said, she knew it was the right thing to do. There would be plenty of time to continue their contest once the Beauty was back on her feet. In fact, it seemed quite unfair to Harriet to keep her husband here in her bed—where he appeared to be quite useless anyway—when he was undoubtedly needed in London.

"Are you sure you would not mind, Harriet?" he asked some time later, after she had pulled the covers up to her chin and turned away to seek her rest. He rolled on his side, and his hand slid over her waist to capture her breast.

Harriet took a deep breath to quell the racing of her pulse. "Of course not," she lied convincingly. "Actually, I would think you a veritable ogre if you stayed. Now be quiet and let me sleep."

She closed her eyes determinedly, and the pressure of his hand on her stilled, although he did not remove it. But Harriet's thoughts were not so much on the disturbing presence of the man beside her, but on the sick woman in London, who must be desperate for the comfort of her lover once more at her side. Harriet would certainly wish for the earl's presence had she been in the Beauty's shoes.

As sleep stole over her, Harriet knew—as surely as if the Beauty herself had spoken to her—that she had done the right thing.

# CHAPTER TEN

# Forbidden Encounter

Lord Kimbalton was halfway back to London before he allowed his thoughts to touch on the events of the previous night.

Nothing in his traditional upbringing, or his comfortable convictions of what a proper wife should be, or his extensive experience with females had prepared him for Harriet. His countess had revealed herself to be quite extraordinary in more ways than one. Harriet, he mused, savoring the taste of her name on his tongue. Yes, his Harriet was a most extraordinary female, and Giles was not sure whether his sense of outrage at her improper behavior was greater than his delight at her uninhibited response to his later demands. But he would not think of that yet, he told himself, although the very act of not remembering that part of their night together was causing a familiar tightening in his groin.

It was his wife's quite inappropriate interest in his mistress that bothered Giles the most. Although he would never admit it, Giles knew himself to be rather conservative in some of his notions. He disapproved of the newfangled custom that was making itself felt among the *ton* of allowing females to have a say in whom they wed. He had disapproved of Harriet's being in such a position, and it offended his sense of propriety that she had even considered rejecting his suit. The knowledge that she had accepted him reluctantly still rankled, and the suspicion that she would have preferred a love match had almost made him draw back from the alliance.

Giles disapproved of love in any form. In his experience, love—or what was glorified by that name among his acquaintances—only led to embarrassing displays of maudlin sentimentality. Giles believed in duty and responsibility, in dignity and family honor. None of these things he cherished appeared to withstand the onslaught of that deranged state people attributed to love. He preferred to call love by its real name because he did believe in pleasure, and the satisfying of lust led to pleasure. As it had last night. The memory of last night brought on a renewed tingling in his groin, and Giles forced his mind back to the problem of Harriet's quite unacceptable interest in Ophelia's illness.

The truth was, Giles finally admitted to himself, after changing horses in Kingston and starting on the last leg of his journey, the stable pattern and familiar fabric of his whole life had suddenly been threatened by a chit who seemed to believe that people took precedence over propriety and tradition. This was quite nonsensical of her, of course, and Giles could not but wonder how he had allowed himself to be swayed by her arguments. As a result of what must have been a momentary weakness, he now found himself rushing back to London to be at Ophelia's bedside. It was outrageous enough that his wife had had the temerity to mention the subject of his mistress at all, but it was far worse that she had shown such genuine compassion for the other woman in her husband's life. It made him distinctly uncomfortable.

Giles had certainly been worried about his beautiful Ophelia himself. Her deteriorated state had preyed on his mind, and he fully intended to return to her as soon as the matter of his bastard brother had been resolved to his satisfaction. But Richard's presence at the Abbey had not been resolved. It had not even been addressed except by Harriet, who had made the odd statement that his brother needed his help. This, too, was obviously more sentimental twaddle. A typical female reaction to a wounded soldier with a handsome face and a glib tongue.

Giles shrugged his shoulders under his modestly caped driving coat and tooled his curricle past a lumbering Mail Coach, which took up more than its fair share of the King's highway. He would deal with Richard eventually, he thought, removing him as far away as possible form the Montague ancestral home. And perhaps he would help him financially, too, if that would please Harriet. The thought of pleasing Harriet was new to him, and reminded him that he must deal with his wife as well. She must never again be allowed to interfere in the smooth running of his life, particularly that part of it occupied by his mistress. He would have a serious talk with her as soon as things returned to normal, he decided with a certain degree of complacency at having set a reasonable course for himself.

She would—indeed she must—learn that a husband's will was a wife's law.

And now that he had settled his affairs to his entire satisfaction—for deciding upon a solution and achieving it were one and the same to him—Giles allowed his thoughts to drift back to last night—particularly to the second part of the night. And to Harriet.

It had been a bizarre experience, that frustrated bedding of his wife, Giles remembered. Perhaps he should have allowed her to take off the blasted night-rail. Perhaps the sight of his wife's nakedness would have carried him through to the consummation. But for some stupid reason, the notion that he could allow Harriet to humiliate herself for his pleasure had deprived him of any desire at all. Even her suggestion that she wished to compare him to Richard had only restored his erection temporarily. And then the insidious memory of Ophelia, abandoned in London when she truly needed him, had crept into his mind to destroy any hope he might have had of enjoying his wife. His panic had increased as his own body had betrayed him. So when Harriet had asked the unthinkable question, shocked as he had been at her audacity and lack of modesty, Giles had admitted the truth. His thoughts had been in London, after all, and the explanation seemed to satisfy Harriet, who promptly told him to get himself back to London.

Then she had turned away and calmly gone to sleep. Giles had not been able so easily to escape his own fears. Sleep had come only gradually, and then his dreams had been filled with nightmares that made him break out in a cold sweat. His wife and mistress had joined forces against him, it seemed, for they danced round him stark naked, teasing him for his failure to rise to the occasion. Then they had both run off, hand in hand, into a dark wood, and he could hear their sweet voices taunting him. And he was helpless to do anything about it; his hands and feet were tightly bound. Only after their voices had faded into the blackness had Giles's bonds miraculously disappeared, and he found himself as hard as a board.

He had woken with a start to find himself in that identical state but with the tantalizing incentive of a soft female bottom pressing into his groin. He had lain perfectly still for what seemed like hours, but the painful throbbing would not subside. In the end he had touched her hip, and then her breasts, first one then the other until his senses rebelled. He listened to her even breathing, reluctant to wake her, yet knowing he would do so. He kissed the nape of her neck and heard her sigh, but she did not wake. She settled more comfortably against him, and Giles thought he would explode. He eased her gently onto her back and explored her body with tentative fingers. Then he kissed her, his tongue tracing her relaxed mouth, until suddenly Harriet opened her eyes and looked up at him, her lips parted in fright. Giles had taken advantage of the moment to invade her mouth.

"Oh, Giles," she murmured when he at last raised his head. "What are you doing?"

He chuckled deep in his throat. "I seem to be seducing my wife," he whispered in her ear before tracing kisses down her neck.

"Couldn't you sleep?" she inquired with such innocence that Giles felt his heart swell with unexpected tenderness.

"No, my love. I was dreaming of you." Which was at least partially true and served its purpose.

She had been immediately intrigued. "Was it a wonderful dream?" she wanted to know.

"This is much better," he murmured, not wishing to lie. He ran his fingers slowly over her stomach and down into her secret places. "Yes," he murmured against her lips as his fingers explored her. "Much better."

"Oh!" she said in a breathless voice. "I promise not to scream."

"Scream?" He paused to raise his head and stare at her in the firelight. "Why would you want to do that?"

"I understand it hurts quite dreadfully," she whispered.

Giles pondered the irrefutability of this fact of life. "I have heard that it sometimes does not hurt nearly as much as you might think," he said, drawing on his meager knowledge of deflowering virgins. "But I really could not say for sure. I have no experience at all with virgins, you see."

"Oh!" she had said again, and Giles wished he had not divulged this secret to her; she would doubtless become apprehensive. But she surprised him again, much to his delight.

"I am so glad," she whispered in his ear. "Now we can discover it together, can't we?"

And discover it they did.

Giles had not known he possessed quite the capacity for tenderness he displayed with his wife that night. And when the crucial moment came, they discovered that the pain was not nearly as severe as Harriet had evidently been prepared for. She had flinched and opened her mouth in surprise, but there had been not even the suggestion of a scream. Then she had smiled at him so sweetly that Giles felt an unfamiliar pain in his chest.

The memory of that moment was so vivid in his mind that his horses had come to a halt before the familiar door of Montague House on Grosvenor Square, and the footman had removed his portmanteau from the back of the curricle, before Giles collected his wits enough to greet the smiling butler who stood ready to usher him into the hall.

For several days after the earl's departure for London, Harriet floated about the house and gardens in such a state of distraction that both Lady Sophronia and the captain remarked upon it.

"Not coming down with anything, are you, child?" her aunt inquired brusquely on the third morning at the breakfast table.

Harriet looked at her aunt in surprise and felt her color rise. "Of course not, Aunt," she responded dreamily. "I feel perfectly wonderful."

And indeed she spoke nothing but the truth, Harriet thought, spreading her second piece of toast with strawberry jam. It was quite wonderful to be rid of the anxiety of being only half a wife. Of being so naive and unsure of herself. And it was certainly wonderful to be awakened in the early hours by a husband who quite obviously desired her. Who had seduced her so gently, and with hardly any pain to speak of. Aunt Sophy had been quite wrong about the pain, Harriet thought. Falling off Greybeard and twisting her leg had been far more painful. One day she would have to tell Aunt Sophy just how wonderful it had been. But not yet, she thought. Her joy in her husband was still too new. Harriet wanted to keep it all tightly cradled within herself, savoring the sweetness of being a woman at last. . . .

"What are you smirking about, Harry?"

Harriet started, and laughed nervously at Richard, who had entered the breakfast room at that moment, his dark hair windblown from his morning ride.

"How was your ride, Richard?" she inquired, ignoring his question. "Is Greybeard behaving for you yet?"

"The brute is still recalcitrant, but I think he is beginning to weary of fighting me. He is the best jumper I have seen in a long time, Harry. I could have used him in Spain, believe me."

"Giles liked him, too," she began eagerly, and then blushed, busying herself with pouring another cup of tea.

"Ah, yes," Lady Sophronia interjected heartily. "His lordship made a quite substantial offer for the horse, but Harriet would not sell."

"I am glad you did not, Harry. I would make you an offer for him myself if I had the blunt."

Harriet smiled. "If you decide to go back to the army, Richard, I shall give him to you as a gift. To help keep you safe."

The captain glanced at her oddly for a moment before accepting the plate of food Carruthers had prepared for him. "I have no intention of returning to the army," he said shortly. "That is if I can persuade my brother to help me get a place of my own. Our father promised me Green Oaks, but he forgot to mention it in his will."

"Green Oaks?" Harriet repeated, intensely disturbed by the bitterness in Richard's voice. "Where is that?"

"Over near Corhampton. Lovely old Tudor manor house with a small estate attached to it. That is sheep country over there, and the place used to be fairly prosperous. I have not seen it in five years, of course. It is a wonder Brian did not sell it off to pay his gambling debts."

Conversation lapsed after that, but Richard's words had given Harriet something to occupy her thoughts other than her own contentment. Her new brother was hurting, and she saw at once that, whether Richard liked it or not, he needed Lord Kimbalton's support to secure his future happiness. Just as the beautiful Lady in London needed Giles to comfort her in her sickness, Harriet mused. Just as she herself needed him . . . The notion of actually needing her husband was a novel one to Harriet, and it took quite a while to admit, even to herself, that she had grown just the tiniest bit dependent on that autocratic man for her happiness.

Shaking off this uncomfortable thought, Harriet asked Richard if he knew where she could obtain some feathered tenants for the lake.

"Swans, do you mean?" Richard wanted to know.

"Oh, yes," Aunt Sophy chimed in. "There always used to be swans on that lake. It specifically says so in all the Guide Books."

"I think swans are out of the question," Harriet observed. "Giles does not like them."

"Well, we do not want to offend the lord of the manor now, do we?" Richard drawled sarcastically. "What about ducks? Old Mrs. Hayes has a brood hatched just last week. I am sure I could persuade her to part with them at a price."

"Ducks!" Lady Sophronia's voice was indignant. "Surely you do not mean to introduce such plebeian creatures to the Abbey, Harriet? What would his lordship say?"

Harriet laughed, and exchanged a wicked grin with Richard. "I think ducks would be just the thing," she said. "Let us go and talk to Mrs. Hayes immediately, Richard."

Mrs. Hayes proved amenable to Richard's persuasion and that very afternoon the new tenants were installed and thriving on the artificial lake, their occasional quacks audible from the open breakfast room window. Harriet was particularly pleased at the sense of vitality the friendly birds contributed to the lifeless body of water.

Two weeks after the ducks became permanent residents of Kimbalton Abbey, Harriet came downstairs one morning to find Aunt Sophy poring over the morning post, a worried frown on her usually placid countenance.

"Oh, dear me," that lady burst out as soon as Harriet entered the room. "I have received some disturbing news, Harriet. Very disturbing indeed. Your Aunt Prudence appears to be quite seriously ill. I have a rather frantic letter from her companion, Miss Burton—quite the scatterbrain she is, I have always thought, but she sounds at her wit's end and begs me to attend Lady Cuthbert as soon as possible." This was uttered in such woeful tones that Harriet crossed the room to put a comforting arm around her aunt's quaking shoulders.

"Whatever am I do to do, child?" she murmured tearfully. "I dislike leaving you alone, love, but I see no other alternative. I know that his lordship has forbidden you to set foot in London, so I shall have to take the stage tomorrow morning and go on my own."

Harriet vetoed her aunt's plans instantly. "You will do no such thing, Aunt," she declared airily. "Of course I will go with you. And the devil fly away with his lordship's silly rules. This is an emergency, as I am sure he will understand. So do not give it another thought, dearest. Leave everything in my hands." She turned to the butler, who had just brought up

her toast. "Carruthers, ask the stables to send round the traveling chaise, if you please. We shall leave in one hour."

"And where are you going, ladies, if I may ask?" Richard
wanted to know, entering the room in the middle of this commotion.

"We are going to London,"' Harriet said unequivocally,
suddenly excited at the prospect of a change of scenery. "And
we are counting on your escort, Richard."

Taking the captain's bemused smile as an acceptance, Harriet set both Lucy and her aunt's abigail to packing the few
clothes they might need for a short stay in the Metropolis, and
an hour later, much to everyone's surprise, they were on their
way.

When the well-sprung chaise drew up in front of Lady
Cuthbert's small but elegant town house on Mount Street,
evening had fallen, and the travelers were received with surprise by the portly butler.

"Welcome to London, Lady Sophronia. And you too, Lady
Harriet," the old man greeted them effusively. "Her ladyship
will be right glad to see you."

"How is my Aunt Prudence, Crofts?" Harriet demanded,
shedding her light traveling coat and removing her gloves.

The butler shook his balding head and sighed lugubriously.
"Not as hearty as we could wish, milady."

When the ladies proceeded upstairs, they found that the butler had not misled them. Lady Cuthbert was indeed still laid up
in her sickbed, attended by a tearful and woefully ineffectual
Miss Burton, but she was a good deal more cheerful than her
companion had led them to expect.

"I had no idea the silly widgeon had written to you, my dear
Sophy," Lady Cuthbert said with considerable chagrin after
she discovered the cause of her sister's unexpected appearance
at Mount Street. "I would have put a stop to it immediately,
you may be sure. My fever was dangerously high, according to
the doctor, but I am feeling a little better today, and he be-
lieves the worst is over."

This piece of information, though certainly welcome news
to the two visitors, proved to be rather an anticlimax. They
had traveled in excessive haste, expecting to find Lady Cuthbert on her deathbed, and here she was, hale if not entirely
hearty.

Lady Sophronia glared crossly at Miss Burton, who

promptly dissolved into tears and rushed out of her ladyship's bedchamber.

Lady Cuthbert shook her head ruefully. "I apologize, dearest Sophy, for dragging you out on a wild-goose chase. But now that you are both here," she went on more cheerfully, "I insist that you spend a week or two with me in Town. I could certainly use the company."

Aunt Sophy privately warned her niece that his lordship would hardly approve of their presence in the Metropolis if he found out, but Harriet had other plans. Although she would not have deliberately disobeyed her husband—at least she liked to think she would not—in coming to London, now that they were here, she saw no harm in spending a few days visiting the shops. Quietly and without any fuss, of course. And naturally she would avoid mingling with the *ton*, where she might run into the earl.

"That is very kind of you, Aunt Prudence," she said quickly. "We would like that very much indeed."

By the end of the week Harriet had not regretted her daring decision. Preferring as she did the quiet country life, she rarely set foot in London, but she soon discovered, from random glimpses of elegant ladies from the front windows of Lady Cuthbert's residence, that her wardrobe was woefully out of fashion. So Harriet gave in to her feminine instincts and spent several delightful mornings at the saloon of one of the less-frequented modistes on Clarges Street. Madame Blanchard was overjoyed at the prospect of gaining a new customer, one furthermore, possessed of a good eye for style and a blithe disregard for cost. Although Madame la contesse adamantly rejected the more daring of her creations, the modiste was more than satisfied with the list of silk and satin evening gowns, afternoon gowns in stripped lustering, a smart blue riding habit, and numerous muslin morning gowns in the newest colors that the countess ordered for prompt delivery.

"Would you care to escort us to Gunther's for an ice this afternoon?" Harriet demanded of the captain one morning at breakfast. "At an hour when the tea-room is less crowded, naturally."

Richard grinned at her and shook his head. "You are dreaming, my dear Harry," he said regretfully. "I would, of course, be delighted to be seen in the company of two such charming ladies, but Gunther's is quite out of the question. Not that Giles frequents the place, I daresay, but too many others do, and one of them might recognize you. Or me," he added wryly. "Only yesterday I ran into the Marquess of Monroyal at my tailor's—"

"Oh, not *that* dreadful man," Harriet interrupted, wrinkling her nose disdainfully.

"You dislike his lordship, I gather?" Richard chuckled. "Monroyal is accounted one of London's greatest catches, you know. Has been for years. All sorts of females have tried to get their hooks into him, but he has grown too wily for match-making mamas and seems to have sworn off matrimony altogether."

"I am glad to hear it," Harriet snapped. "He is also one of the world's greatest rogues. I am sorry that he seems to be one of Giles's cronies."

Richard raised a dark eyebrow. "Cronies are they? That's odd. I would have thought the marquess, notorious rakehell that he is, might find Giles rather dull." He grinned at Harriet's sudden frown. "Do not bite my head off, love. Giles is a lot of things, but reckless rogue and wicked womanizer he certainly is not." He looked pensive. "I wonder what they see in each other?"

The subject did not interest Harriet, and she waved it aside. "What about Mr. Cross's Royal Menagerie, then?" she asked innocently.

Richard gaped at her. "You cannot mean to drag me through that place, Harriet?" he groaned. "It is always crowded with Cits and their families gawking at the wild beasts. Spare me, I beg of you."

It was Harriet's turn to laugh. "Where would *you* like to go this afternoon, Aunt?" she inquired. "That is if Aunt Prudence can spare you for a few hours?"

Lady Sophronia shook her head. "I think I had better stay to keep Pru company," she said. "That Miss Burton is a bird-brained twit who is worse than useless in the sickroom. Pru-dence is feeling much better, of course, but she still gets restless in the afternoons. But if you happen to go near Hatchard's Bookshop, you might get Mrs. Radcliffe's latest novel. I could read it to Pru in the evenings." She looked at Harriet hopefully.

"What a splendid idea!" Harriet exclaimed. "I had planned to visit Hatchard's anyway. We can do so this afternoon, can we not, Richard?"

When the captain looked at her dubiously, Harriet laughed.

"Please humor me in this, Richard. Hatchard's has always been one of my favorite places."

"Unfortunately, half the *ton* feels the same way, Harriet," he warned. "Are you sure you want to risk it?"

"The risk will be minimal if we go early, before the fashionable hour for promenading. I promise not to spend more than ten minutes there," she wheedled.

In the end Richard capitulated, and two o'clock found them ascending the shallow steps to the famous bookshop.

"Ten minutes only," Richard reminded her. "I shall take a look at the newspapers."

Harriet went straight to the section where new books were displayed, and soon found the Radcliffe novel she sought. There were several others whose titles tempted her to browse through them, particularly a volume of poetry called *Childe Harold* by Lord Byron. She opened the slim book and was immediately caught up in the somber tenor of the author's words. She read on, oblivious of the murmur of voices around her, until the sound of a familiar name interrupted her concentration.

"Yes, indeed, Mrs. Brooks," the unctuous clerk was saying to a tall, slim lady in an elegant pale blue walking gown of expensive lustering, trimmed with darker blue around the collar and hem. "The book you ordered came in yesterday. Shall I wrap it for you, ma'am?"

"If you will, please," the lady replied in a softly musical voice that struck Harriet as infinitely sad. "I wish to look at your new arrivals, while I am here."

Brooks? Harriet thought absentmindedly. Where had she heard that name before? The lady's hair was of the palest gold, the palest Harriet had ever seen, and that, too, seemed somehow familiar.

"Over there, Mrs. Brooks," the clerk indicated the table where Harriet stood before hurrying away on his errand.

And then the blonde lady turned towards her, and Harriet drew in a sharp breath, shocked at the flood of memories which came rioting through her mind.

"Ophelia!" she exclaimed ecstatically. "Ophelia Weston! No, it is Brooks now, of course, but to me you will always be Ophelia Weston." She stepped forward eagerly and clasped the lady's limp hands in hers. "Oh, my dear, dear friend, I simply cannot believe it," she continued, unable to resist giving the tall, beautiful creature an enthusiastic hug. "It's been years since I've thought of those days we shared in Miss Harrow's Seminary. And what wonderful times they were, Ophelia. I cherish those memories and regret we lost touch when you married Roger and followed him to Spain."

She glanced curiously around the shop. "Are you both home on leave, Ophelia? Tell me where you are staying and I will call on you. We have so much to catch up on, dearest."

Harriet felt the cold hands jerk spasmodically in hers and looked up at her tall friend, shocked to see the lovely face lose several shades of what little color it had.

"Oh, Harriet, Roger was killed in Spain six years ago," Mrs. Brooks said simply, her violet eyes filling with tears.

"Oh!" Harriet murmured, horrified that she had opened old wounds. "I am sorry, Ophelia. I didn't know. All this time I thought you were both in Spain." Her voice trailed off.

Ophelia was looking decidedly peaked, Harriet thought, giving her friend's cold fingers an encouraging squeeze. "But now that I have found you again, my dear," she continued, determined to make up for her gaffe, "we simply must not lose touch, must we? I am staying with my Aunt Prudence, Lady Cuthbert, you know. Do come back with me for a cup of tea, Ophelia. Aunt Sophy is with me. You remember Aunt Sophy, don't you, dear? And also Captain Richard Montague, whom you won't know. He's my husband's brother, and he is about here somewhere." She glanced about the room, which suddenly seemed to be more crowded than she remembered. And people seemed to be staring, quite rudely in fact.

"Montague?" Mrs. Brooks murmured disjointedly, her fingers trembling uncontrollably. "Did you say Montague, Harriet?" She swayed noticeably, and Harriet grasped her arm, fearful that the fragile beauty was about to swoon.

"Yes, Richard Montague. He is recently returned from the war and staying with us down in Hampshire." She regarded Ophelia with growing alarm. "Are you feeling unwell, dear? You look so pale."

"Yes, that's it," Ophelia murmured faintly, clutching at Harriet's hand as if to draw strength from it. "I have been feeling perfectly rotten for several months now. Since before Christmas actually. I thought I was a little better this morning, but I can feel the megrim coming back."

"Let me take you home, Ophelia," Harriet urged. "Ah, there is Richard. He will take care of everything."

But to her dismay, Richard looked rather grim when he came up to them and made a stiff little bow to Mrs. Brooks, ignoring Harriet's attempts to introduce them. "We must leave immediately, Harriet" he said in a strange, tight voice, which sounded uncannily like his brother's. He took her none too gently by the elbow and inclined his head briefly to Ophelia again, before turning towards the door. "Come on, Harriet," he whispered between clenched teeth. "If we don't get out of here this instant, there will be the devil to pay, believe me."

Harriet was nonplussed. Had everyone run mad? she wondered. Richard was behaving very strangely, and Ophelia looked as pale as one of the ghosts that, according to the Guide Books, were supposed to haunt the Long Gallery at the Abbey. She turned her gaze back to Ophelia and noticed her friend's eyes, wide with shock, staring in horror at someone who had just stepped into the room.

There was a moment of deafening silence, and then the cluster of patrons standing by the bow window broke into an incoherent jabber of avid conversation. Harriet had the disagreeable sensation that they were, for some obscure reason, talking about her.

She turned towards the door, and her own breath caught in her throat for so long she thought that she must surely swoon herself.

Lord Kimbalton's cool gray eyes flickered over the scene before him, and Harriet saw his features abruptly freeze into a marble mask.

"Oh, God," she whispered under her breath. "It is Giles!"

"How incredibly perceptive of you, my dear," Richard whispered back, his jaw set in a rigid line.

To Harriet's eternal mortification, the earl casually took a jeweled quizzing glass from his waistcoat pocket and held it up to his right eye. She felt Richard's fingers tighten painfully on her arm, and Ophelia moan something quite unintelligible behind her. Harriet herself would gladly had slapped the odious brute, but Richard held her in an iron grip.

"A most edifying picture, to be sure," the earl murmured in a voice more deadly than any Harriet had ever heard him use.

She heard Richard swear viciously under his breath, and then she was walking, propelled by the captain's merciless grip, past her husband, out of the door, and down the steps.

It was not until she turned to face Richard and saw the compassion in his eyes that Harriet began to have an inkling of what had just occurred. The suspicion was too terrible to contemplate, of course, but could she ignore the truth that she read in Richard's gray-blue eyes?

Good God! she thought, her spirits descending to the very bottom of her soles. She had made a mull of things again!

# CHAPTER ELEVEN

# *Harriet Intervenes*

Lord Kimbalton drew himself up to his full height and raised his quizzing glass. He glared contemptuously at the group of interested patrons in the bow window until they turned away, smirks still on their faces. He could do little to mend that, Giles thought in a cold fury, but he could at least brush through this highly embarrassing situation with some shreds of his dignity intact.

He turned back to Ophelia, who was leaning heavily against the counter, ignoring the neatly tied parcel the clerk held out to her. Predictably, the widow had gone all to pieces, Giles saw with a flicker of annoyance, which he quickly suppressed. Ophelia had always been easily alarmed and lacked even the slightest hint of assertiveness or fortitude. This docile characteristic had been one of the traits that had initially attracted him to the Beauty, the earl remembered. He had enjoyed her absolute submissiveness to his better judgment, and her unfailing willingness to be guided by him in all things.

Quite unlike Harriet.

The thought of his wife caused a fresh wave of fury to sweep over him. Was a man to have no relief from this everlasting feminine meddling in his affairs? His jaw muscles clenched at the recollection of the infuriating scene he had just witnessed. What in Hades was Harriet doing in London anyway? And why must she pick out the one female in the entire town with whom she should never have associated? Well, she would soon learn that she had passed beyond the line of what he would tolerate in a wife. In *his* wife. He ground his teeth in frustration.

"Steady on, old chap," a familiar voice drawled at his elbow, distracting Giles from his murderous thoughts of what he would do to Harriet when he got his hands on her. "That was quite a performance the Montagues put on there. Vastly more entertaining than MacBeth, I can assure you. But don't

frown so, Giles, you are terrifying our beautiful Mrs. Brooks
out of her wits."

Giles swung round and glared at the Marquess of Monroyal,
who appeared not to notice the simmering hostility. "Stay out
of this, Monroyal," he muttered. "And where were *you* when
this debacle started?" he added, giving the marquess a level
look. "Could you not have done anything to prevent my wife
from making a spectacle of herself?"

The marquess laughed cynically. "Oh, no you don't, old
man. It's no use trying to shift the blame to me. I never interfere between a man's wife and his mistress. Wild horses could
not induce me to venture on those troubled byways." He
laughed again, and Giles felt a sudden urge to darken his
friend's daylights. "You have no doubt heard the old adage
about making one's bed and lying on it. Seems most appropri-
ate to me," the marquess chuckled wickedly. "Perhaps you
should take it to heart, old man."

"Don't preach to me, my lord. My temper is wearing mighty
thin, and you could catch cold."

The marquess shrugged his elegant shoulders and strolled
away, while Giles turned his attention back to Ophelia, who
appeared on the point of swooning. Once again Giles felt the
prick of impatience, which he ignored. He stepped up to the
counter and took the parcel from the gangling clerk, whose
nose was twitching with excitement.

Giles paid for the book and offered his arm to Ophelia, who
took it hesitantly. "Come along, my dear," Giles said, forcing
himself to speak gently. Ophelia's eyes were wide and glazed
with shock, he noticed, and her distress caused him a tremor of
anxiety not unmixed with impatience.

He led her out of the establishment and down the shallow
steps to where her closed carriage awaited her. As he handed
her into the vehicle, Giles noticed a tear edging its way down
her chalk-white face, and he cursed under his breath. If Harriet's imprudence had caused a setback in Ophelia's delicate
health, she would pay dearly for it, he thought, glancing
around to see if the culprit was still in sight.

He spotted his brother trying, without much success, to get
Harriet into a carriage a little way up the street. Leaving Mrs.
Brooks with the curt admonition that he would be back
shortly, Giles strode purposefully in their direction. He saw his
wife's hazel eyes open wide at the sight of him, but not from
fright, he noticed with annoyance. Any normal female would

be cowering in the face of his rage, as Ophelia was doing even at this moment. But Harriet showed no sign of feminine trepidation as he came to a halt and glared down at her. Instead, she had the audacity to address him as though he were some particularly repulsive monster.

"Oh, Giles, it was odious of you to frighten Ophelia out of her wits with that monstrous frown of yours. You must not blame her for this quite dreadful coincidence, you know. I should not have been in Hatchard's at all, as Richard has already told me. But—"

Giles felt his face go rigid. "How do you know her name?" he said slowly and distinctly, his voice trembling with fury.

"Oh, because we grew up together, of course," his wife replied impatiently, as though he were some halfwit who must have everything explained to him. "I've known Ophelia Weston for years; we went to school together in Bath. When I saw her again, I was overjoyed. I didn't know of course that Roger was dead or that . . ." she paused, her eyes clouding angrily— "I did not know about . . . that you had . . . that she was . . ." She stumbled to a halt and merely glared at him, the golden flecks in her eyes dancing angrily.

Giles saw with a glimmer of satisfaction that even his outspoken wife could not quite bring herself to say what was troubling her. His lips twitched into a thin smile. "That she was what, my dear?"

Harriet's chin went up, and Giles instantly wished he had not provoked his wife.

"You know perfectly well, you beast," she spat at him. "Oh, you are truly reprehensible! How *could* you take advantage of a lovely creature like Ophelia? You are despicable and selfish and an odious bully. Does nothing matter to you at all but your own convenience?" she cried, her voice quavering with the force of her emotions. "I *hate* you!" she choked, and whirled away to clamber into the carriage without waiting for Richard's assistance.

The earl felt the color drain from his face. He could not believe his ears. He stood for a full minute staring into his brother's startled blue-gray eyes. Giles was surprised to see a glint of sympathy there, rather than the cynical amusement he would have expected from Richard. With a mighty effort, he pulled his wits together.

"Take that harridan back to Montague House, if you will," he said in a toneless voice. "I shall deal with that disgraceful display later." Without another word, he strode over to the other waiting carriage.

Silently, he climbed in beside a softly weeping Ophelia. He was unused to these theatrical displays of emotion and his wife's inexplicable burst of invective had unnerved him far more than his mistress's restrained tears.

"*Please*, Giles, do not take your anger out on Harriet," Ophelia surprised him by murmuring as the carriage lurched into motion. "If anyone deserves your disgust, it is I, my lord. I should not have gone there, and indeed would not have done so had I but known . . ." She paused to catch her breath. "It was all a terrible mistake. Harriet has always been like a sister to me, and I could not bear to repulse her when she appeared so glad to see me. I simply could not do it, Giles," she sobbed, her beautiful face unmarred by the tears that trickled down her cheeks.

The notion of the two females in his life defending each other against his justifiable wrath, which had yet to fall on either of them, would have amused him under any other circumstances. As it was, Giles felt only a growing frustration at the events which had shattered the calm surface of his life. And it was all Harriet's fault, he could see clearly. Had she been the obedient female her brother had touted her to be, none of this highly unsettling rumpus would have occurred, he thought savagely, clenching his fists at the necessity of waiting another hour before he could vent his wrath on her disobedient head.

A sob escaped the woman at his side, and Giles realized that Ophelia must imagine his wrath was directed at her. He reached for her slim gloved hand and held it in both of his. "Do not distress yourself, my dear," he said kindly. "It is not your fault that the countess saw fit to disobey my express orders not to set foot in London. Neither is it your fault that she happened to be in Hatchard's when you went there. Do not tease yourself on her account," he added grimly. "When I have finished with Lady Kimbalton, she will know precisely how I expect my wife to conduct herself in future. She will not disobey her lord again, my dear, that I can guarantee you."

These assurances, which Giles had intended as comforting, resulted in a fresh outbreak of tears.

"Oh, dear!" Ophelia cried in an anguished voice. "You are going to beat her, Giles. I just know you are. I cannot bear the thought." Mrs. Brooks covered her face with her hands and sobbed disconsolately.

The earl gazed on this disturbing spectacle with amazement mixed with impatience. He tried to put a supporting arm around his mistress, but Ophelia shrank from him.

"The devil take it, Ophelia," he exclaimed impatiently. "I am not going to beat anybody. Whatever gave you that bacon-brained notion? Come, my dear," he added, forcing himself to subdue his temper. "Dry your eyes. We are about to arrive, and you would not want Stevens to see you in such a state, would you? He might think I have beaten you, which you know I never have and never will."

It took Lord Kimbalton a full hour to restore his mistress to her usual quiet demeanor, and it was not until he had seen her ensconced on the rose settee in the Chinese drawing room, with a warm rug tucked around her, and taken several cups of tea with her, that Giles was able to take his leave.

When he arrived at Montague House, Giles's fury had abated somewhat, but he still intended to give his errant wife the rough edge of his tongue and send her packing back to Hampshire. Upon being informed that Captain Montague awaited him in the library, Giles felt his hackles rise again. If Richard had the audacity to say one word about his handling of the unfortunate encounter at the bookshop, Giles would have him thrown out of the house. He had endured enough meddling for one afternoon, enough invective from his wife, and quite enough tears from his mistress to last a lifetime. He would not endure interference from his damned brother.

He strode into the library quite prepared to tell Richard he might take his advice elsewhere.

"Well?" he demanded without preamble. "What is it now?"

"It is Harriet, of course, who else?" his brother responded with equal brevity.

"I do not need your assistance to discipline my wife," he said curtly. "I shall deal with her in a moment. Now what do you . . ."

"She ain't here," Richard drawled laconically.

Giles paused to digest this piece of unexpected news. "Where is she?" he demanded, his voice registering his frustration.

Richard grinned wryly. "She is staying with her aunt, Lady Cuthbert, on Mount Street," his brother replied.

The earl ground his teeth. "I thought I told you to bring her here, damn it."

"You did. But have you ever tried to argue with Harriet

when she has her mind set on something? An entirely fruitless
exercise, as no doubt you already know. She expressed a distinct aversion to your tyrannical starts, as she called them, and
refused to set foot in this house. Short of dragging her in bod-
ily, which I did not think you would appreciate, I could not
budge her."

Giles glared at his brother for several moments before he
could trust himself to speak.

"Mount Street, you say?" he growled. "I shall go over there
and drag her back myself." He turned towards the door, but
Richard's quiet chuckle stopped him.

"Do you really think Harriet will receive you, old man?"

"Of course, she will receive me. I am her husband," Giles
replied icily. The mere suggestion that his wife could deny
herself was unthinkable. He stalked out of the library, followed by Richard.

"I do not require an escort, Richard," the earl said coldly. "I
can handle this matter perfectly well on my own."

Richard seemed unfazed by his bluntness. "I am racked up
there, too," he explained as the two men walked down the
steps together. "So I shall drive over with you if you do not
object."

Giles had barely settled himself into his carriage when another unpleasant thought occurred to him. "Why did you not
come to Montague House?" he demanded.

Richard regarded him oddly for a moment. "I did not think I
would be welcome there, brother," he said with a crooked
smile.

Giles stared at his younger brother for several long moments
before he looked away self-consciously. "That is poppycock,
and you know it," he said gruffly. But they both knew differently, of course. Giles had told his brother in so many words
that he was not welcome at the Abbey. Could he really blame
Richard for not feeling welcome at Montague House?

The drive to Mount Street was accomplished in silence.
Giles was uncomfortably aware that his neatly arranged life
had suddenly taken on the appearance of a melodrama, and
that he had become the villain of the piece. This troubled the
earl more than he cared to admit, for he had always considered
himself a fair and tolerant, independent and self-sufficient
man. The scandalous scene in the bookshop had upset the delicate balance of his relationships with those closest to him, and
Giles felt inexplicably bereft of emotional support. Emotional

support? he repeated to himself, aghast at the notion that he could be touched by such maudlin sentiments.

But it was true, he admitted wryly. The comfort and pleasure he had been accustomed for the past four years to find with his mistress seemed to have evaporated. Ophelia had turned into a watering-pot, and Giles had not been in her bed for over two months. And his brother had just admitted to avoiding the family residence because he did not feel welcome there. And as for Harriet . . . Giles had evidently alienated his wife, too, although how this could have happened when he was in the right, and she definitely in the wrong, he could not fathom. And now here she was avoiding him, running off to her aunt's when she should be in Montague House, *his* house, where *his* wife belonged.

Harriet, he thought. Why the devil could she not behave like the dutiful wife she had been last month, when he had visited the Abbey. The memory of that extraordinary night Giles had spent in his wife's bed flooded back to soothe his battered spirits, and he suddenly felt a terrible, quite irrational need to hold Harriet in his arms again. The feeling was so acute that he actually experienced a constriction in his chest.

As the coach drew up before Lady Cuthbert's residence, the earl suddenly made up his mind. He would not say a single word of criticism to his wife. He would forgive her for her outrageous behavior, her disobedience, her quite dreadful language, her association with Ophelia, her brazen defiance. He would overlook all of this and take the wench back to Hampshire where she should be. And he would stay with her for a week or so, until this whole episode faded into the past. They would take up where they had left off a month ago. The thought of that most agreeable part of his plan gave Giles's heart a lift as he stepped from the carriage and ran up the steps. He would get a child on her, he thought with sudden inspiration. That would keep her quietly at home instead of complicating his life in London.

And then he would do something for Richard. He was not sure what, but he would find something. Ophelia would regain her health and strength, and life would return to normal.

Having organized the future to his entire satisfaction, Lord Kimbalton rapped impatiently on the heavy door with his cane.

"Tell the countess that Lord Kimbalton is here," Giles commanded as soon as the butler appeared. He stepped into the hall and removed his beaver. The butler gazed at him impassively.

"Their ladyships are not receiving this afternoon, milord," he said stiffly. "The countess has retired to her rooms with the megrim, milord."

"Tell her ladyship I am here, nevertheless," Giles repeated icily.

The butler regarded him with indifference. "I beg your pardon, milord. I have strict orders not to admit anyone."

The earl turned around to find Richard standing in the doorway, regarding him silently. Very deliberately, he replaced his beaver.

"Inform her ladyship that I shall return tomorrow morning," he said stiffly to the butler over his shoulder. "And I shall not be denied."

"Very well, milord."

After a long, piercing look at his brother, Giles strode past the butler and down the steps without another word.

No sooner did Harriet receive word from Richard that his brother had quit the premises than she dashed off a note to Ophelia, begging her friend to receive her immediately. When she cornered Richard in the library to wheedle Ophelia's direction from him, she encountered strenuous opposition.

"Giles ain't going to like it, Harry," Richard protested. "Bound to kick up the devil of a dust if he finds out I gave it to you. And I am in his bad books already, you know."

"Pooh!" Harriet responded impatiently. "There is no reason for him to know. And if Peter were here, he would give it to me instantly. In fact, he would offer to escort me there himself," she added hopefully.

"Well, he ain't here," Richard pointed out unnecessarily. "And do not think you can cozen me into one of your birdwitted schemes, because you will catch cold there, my lass."

"All I want to find out is the best time to call on her," Harriet explained, quite as though she were planning a drive in the Park instead of a call on her husband's mistress. "But perhaps you can help me with that. What time do gentlemen usually visit their mistresses, Richard? Can you tell me?"

Richard regarded her in pained astonishment. "No, I certainly cannot, you outrageous chit!" he exclaimed. "And besides, I ain't got the kind of blunt it takes to keep a ladybird, so I would not know."

It was Harriet's turn to stare at him after this revealing statement. "Do you mean to tell me, Richard, that you have never—" She clapped a hand to her mouth in sudden embarrassment. "I do beg your pardon," she muttered at his crack of laughter. "I did not mean what you seem to think," she added, her hot flush of color giving the lie to her words.

"It is a jolly good thing Giles ain't here to listen to that remark, my girl. He would doubtless fly into high dudgeon."

After arguing that Mrs. Brooks would probably not wish to receive a call—even from an old school friend—this late in the afternoon, and promising not to do anything without consulting him, Harriet finally wrung the information from Richard. She sent the note with a footman, with instructions to wait for an answer. Ophelia's response, on expensive pressed paper redolent with the scent of violets, sounded just as muddled and melodramatic as the young Beauty Harriet had known and loved so many years ago. Ophelia begged her friend, under pain of death, not to do anything rash, but added the interesting rider that his lordship rarely visited her before eight of the clock.

This was all Harriet needed, and less than ten minutes later she had cajoled Richard into escorting her to Curzon Street. Although the captain adamantly refused to come into the house, Harriet had little trouble in extracting his promise to fetch her away before eight o'clock.

"For if Giles finds me here," she half teased, half threatened him, "there will be the devil to pay, and it will be all your fault, Richard. You would not wish my untimely death on your hands, now would you?"

Without waiting for the captain's answer, which—from the wicked gleam in his eyes—she suspected might not be at all flattering, Harriet tripped happily up the steps and into the hall, overcoming the butler's reticence with the information that Mrs. Brooks was expecting her.

If Harriet had any qualms about her reception at Curzon Street, these were quickly dispelled by her friend's enthusiastic greeting.

"My dearest Harriet," Ophelia exclaimed tearfully as Harriet crossed the room in a rush and flung her arms about the Beauty's slender shoulders in a hug that left them both breathless. "I am so glad we have this last chance to talk before we must part forever," Mrs. Brooks murmured as soon as the butler had been sent off to bring up the tea-tray.

Harriet plunked herself down in a rose brocade armchair and pulled off her gloves. "What balderdash are you talking, Ophelia?" she demanded in astonishment. "We have only just found each other again after all these years. How can you say that we must part?" She untied the ribands of her modish new bonnet and threw it carelessly onto a nearby table. "Besides, I have so much to tell you, dearest," she added affectionally. "And I have had the most wonderful notion, Ophelia, you cannot imagine . . ."

"Oh, I think I can, Harry," the Beauty sighed gustily and dabbed at her lovely eyes with a scrap of lace. "You always were full of hare-brained plans that invariably got us into the most dreadful pickles." She shuddered gracefully. "I can still remember the time you smuggled that stray kitten into our room, do you recall? I think you would still have the mangy little creature had Miss Harrow not chanced to come by when the pesky thing was stuck at the top of the curtain."

"Oh, yes," Harriet interrupted eagerly. "I have not thought of poor, sweet Whiskers in years. He did love to climb up those dreadful mauve curtains old Sour Face was so proud of. It was unfortunate that she came in at the very moment Whiskers jumped down." She giggled at the vividness of the memory, and Ophelia smiled.

"And I suppose you are going to claim that it was also unfortunate that the dratted cat jumped down on Miss Harrow's shoulder?"

Harriet laughed outright. "Of course it was. And I shall never forget the expression on the old harridan's face when Whiskers came flying out of nowhere and perched quite happily on her shoulder."

"Naturally," Ophelia remarked with a smile. "That is the sort of thing you would remember, Harry. All I recall are the pages and pages of Latin verbs she made us copy out as punishment for . . . what did she call it?"

"Conduct unbefitting females of gentle birth," Harriet pronounced in a stilted, high-pitched voice, which caused both ladies to dissolve into gales of laughter.

After the butler had come and gone with the tea-tray, and both ladies sat sipping their China brew, Harriet bluntly broached the subject that had bothered her since their encounter in Hatchard's.

"How did you become so weak, Ophelia? You never were

sickly as a child. Was it something you brought back from Spain?"

Ophelia sighed and set her cup down with trembling fingers. "It cannot have been anything like that, Harry," she said in a tired voice. "For I was perfectly fine when I came back to England after . . . after Roger died. And then a year ago last winter, I caught this terrible cold that simply wouldn't go away. It turned into influenza last December, and I truly thought I was going to die."

Harriet gasped, remembering the urgency with which her husband had departed the Abbey last Christmas. He must love the Beauty very much to rush to her bedside with such speed, she thought with a sinking feeling in the middle of her stomach. But how could she blame him? she wondered. Ophelia was, if anything, more beautiful and appealing than she had been at sixteen. Harriet had always envied her friend's ethereal loveliness, and had paid scant attention to Ophelia's assurance that she would grow up to be beautiful, too, one day. That day had not yet come, she thought wryly, remembering the gangling chit of fifteen who had practiced romantical, languishing poses for hours before her cheval mirror. Rather than converting her magically into a smaller version of Ophelia, this posturing had made her look rather silly, and Harriet had finally abandoned the youthful illusion she had treasured secretly for many years of being a fairy princess in disguise. When she finally admitted to herself that the disguise she had hoped to shed miraculously when she emerged as a golden image of Ophelia was no disguise at all but the real Harriet Egerton, she had been oddly relieved.

And now, as Harriet gazed fondly at her friend, she realized that it had all been for the best. She would have made an ungainly Beauty, since she had never learned to languish convincingly, nor could she flutter her eyelashes with any degree of competence. And when she cried, her eyes turned red and puffy, whereas the tear that was inching its way down Ophelia's alabaster cheek made her appear, if that were possible, even more beautiful and fragile. She could understand how Giles had been captivated, but he should not have taken such nefarious advantage of the Beauty's helplessness, she thought. He should have married Ophelia and raised beautiful babies and lived happily ever after with his fairy princess in his Guide Book castle.

Harriet shook herself out of these mawkish ruminations. It

dawned on her that nothing had happened as it did in romantical novels. The earl had not married the fairy princess, he had
married Lady Harriet Egerton, a choice he had made while
seeming of sound mind, and without any undue coercion from
her. This thought sank in slowly, cheering Harriet no end as it
did so.

"Well, you did not die," she remarked prosaically. "So do
not cry, dearest. You know it only makes you mopish. We
must think of something that will help you to get completely
well again. What does your doctor advise?"

"Dr. McIntyre suggested that it might be the putrid air in
London that is affecting my lungs," Ophelia replied in her musical voice. "He said that a change of scenery might do wonders, but of course that is impossible." She waved one slender
white hand dismissively.

"Why is it impossible?" Harriet demanded. "And what does
Giles say?"

Ophelia stared at her in horror, her lovely eyes brimming
with tears again. "Oh, I wouldn't dream of burdening his lordship with such ideas," she whispered. "And I forbade Dr.
McIntyre to mention it to him."

"Are you telling me that Giles does not *know*?" Harriet
could not believe her ears. How like dear ineffectual Ophelia
to dither about when definite action was called for, she
thought.

The Beauty shook her head. "You do not perfectly understand, Harry. I could never suggest a stay in Bath or Brighton
to his lordship. For one thing, it would inconvenience him terribly. And for another, he would think that—"

"And who cares a fig for his lordship's convenience?" Harriet burst out indignantly. "You are sick, Ophelia, and you
must consider what is right for you. Do not bother your head
with what Giles thinks." She paused in the middle of this
tirade when her friend clasped her hands together and wrung
them, moaning piteously.

Harriet gazed at her, nonplussed, until she recalled that
Ophelia would always weep—which she did very prettily—
rather than fight. Even in their childhood days, the Beauty had
left the fighting, the planning, the arguments, the daredevilry
to her more intrepid companion. Harriet poured out their second cups and sat down to savor hers, while Ophelia regained
her composure.

"I did not mean to overset you, dearest," Harriet said after a while in a coaxing voice. "But I know from experience that men will ride roughshod over us poor females unless we show a little gumption."

Ophelia smiled faintly. "As I recall you always had plenty of that, Harry. I envied you terribly, you know."

"You envied *me*?" The notion was so preposterous that Harriet was momentarily diverted. "Well, the fact remains, dear, that if you do not make a push to exert yourself, Giles will do nothing about it, will he?"

Ophelia looked dubious. "I suppose so," she began. "But I don't think I could—"

"It doesn't signify," Harriet interrupted brightly. "Because I have a marvelous idea that will solve everything." She looked expectantly at her friend, but Ophelia only appeared to shrink further into the cushions of the settee, as if she could escape the avalanche of Harriet's enthusiasm.

"Don't you want to know what it is?" Harriet demanded impatiently.

Ophelia nodded weakly. "Of course, dear."

"You shall come back to Hampshire and stay with me, dearest," she exclaimed triumphantly, ignoring a nagging voice at the edge of her consciousness that hinted at dire consequences. "Country air is just what you need, and we will have you back on your feet again in no time." She beamed at the Beauty, who seemed to be bereft of speech.

"You cannot be serious, Harry?" she whispered after a considerable pause. "You must be quite mad! Tell me that this is merely another of your Banbury tricks. You cannot have considered what his lordship would say to such a scheme. I tremble to think of it."

Harriet let out a peel of delighted laughter. "That won't signify in the least," she began. "If we have to, we can always sneak away in the middle of the night. Richard can escort us." She chuckled at the thought of the captain's face when she informed him that he was to help his brother's wife and mistress abscond in the middle of the night.

It was then that she noticed that Ophelia's beautiful violet eyes had opened to their full extent, and were glazed with fear. She appeared to be gazing at a point just beyond Harriet's shoulder. Harriet glanced apprehensively at the clock on the mantel, but it was not yet six of the clock. The earl would not be there for another two hours, she thought, ignoring the prickling sensation snaking its way down her spine.

"And just where is my esteemed brother to escort you, my dears?"

Harriet closed her eyes as the ice in her husband's voice seemed to cut right through her. Then she opened them in time to see Ophelia's long lashes flutter bewitchingly, her violet eyes close gently, and her head sink back on the cushions in a deep, graceful swoon.

Her own momentary terror subsided instantly, and Harriet jumped to her feet, swinging round to face the enemy.

"Now look what you have done, you nodcock!" she exclaimed furiously. "You have frightened poor Ophelia quite to death."

# CHAPTER TWELVE

# Ménage à Trois

Lord Kimbalton stood transfixed on the threshold of his mistress's Chinese drawing room, his gaze riveted on the fiery, diminutive figure of his wife.

"What the devil are you doing *here*?" he roared, quite beside himself with fury. His initial decision to remain calm and coldly aloof in the face of his wife's fresh outrage dissolved as abruptly as snow in August at the hoyden's accusation that he was somehow to blame for Ophelia's prostration.

Harriet merely looked at him pityingly. "There is no need to shout, my lord," she remarked. "You have caused poor darling Ophelia quite enough trouble already without adding to her distress by—"

"I was informed that you had retired to bed with the megrim," Giles interrupted savagely, suddenly recalling his uncomfortable confrontation with Lady Cuthbert's butler.

"Yes, I know," she said quietly. "It was very considerate of you not to order me dragged from my sickbed to receive you, my lord."

Harriet smiled faintly, and the earl bristled at the double-edged compliment. She had come too close to the truth for comfort, he realized, for he had indeed contemplated forcing his way upstairs to his wife's room. He had wanted to tell her that he was willing to overlook her appalling lack of decorum and outright disobedience. He would forgive her—although it went against all his principles to do so—if she promised to be entirely governed by him in the future; if she would accompany him back to the Abbey and settle down as a dutiful wife, in his house, in his bed. The thought of Harriet in his bed distracted him, and he let his gaze stray to her lips and drift down her body, remembering the exciting and quite unexpected sensuality she had revealed to him that night.

With considerable reluctance, Giles pulled his erotic thoughts away from his wife. God's truth, he thought disgust-

edly, he was acting like a cursed Johnny Raw. The sudden jolt
of raw desire the memory of that night with his wife conjured
up so vividly came as a shock to Giles, who had always fancied himself free from the unruly dictates of youthful passion.
The sort of lustful urge that had inexplicably overcome him at
the sight of his wife was quite beyond the pale. No gentleman
ever thought of his wife, the mother of his children, with anything less than respect and utmost consideration. Those animalistic impulses to which men were naturally prone should
be diverted into less respectable channels, he reminded himself
grimly. It was unthinkable to confuse a man's wife with his
mistress, and he was in imminent danger of committing that
unpardonable sin.

"I am not quite the monster you seem to think me, Harriet,"
Giles said in gentler tones, although at that moment he knew
himself to be closer to that irrational state than he could remember.

"Perhaps," she replied noncommittally, but Giles could have
sworn, from the pale pink that flooded Harriet's cheeks, that
his wife's thoughts had taken a warmer direction.

A plaintive moan from the supine figure on the rose brocade
settee brought the earl's mind back to the present, and all ten-
derer thoughts of his wife cooled instantly.

"You have not answered my question, Harriet," he said
tersely.

Harriet, who had turned to sit beside Mrs. Brooks, shot him
a caustic glance. "If you mean the *What the devil are you
doing here?* question, my lord, I should think that must be obvious. I am drinking tea with my dear school friend Ophelia
Weston." She arranged Ophelia's delicate head more comfortably on a pink cushion. "Would you care for a cup, my lord?"
Harriet added, quite as though she were in one of London's
fashionable drawing rooms instead of serving tea in his mistress's house.

Giles ground his teeth.

Was there no limit to this chit's temerity? he wondered,
feeling quite put out by the sudden upheaval of all his plans.
He had spent a particularly frustrating evening after leaving
Mount Street, torn between the desire to wring his wife's de-
lectable neck, and the unexpected urge to cease being the villain in her life and persuade her that he was quite prepared to
forget the entire episode. After a tiresome hour or two at
White's spent playing hazard with several of his cronies,

among them the Marquess of Monroyal, who quizzed him unmercifully about the scandalous encounter in the bookshop, Giles had thrown up his hands in disgust. On impulse he had walked over to Curzon Street with the express purpose of spending a quiet evening with his mistress, only to discover her drinking tea with his wife as though it were the most natural thing in the world.

Giles ignored Harriet's facetious invitation and strode nervously about the room. He was at a loss as to how to proceed, a state of affairs that was disconcertingly new to him. His first impulse was to drag Harriet back to Montague House with him and consign her to his mother's care. The dowager would be delighted, and would certainly take it upon herself to see that Harriet behaved appropriately. Since the earl had informed his mother of his marriage to Lady Harriet Egerton, the dowager had ceased her campaign to throw eligible chits in his path, but had developed an equally tiresome new obsession. The new Countess of Kimbalton must be introduced to the *haute monde*, the dowager informed her son at least once a day, and who better to undertake such a task than the earl's mother?

The earl grimaced. He was unaccountably reluctant to throw Harriet into his mother's clutches, although it might be interesting to watch the battle of wits that was sure to ensue. Unfortunately, he had walked to Curzon Street and would have to take the carriage he kept here for Ophelia's personal use. The notion was somehow distasteful.

At that moment he heard a pathetic sigh and turned to find Harriet applying sal volatile to a protesting Ophelia.

"Come along, dear," she was saying in a no-nonsense voice to the reclining Beauty. "Sit up and drink this tea I have just poured for you. You cannot loll around any longer, Ophelia. There is too much to do. His lordship is here, and we must discuss our plans with him."

Ophelia gave a tiny shriek of horror as her violet glance settled on Giles, and she subsided against the cushions, closing her eyes.

Harriet shook her friend impatiently. "Don't be a peagoose, Ophelia. You do wish to get well, do you not? Well, then you must be strong, dear. I am sure his lordship will be reasonable when he hears what the doctor had to say."

Giles ceased his pacing at Harriet's words and came to a halt beside the settee. "What is this prattle about the doctor?" he demanded, worry making his voice sharp.

"Oh, do not, I beg of you, Harriet, do this to me," Ophelia whimpered in a faint voice. "I cannot bear it, dear. I shall die of mortification."

"Fiddle!" Harriet responded calmly. "One does not die of mortification, dear. It only appears that way. Now, are you going to tell his lordship our plans?" She paused expectantly, but when the Beauty merely sighed and closed her eyes, Harriet continued implacably. "If you are craven, I shall do so myself. Do you wish that?"

"By all means do so," Giles broke in impatiently. "What the deuce is this plan you mentioned?"

"Nothing that you could not have thought of yourself, my lord," Harriet replied acerbically. "Dr. MacIntyre has informed Ophelia that the London air disagrees with her. And like the silly goose she is, she refused to tell you. She was afraid it would *inconvenience* you, my lord."

Giles bristled at the sarcasm in his wife's voice, but the reproach in her gaze made him uncomfortable. Had he perhaps been unduly concerned with his own convenience? he wondered. The notion was new to him, and Giles felt vaguely uneasy.

"And what precisely do you mean by that?" he demanded sharply.

Harriet looked at him pityingly once more, and Giles had the strange sensation that he had been judged and found wanting. The feeling was not at all pleasant, nor what he was accustomed to.

"You really do not know, do you?" she said, more a statement than a question. "Then allow me to enlighten you, my lord."

The Beauty gave a pathetic moan. "Harriet, please . . ."

"Hush, dear," Harriet said bracingly. "Do not worry your pretty head over this, Ophelia. I intend to take care of everything. I shall ask the housekeeper to make up a cup of tisane for you. It will—"

"Will you get to the *point*," Giles interrupted, exasperated at his wife's penchant for prevarication. "What is this confounded plan?"

"Ah, yes." Harriet's hazel eyes fixed themselves on him, and Giles imagined he saw a flicker of apprehension in them. "Would you not sit down, my lord?" she said with unexpected politeness.

Giles was instantly wary. "I can only suppose you are about

to heap yet another outrage on my head," he muttered testily, ignoring the invitation.

"Oh, nothing of the sort, my lord. You are off the mark if you believe me capable of . . . capable of . . . " She hesitated, and Giles found himself grinning wolfishly at his wife's discomfort.

Harriet blushed and then continued in a defiant rush. "I have conceived the happy notion of inviting Ophelia to spend some time with me in Hampshire, my lord. The warm weather and country air will do wonders to restore her health and I shall enjoy the company."

"You did *what*?" Giles roared, spluttering in disbelief. He felt his face slowly turning pale as the import of his wife's words sank in. He stared at Harriet in consternation, unable to control the tide of fury which threatened to engulf him. "Did I understand you to say that you have invited Mrs. Brooks to Kimbalton Abbey?"

Harriet's chin went up defiantly. "Yes, my lord, I have," she replied, meeting his gaze squarely. "And she has accepted," she added with an air of finality.

"I will not go, Harriet," the Beauty protested weakly from the settee, fresh tears springing to her violet eyes.

"Oh, yes, you *will*, you silly peagoose," Harriet said forcefully. "Even if I have to drag you down to Hampshire myself."

"No, you will *not*!" Giles heard himself shouting, quite beside himself with rage. He could not understand why his wife aroused such violent emotions in his breast. The earl had always considered his nature to be phlegmatic, immune to the passions which so often drove his friends and acquaintances to dangerous extremes, such as indulging in fisticuffs, or fighting duels, or falling in love. After his accession to the title, Giles found that he rarely needed to raise his voice. When he did, people wilted before his cool authority, and he had grown accustomed to overcome opposition with the mere raising of an eyebrow. But for some reason, Harriet touched an irrational side of him Giles never knew existed, a hidden well of emotion which flared at the first sign of defiance in those expressive hazel eyes of hers.

Giles drew a deep breath to control his anger.

"Oh, Harriet, I warned you how it would be!" The Beauty's feeble shriek distracted Giles, who frowned at her impatiently, causing her to crumple into a quivering heap of distraught emotions.

Harriet patted her friend absentmindedly on the shoulder and turned to glare at the earl. "I must ask you again to keep your voice down, my lord," she snapped. "No doubt they can hear your brawling down in the kitchen."

"I can vouch for that, my dear Giles," a voice drawled from the doorway, and the earl spun around in time to see his brother stroll nonchalantly into the room, a wide grin on his face.

Harriet swept over to grasp Richard's hands impulsively. "Oh, Richard!" she cried. "I am so glad you are come. Giles is being quite impossible again. Can you believe that he refuses to let me invite Ophelia down to Hampshire for the summer?"

For the first time since his arrival at Curzon Street, Giles felt a glimmer of amusement. His brother's face registered a spectrum of emotions, ranging from astonishment and shock to incredulity and embarrassment. Richard raised his eyes from Harriet's upturned face and stared blindly at the earl.

Giles smiled grimly. At least he now had an ally in his stand against this insanity his wife was determined to unleash in the ordered pattern of his life. It was only much later that it occurred to Giles that he had never considered Richard an ally before.

The notion was oddly comforting.


The following afternoon Harriet found herself in the earl's elegant, well-sprung chaise traveling in the direction of Hampshire with all the speed a gentleman of wealth and fashion might expect from his highly bred cattle. Her return to the Abbey was not in itself unexpected, for Harriet knew she could not hold out forever against the earl if he insisted upon exercising his authority. What did surprise her—and caused her an inordinate amount of pleasure—was the fact that besides herself and Aunt Sophy, the third occupant of the coach was Mrs. Ophelia Brooks.

Harriet glanced once again at the snugly cocooned figure reclining drowsily in the opposite corner. Giles was obviously not taking any chances with his mistress, Harriet noted with a stab of something alarmingly like jealousy. When the crested coach had drawn up before Lady Cuthbert's house on Mount Street at the unprecedented hour of one o'clock that afternoon, the surprise passenger had obviously been accorded all the benefits of the earl's wealth to ensure a comfortable journey. The rugs that swathed her slim figure were of the finest English wool, she was surrounded by soft cushions, and hot bricks had been provided for her small feet. Ophelia had also been accompanied by a fiercely protective and highly voluble abigail who evidently expected to ride in the carriage with her mistress.

Pushing her ungenerous thoughts aside, Harriet smiled at the memory of the abigail's consternation when she had been forcibly ejected from the vehicle by a sturdy footman. Although her knowledge of the Spanish language was limited, and Santa seemed either unwilling to speak English or incapable of doing so, Harriet had managed to convey her instructions with the aid of her aunt's footman, and the abigail was now firmly ensconced in a second carriage with the rest of the servants.

By the time the coach had passed Richmond, Ophelia had fallen into a deep sleep, and Lady Sophronia—who had accepted the visit of her niece's school friend to Kimbalton Abbey without a blink—nodded over one of Mrs. Radcliffe's latest novels. Harriet let her thoughts drift back to the previous evening when Richard had come to Curzon Street to rescue her—as he had later confided—from the dragon. He had been too late, of course, and had seemed as startled as his brother at Harriet's suggestion of inviting Ophelia to the Abbey.

Rather than take her side in the violent argument that had ensued, Richard had surprised and annoyed Harriet by unexpectedly supporting the earl's claim that the presence of Mrs. Brooks at the Abbey would incite scandalous rumors among the gabble-mongers of the *haute monde*. A gentleman simply did not invite his mistress to stay under the same roof as his wife at his ancestral home, Richard had pointed out stubbornly. To do so would be to break one of society's most stringent rules. No wife should lower herself to acknowledge the existence of her husband's light-of-love. In fact, the whole argument they were engaging in was, Richard had insisted, much to Harriet's chagrin, highly improper and should never have occurred at all.

Harriet had pouted and stamped her foot, teased and wheedled, but both men had remained adamant in their refusal to sanction her ramshackle start. In the end, she had taken her reluctant leave of Ophelia, who had fallen in and out of unconsciousness so many times during the heated exchange that Harriet had lost count. She had ignored her husband and swept out of the house and into Richard's carriage in high dudgeon.

To her utter amazement and chagrin, Lord Kimbalton had
entered the carriage with the captain and settled himself beside
her. Upon their arrival at Montague House, her husband had
asked her, mildly enough considering the violence of their recent exchange, if she would gratify him by coming inside to
make the acquaintance of his mother, the dowager.

So incensed was she at the obtuseness displayed by both
gentlemen, that Harriet replied instantly, without a thought for
the consequences.

"And if I do not wish to do so, doubtless you will drag me
into your house by my hair, my lord," she said icily. "All you
ever do is ride roughshod over everyone's sensibilities," she
added, quite carried away by her sense of ill use.

The earl had gone quite still for a moment, and the suggestive glitter in his gray eyes had faded abruptly. "Hardly by
your hair, my dear," he drawled in a neutral voice, reaching
for her hand. Harriet had imagined the worst and gone rigid,
but he had laughed humorlessly and merely raised her fingers
for his kiss. And without another word he was gone, and Harriet had been left with an odd sense of loss.

"Oh, dear," she murmured as the carriage resumed its way
to the house on Mount Street. "I think I may have made things
worse."

"That was not exactly well done of you, Harry," Richard re-
monstrated mildly. "I believe a show of wifely obedience
might have been wiser."

The knowledge that the captain was probably correct did
nothing to improve Harriet's mood. "Are you saying I should
have gone with him meekly, like some weak, spineless creature?" she demanded stiffly.

"I imagine that meekness might be rather appealing to a
man like Giles, especially in a wife." The captain grinned
wryly. "And it was within his rights to drag you inside, as you
must know, Harry."

"Well, I am not meek," Harriet snapped, now thoroughly
annoyed at herself for her churlish behavior. "He has Ophelia
for that," she added waspishly, regretting her words as soon as
they were uttered.

"I am sure Giles has noticed that fundamental difference between you and Mrs. Brooks," Richard remarked dryly, and the
devastating honesty of this observation made Harriet flinch.

She was silent for a long time. When she spoke again, her
voice held a note of anxiety. "Do you really believe that,

Richard? About Giles preferring meek females? Do *you*?" she added impulsively.

"No, I do not prefer meekness, as it happens," the captain replied lightly. "But I am not Giles, my dear." He regarded her speculatively for a moment. "If you want to know what I really think, Harry, I shall tell you. I believe that you have shaken up Giles's staid and comfortable world with a vengeance. You have added a maelstrom to his placid existence, so to speak. He is naturally disconcerted, even alarmed, to discover that the two females in his life, who should never be spoken of in the same breath, are in fact bosom bows. I will have to admit it startled me, too."

"That is not my fault," Harriet retorted.

"True enough, my dear. But are you really surprised that poor old Giles has been thrown into high fidgets?"

Harriet sighed gustily. "I just do not understand him, Richard," she complained.

Richard laughed. "I daresay you are a total enigma to my brother, too, my dear."

"Now that I cannot believe," Harriet protested hotly. "I am a very ordinary sort of female—" she began.

Richard cut her short with a great guffaw of laughter. Before Harriet could discover what caused this unflattering hilarity, the coach came to a halt before her aunt's house, and an anxious butler opened the door to inform them that the first dinner gong had already sounded.

The following morning, Harriet had received a curt note from the earl, announcing that his carriage would call for her promptly at one o'clock to carry her back to Hampshire. He made no mention of Ophelia, so it came as a complete surprise to Harriet when the beautiful widow made her presence known.

"I daresay Giles is not such a care-for-nobody as he pretends to be," she remarked to her friend, glancing eagerly about to see if her husband had accompanied the carriage.

He still had not put in an appearance by the time the two ladies from Mount Street were ready to depart, and Harriet cast a despairing glance at Richard, who was already mounted on Greybeard.

"What is keeping your brother, do you suppose?" she inquired anxiously.

Richard regarded her for a moment or two before he replied with an attempt at nonchalance. "Do not look for Giles, my

dear Harry. He informed me that he would remain in London
at least until the end of the Season to escort his mother about.
But never fear, my dear, you will be quite safe with me."

Without another word, Harriet climbed into the carriage and
hid her disappointment by fussing over her aunt and ejecting
the belligerent abigail Santa from her position next to Ophelia.
It was only after they had been on the road for nearly an hour,
and the other two passengers had relaxed into somnolence,
that Harriet allowed herself to think of Lord Kimbalton's cow-
ardly desertion. He could easily have ridden, she thought mul-
ishly, if he had not dared to travel in a closed carriage with
two females whose combined proximity seemed to offend his
sense of propriety. Couldn't he? The fact that he had chosen
not to accompany the ladies at all brought Harriet to the unpleasant realization that her husband was deliberately avoiding
her.

This conclusion hurt more than she had anticipated. And
worse yet, the earl's absence did not seem to bother Ophelia in
the slightest, Harriet noted unhappily. Which could only prove
that the Beauty was far more confident of the earl's regard
than his wife. At least, that was the only conclusion Harriet
could come up with, and it failed miserably to improve her
mood.

Could it be, she asked herself—after they had changed
horses at Kingston and taken to the road again—that Lady
Harriet Egerton had done the unthinkable and lost her heart to
a dictatorial, insensitive, oaf of a man who obviously did not
care a fig for her?

The notion had a lowering effect on her already tense
nerves, but the more Harriet considered the unpleasant possibility, the more she had to admit that it might well be true.

A month later, Harriet was still trying to convince herself
that Giles Montague had not captured her foolish heart, and indeed never would do so. The notion was simply too preposterous, she told herself at regular intervals during that first month
back at the Abbey. Harriet Egerton had far too much common
sense to allow herself to be overcome—like a silly chit fresh
out of the schoolroom—by the emotions afflicting the heroines
in those highly improbable melodramas Aunt Sophy was constantly reading. But then how could she explain the odd sense
of incompleteness she felt? Harriet often wondered. Or the
quite uncharacteristic pettishness which assailed her as Ophe-

lia showed increasing signs of recovering her health and glittering good looks. Harriet could find no satisfactory answer.

"Is something bothering you, Harry?" Ophelia inquired one sunny morning as the two ladies strolled along the brick path in the new rose-garden behind the house.

Harriet stopped to snip a faded pink blossom and threw it into her basket. She was doing what she liked best in the whole world, tending her rose-trees, yet at her friend's words, Harriet became aware that even here, in her beloved rose-garden, she was not as carefree as she had been before her visit to London. The sparkle had gone out of her life.

"It so happens that I am feeling particularly well today," she lied with only a faint twinge of conscience. Harriet had developed a talent—if not a liking—for stretching the truth during the past month in order to fob off all such good-intentioned questions regarding her health. She cut a long-stemmed red bud and added it to the others in Ophelia's basket.

"I think we have enough roses for the Great Hall," she added, anxious to divert the topic of conversation. "Shall we have time to arrange them in the flower room before nuncheon, do you suppose?"

Harriet was particularly pleased with her flower room, one of the changes she had made in the Abbey by converting a small space next to the stillroom into a convenient place to arrange her roses. By adding running water and a number of wide shelves to hold the variety of vases and bowls she had collected from all over the house, Harriet had created a working nook for herself isolated from the bustle of the kitchen staff. Gathering and arranging her flowers was a hobby Harriet shared with Mrs. Brooks, who had had little opportunity to indulge such rural tastes at Curzon Street.

As the two ladies emerged from the flower room, having dispatched two footmen to the Great Hall with the freshly arranged bowls of roses, they encountered Captain Montague, who was, Harriet saw immediately, in very high gig indeed.

"What has happened to give you that smug expression, Richard?" Harriet teased him. "You look positively replete with good tidings."

Richard grinned companionably at her and pulled a sheet of paper from his pocket. "I was coming to find you, Harry, because I have received word from Giles this morning."

Harriet felt a pulse start singing in her veins. "Is he coming

down to Hampshire after all?" she demanded, conscious of the
hopeful note in her voice.

Richard shot her a quick glance, then shook his head. "He
does not say anything about that. He wishes me to meet him at
Green Oaks tomorrow. Apparently, Giles has been there for
the better part of a week."

"Oh, what a wretch he is," Harriet said dispiritedly. The
news that her husband had come to the neighborhood without
stopping at the Abbey only reinforced her suspicion that he
was avoiding her. She took the letter Richard held out to her
and looked eagerly down at the autocratic scrawl, as if she
could discover a more personal message there.

"What is he doing at Green Oaks?" she asked curiously
when the earl's note failed to reveal any comfort to her aching
heart. "And why does he want you to go there, Richard?"

"Giles was never one to explain his actions, Harry. You
should know that. No doubt I shall find out in good time."

"I think we should all go," Harriet burst out impulsively. "It
would make a comfortable outing if we left early in the morning. What do you say, Ophelia?" She gazed at the widow, who
blushed and cast an anxious glance at the captain.

Harriet had expected the Beauty to endorse the idea with enthusiasm. After a month's absence, she reasoned, Ophelia
must be eager to be reunited with her lover. Harriet experienced an acute sinking feeling every time she thought of her
husband as another woman's lover, but she had forced herself
to be sensible about this ménage à trois she had promised to
countenance when she had accepted the earl's offer. The discovery that Giles's mysterious lady was her childhood play-
mate Ophelia Weston had been a severe shock, even for
Harriet, but she had been sensible about that, too. Or at least
she had tried very hard to be. It might have helped had Ophelia
been the kind of female Harriet had expected a mistress to be.
If she had been brazen, and coarse, and greedy, Harriet could
have accepted her breathtaking beauty. But Ophelia was none
of these things. She was sweet, amiable, unassuming, and dis-
tressingly vulnerable. In short, she was the dear, silly Ophelia
Harriet remembered so well from the old days. How could she
resent such a woman when she loved her so dearly?

"I rather think not, Harry," Richard cut in laconically. "This
is hardly a social call, my dear. No doubt Giles has some estate business he wishes to discuss with me. He would doubtless have my hide if I turned up with three females in tow."

"How horrid you are, Richard," Harriet protested crossly. "You are getting as bad as Giles for spoiling our fun." She thrust the letter back at him and flounced off to the dining room, where nuncheon was laid out.

Without Richard's amusing company, the next day seemed to drag by on leaden feet and by midafternoon, Harriet wanted to scream with frustration. Her thoughts had gone off early that morning with the captain, who had ridden down to Corhampton on Greybeard, and although she had suggested rather obliquely that it might be nice if Lord Kimbalton accompanied his brother back to the Abbey, she had little expectations of him doing so. She had not set eyes on her husband in over a month, and her conviction that he was deliberately avoiding her grew painfully stronger as the days went by.

After enduring a prolonged call by Lady Hawthorn and her three aging daughters, during which her ladyship made every possible effort to pry the last particle of information out of the Abbey ladies concerning Lady Kimbalton's dear friend, Mrs. Brooks, Harriet could stand it no longer. As soon as the Hawthorn carriage disappeared down the driveway, she slipped out the back onto the flagstone terrace, and set off in the direction of the gazebo, scene of her ill-fated acceptance of the earl's suit.

The last daffodils—planted with such care last autumn on the grassy slope—had faded, but the delicate pink roses Harriet had set out all around the trellised structure had thrown up caressing arms of greenery to embrace the latticed walls and reach up to shroud the pagoda roof. Harriet found their simple blossoms quite enchanting, and the effect was exactly as she had planned it, a sort of ordered wilderness. Now, if only Giles were here to share it with her. . . .

But enough of that, she told herself firmly, mounting the steps into the cool interior. Could it have been only last September that she had stood over there at the window embrasure gazing out at the countryside that had reminded her so much of Lark Manor? With a slight tremor Harriet recalled the excitement she had felt at the kiss that had never happened. His lips had been so warm and seductive on the palm of her hand. Without conscious thought, Harriet glanced at her hand. The memory of the earl's kisses was so vivid she expected to find the visible imprint of his lips there. But there was nothing. She sighed.

The sound of steps behind her made Harriet freeze. Her

heart leaped wildly, but when she whirled around it was only Ophelia standing in the doorway, elegant parasol in hand.

"Harriet!" her friend exclaimed anxiously. "I saw you crossing the park and wondered what you were up to. Is something bothering you, dearest?"

Disappointment settled upon Harriet like a cold fog, extinguishing the brief euphoria that had swept over her. Without quite knowing how it happened, she felt a warm dampness on her cheeks, and then she found herself clasped tightly in Ophelia's arms, sobbing jerkily and mumbling incoherently in a voice she did not recognize as her own.

"There, there, love," Ophelia murmured softly, stroking her hair soothingly. "Sit down over here, Harry, and tell Ophelia all about what has so upset you, dear."

"It is nothing. Really," Harriet responded automatically in a choked voice, allowing herself to be led to the wooden bench beside the table. "I am being maudlin. Pay no heed to me."

"It is Giles, is it not?" Ophelia said quietly, laying her pink parasol on the rough table. She gathered her skirts and sat down beside Harriet. "You are worried about Giles. Am I right?"

Harriet swallowed hard and fumbled in her pocket for a handkerchief. But of course she had forgotten to bring one. She never cried. Ophelia pulled one from her reticule and handed it to Harriet. It was a filmy lace confection redolent with the faint scent of violets, and the sight of it brought fresh tears to her eyes.

"Tell me, dearest," Ophelia insisted gently. "Is it Giles?"

Harriet shook her head vigorously, vowing to have her tongue cut out before she admitted to Giles's mistress that she harbored an impossible *tendre* for her own husband.

"Of course it is, Harry," the Beauty said. "I am not blind, child. Do you think I have not seen what is going on in your heart?"

Harriet sat up and glared at her friend. "That is a bag of moonshine, Ophelia, and you know it," she said crossly. "Why should I feel anything for that odious man who avoids me so openly? Can you tell me that? Only a flat would be *that* stupid."

Ophelia clasped Harriet's hands in hers and squeezed them gently. "You are a silly peagoose, Harry, truly you are." She laughed softly, and Harriet cringed at the sound. Was her childish infatuation so obvious that she had become a laughingstock to her friend? she wondered, appalled and intensely humiliated at the thought. So sunk in misery was she that Harriet almost missed the Beauty's next words.

"You have it all wrong, dear. It is not *you* his lordship is avoiding, so disabuse yourself of that nonsensical notion. He is avoiding *me*, Harry. I could have told you that in London before we set out to come to Hampshire. I thought you knew."

Harriet stared at her friend in disbelief.

"That cannot be true," she said stiffly. "Giles would not do that to you, Ophelia. He loves you!" The Beauty would never know what it cost her to say these words, but Harriet could not abide hypocrisy.

Ophelia opened her lovely violet eyes in amazement. "Now you really are being absurd, dearest," she protested. "Wherever did you get that Banbury tale?"

Harriet's chin went up stubbornly. "I have seen it with my own eyes," she declared. "He dotes on you."

"You have only seen what you wanted to see, Harriet," Ophelia said seriously. "Giles is quite incapable of loving me, and I am vastly relieved that he does not. It would be most uncomfortable, believe me."

Harriet stared at her uncomprehendingly. "Do you not love *him*, Ophelia?" she asked bluntly, unable to accept what her ears were hearing.

The Beauty smiled sadly. "No, dear. My love died six years ago with Roger. I have yet to experience any desire to give my heart to another."

This revelation, spoken with such obvious sincerity, went straight to Harriet's heart, and she burst into fresh tears and flung her arms around her friend. It was some time before she realized that the Beauty's eyes were also damp.

"What must we look like," she whispered in a watery chuckle after some time had elapsed. "We have become two watering-pots. I am glad nobody is here to see us." She examined Ophelia's lovely face, unmarked by the flow of tears. "If what you say is true, Ophelia, and you do not have any affection for Giles—"

"Oh, I never said I do not hold him in affection, Harry. I do, you see. Giles has been most considerate in his dealings with me. I was practically penniless when I came back from Spain. It took what little money I had to bring Roger back to England and bury him in his family plot. He was not on speaking terms with his brother, the present owner of Brooks Manor, but

Roger loved his home and would have wanted to lie there with his mother, whom he adored. It was the last thing I could do for him."

Ophelia paused, and Harriet looked at her expectantly. "And after that you returned to London?" she prompted.

"Yes. I had run into your brother, the viscount, in Paris, and as you know, Peter and Roger were fast friends. Your brother helped me with the arrangements and accompanied me back to London. Later he introduced me to Giles, and it was not long after that his lordship offered me a very . . ." She paused again. "A convenient arrangement. Giles has been so kind to me over the years, Harry. Kind and very generous. I shall miss him."

"Miss him?" Harriet repeated, unsure that she had heard aright. "Of course you miss him, dear. But you will soon be well enough to return to Curzon Street and—"

"Oh, no!" the Beauty exclaimed with more than her usual force. "I have been meaning to tell you, Harry. My sister Elizabeth is recently widowed and has asked me to make my home with her in Bath. She does not know what I have become, of course—"

"Never say that Giles has cast you off!" Harriet exclaimed in horrified tones. "The wretch will pay dearly for it, I can assure you."

Ophelia laughed with genuine amusement at this, and Harriet gazed at her curiously. "It is a good thing the gentlemen are not here to listen to you talk that way, my dear Harriet. Giles would surely have a fit of apoplexy, and even Richard, who is considerably less prudish than his brother, would doubtless take you to task for harboring such indecorous thoughts."

Harriet felt stunned. "But what will Giles do if . . . if . . ." She found it difficult to finish her thought. "If you go away?" she finally stammered, feeling a warm flush invade her cheeks.

"I imagine he will spend a good deal more of his time here in Hampshire," Ophelia said calmly. "I fancy he will soon find out—if indeed he has not already done so—how fortunate he is to have married you, Harry."

Harriet lowered her eyes to the delicate handkerchief clutched in her fingers. It was damp and wrinkled, much as she was herself, she mused. Ophelia's words rang in her ears, but Harriet steeled herself against them. The Beauty was merely being kind; there could be no truth in what she said. More likely than not, Giles would fly into one of his black rages when he discovered that his beautiful mistress had left him.

Harriet had difficulty imagining anyone wanting to leave Lord Kimbalton. She herself would be quite incapable of doing so, she realized with sudden foreboding. She was tied to him more firmly than she could have believed possible. Now if only she could learn to be the meek female Richard said his brother might prefer, perhaps she could bind Giles to her, too. Perhaps he really would spend more of his time at the Abbey. Perhaps he would not scowl at her quite so much. Perhaps . . .

Unaccountably cheered by this train of thought, Harriet vowed to practice meekness with a vengeance.

# CHAPTER THIRTEEN

# Green Oaks

Lord Kimbalton stood at the open French windows in the downstairs parlor and gazed out across the modest park at Green Oaks. The grass had been almost knee-high when he had driven down from London over a week ago to inspect the small manor house he had not visited since his accession to the title. The estate had always been trouble-free and productive, and he had been content to leave its management in the hands of his father's old steward, Matt Foreman, just as he trusted Henry Mulligan to tend to the everyday running of Kimbalton Abbey.

As he stared out at the freshly scythed grass, Giles wondered if perhaps he had been too lax in his care of his patrimony. It had seemed so convenient to follow in his father's and brother's footsteps, and spend most of his time amusing himself in London while the Montague estates apparently faired well enough to produce the income he needed to sustain his chosen way of life. Now he was not so sure that his choice had been a wise one.

The first indication that anything was amiss came as his curricle swept between the yellow stone pillars that guarded the entrance to Green Oaks. The gravel driveway had seemed woefully untended, and the grass on either side looked more like an abandoned meadow than the park of a gentleman's manor. Unable to raise anyone at the front door, Giles had driven round to the stable-yard only to find it, too, deserted except for a liver and white hound, which looked like an offspring to those his father had kept at the Abbey years ago.

A shout had brought a tousled lad ambling out of the stalls. The lad's demeanor changed only slightly when he saw the earl standing impatiently beside his curricle. The head groom, Giles soon learned from the garrulous stable-lad, had been gone since morning to Corhampton to have Mr. Foreman's mare shod. Giles also learned that his steward was laid up with ague, and that the cook had given her notice a month ago, claiming that she refused to share her kitchen with rats.

"Rats?" the earl repeated, startled out of his ill humor.

"Aye, guvn'r," the lad confirmed with a wide grin. "Kicked up the devil of a dust, she did. I told 'er the beasties wouldna 'urt 'er none, but she packed up and loped off anyways. Good riddance, I say, guv. The mort dinna cook worth a sow's baby." He regarded the earl with eyes that were far too knowing for his age, Giles thought, and showed an alarming penchant for saucy talk.

"Be ye wishful of me un'itchin' yer cattle, guv?" the urchin asked with no discernible sign of bashfulness.

The earl nodded. "Where is Foreman?" he demanded.

After following the lad's lackadaisical directions, Giles discovered his steward in the tiny parlor of his cottage, reclining in an old armchair that had seen better days. The old man struggled up hastily when the earl poked his head into the low-ceiling room, but Giles motioned him to remain seated.

An hour later, he emerged with a thoughtful expression on his face. Things appeared to have slipped badly since the steward had contracted a nagging inflammation of the lungs last Christmas. Fearful of losing his position, the old man had struggled to manage the estate from his sickbed rather than confess his ill health to the earl.

As he rode around the estate the next morning, after a makeshift breakfast provided by one of the two maids who remained on the premises, Giles realized that his decision to deed Green Oaks to his brother could not have come at a better time. The decision had not been easy to make. On one hand, his instincts as the title holder to maintain the Montague holdings intact weighed heavily with him. On the other, Harriet's accusations and his own newly emerging awareness of his brother's dilemma—Richard's fierce attachment to the Montague heritage with no legal claim to any part of it—had touched him deeply. His man of business had attempted to dissuade him, but the solicitor's ill-concealed contempt for Richard's illegitimacy had triggered an unexpected surge of anger in Giles, and he had signed away the property with a satisfying flourish.

The gift of Green Oaks would right some of the old wrongs, he thought. It would acknowledge his brother as a true Montague, and give him the independence a man needed to hold his head up. Giles was pleased with his decision, but the seedy appearance of the estate had caused him to send for Richard sooner than he had intended.

The sight of a grey horse cantering up the driveway jerked Giles out of his reverie, and he strolled out into the hall, where an ancient footman was already holding the door wide. The appearance of Greybeard brought Harriet to mind, but for some odd reason he resisted the urge to ask Richard if his wife had sent a message for him. Instead, he clapped his brother on the shoulder and took him into the small library for a brandy.

Later, as the two men rode around the estate discussing the different projects that needed attention, Giles found himself increasingly uneasy about Richard's reaction to the proposed gift. Perhaps he should have consulted his brother before making out the deed, he thought, uncomfortably aware that once again he had acted arbitrarily. He wished, quite irrationally of course, that Harriet were here to tell him how to go on. Once again he heard her accusing him of riding roughshod over everyone in his path, and he glanced uneasily at Richard.

The thought still bothered him as he poured their brandy after dinner that evening, and Giles wondered how he could broach the subject without sounding autocratic.

"Do you agree with my wife that I ride roughshod over people's sensibilities?" he asked abruptly before he lost his nerve.

Richard looked at him in surprise, a grin tugging at his lips. "Harriet does tend to get right to the heart of the matter, doesn't she?" he drawled noncommittally.

"But is she right in her assessment of my character?" Giles insisted.

After a slight pause, Richard shrugged. "Yes," he said bluntly. "I think she is right in this case. And Harry is in a position to know, after all," he added in a flat voice.

"So are you," Giles said with equal bluntness.

Richard let out a cynical laugh. "Yes, brother, I am at that," he drawled. "But I doubt you invited me here to ask my opinion on your character."

Giles held his brother's blue-gray gaze steadily for several moments. Then he shrugged. "No. I would like your opinion on something quite different." He opened a drawer in the dusty escritoire in the corner and drew out the transfer he had signed in London. "Here," he said casually, handing the legal papers to his brother. "I am thinking of disposing of Green Oaks and would like you to read this and tell me what you think."

Richard stared at him, shock and anger warring in his expression. "What the devil does it matter what I think?" he exclaimed harshly. "The place is yours. You can dispose of it any damned way you please." He threw the deed down on a small table, raising a cloud of dust.

Giles took up the papers and held them out again. "I would nevertheless be obliged if you would read it through, Richard. Please," he added as the mulish look on his brother's face deepened.

Richard automatically reached for the deed, looking down at it as though it might bite him. "Oh, very well," he said ungraciously, flinging himself into a leather chair beside the empty hearth.

Giles leaned an elbow on the mantel and gazed down at his brother, his nerves tensed. Richard read carelessly at first, but suddenly he stiffened and he went back to the beginning, reading slowly, as if unsure of the meaning. When he came to the end of the document, Richard sat for a long time staring at the flourish of the earl's signature.

"I presume this is for Harriet's benefit?" Richard said expressionlessly, after an interminable silence.

Giles stared in astonishment. "What?" he said stupidly.

Richard grimaced. "I assume this magnanimous act is designed to impress your wife," he said contemptuously. "Well, I don't want any part of it, thank you very much."

Giles had a blistering rebuke on the tip of his tongue, when he stopped abruptly. He shut his mouth and stared at his brother's angry face, an odd thought flickering at the back of his mind. What exactly was Richard asking? he wondered. And then the answer came to him, slowly and tentatively, but he knew that it had to be right. His brother wanted confirmation that Giles was making this transfer for the right reasons. But what were the right reasons? Giles wondered anxiously. He was not even sure he knew the answer himself.

"No," he said slowly, choosing his words carefully. "This is not to impress anyone, least of all Harriet. She did put the idea into my head, I'll admit that. When she called me autocratic." He stopped and took a drink of brandy. Richard's expression had not changed. His face was set in a cynical mask.

Giles tried again. "It is much more than that," he said, searching for the explanation which eluded him. "Actually I did it for both of us. Primarily for you, of course, but also for me—"

"Made you feel good, no doubt," Richard interrupted sarcastically. "Like handing out alms to the needy."

Giles bristled. "Do you have to be such a . . ." He stopped abruptly, horrified at what he had almost uttered.

"A bastard? Is that what you almost said, brother? Well, I am a bastard, of course, so you are quite right there." The bitterness in his brother's voice tore at Giles's heart.

"You are also a Montague," he snapped. "And it is high time you started acting like one instead of sniveling over what cannot be changed." He paused, then added in a softer voice, "I have also settled ten thousand pounds on you so that you can make this place productive again. It used to bring in two or three thousand a year. Sometimes more."

Richard stared at him with a strange expression, his anger gone. "You will swear to me that Harriet had no hand in this? She did not badger you to do it?"

"How could she?" Giles responded, his heart suddenly light. "I have not seen the disobedient wench in over a month."

His brother laughed at that, and Giles could feel the atmosphere relax between them. "More fool you, brother," Richard said bluntly, his eyes dancing with a message Giles could not misunderstand.

"Fill up the cups, Giles," Richard demanded jubilantly, holding out his glass. "I would like to propose a toast.

"To Harriet," he exclaimed, raising his glass and meeting his brother's eyes. "A disobedient wench who is worth a dozen of the others."

Giles lifted his own glass, and as the crystal touched his brother's, he felt that between them, Richard and Harriet had changed the direction of his life.

"To Harriet," he echoed, suddenly filled with an irrational longing for his disobedient wife.


"Promise me you will write often, Ophelia," Harriet admonished her friend for the umpteenth time since the Beauty had come downstairs in her traveling clothes. Her valise and bandboxes were already lashed to the roof of the Kimbalton chaise, which stood waiting at the front door, but Harriet had been unwilling to let her friend go without one last good-bye.

"Of course I shall write, Harry. No doubt Bath will be full of quizzes at this time of year, and I shall have no end of stories to relate about their oddities. You may count upon it, dear. And you must answer all my letters as you promised."

"I shall indeed," Harriet replied, marveling—as she had so often during these last few days of Ophelia's stay—at the radiant loveliness of this woman who had burst into her life again under such strange circumstances. She hated to part with her, yet if what Ophelia had said was true, she would have to do so if she ever wanted to see her husband again. Harriet still found it well nigh impossible to believe that Giles did not love his beautiful mistress. His ex-mistress, she reminded herself, not without a flicker of something like relief, which she quickly suppressed. She wanted to believe it, of course. Her spirits rose miraculously whenever she considered the possibility that Ophelia might be right, only to be cast down again when her common sense told her that a man would be a fool not to lose his heart to such a Beauty.

"And I shall expect you to visit me again before the end of the summer. Now, do not argue with me, Ophelia," she continued hastily as the Beauty's face clouded. "I shall not take no for an answer, you know. And if you do not come, I shall travel to Bath to see you."

"That would not be at all wise, my dear," Ophelia said gently. "You cannot have considered the consequences."

"I do not care a fig for the consequences," Harriet exclaimed hotly, pacing up and down the new Aubusson rug in front of the empty hearth of the Great Hall. "And do not mention Giles to me, Ophelia, for I do not care what he thinks either. I shall not give you up just because that odious, stiff-necked man orders me to do so. I simply will not."

"At odds with Giles again are you?" a jocular voice said from the doorway. Harriet spun around as Viscount Bridgeport strolled into the room.

"Peter!" she cried ecstatically, rushing over to embrace her brother. "What a wretch you are not to let me know you were coming." She drew him forward to meet her friend when she remembered that Peter and Ophelia's husband had been comrades in Spain. "You remember Ophelia Brooks, don't you, Peter? She has been spending a few weeks with me."

There was an uncomfortable silence, and Harriet realized with a shock that both her brother and the Beauty showed signs of intense embarrassment.

"Mrs. Brooks? Of course I know Mrs. Brooks," the viscount said in an oddly stiff voice. "How do you do, ma'am? I had not expected . . ." He colored and his question trailed off.

"You had not expected to find me here. Is that what you

were about to say, my lord?" Ophelia murmured without rancor. "As you see, I am about to leave for Bath to join my sister."

Harriet immediately came to her friend's rescue. "How could you be so inconsiderate, Peter?" she exclaimed heatedly. "Ophelia is a dear friend of mine, and I will not have her insulted in my home. Even by *you*," she added belligerently.

The Beauty laid a gloved hand on Harriet's arm. "Hush, dear. His lordship is quite right to be shocked at my presence here. You are always so quick to fly into the boughs, Harry. But only consider what the London gossips would say if they knew I was here with you. It would create a very disagreeable scandal, I can tell you. Please, your lordship," she continued, turning to the viscount, "I beg you to use your influence with your sister to convince her that our association cannot continue."

"Fiddle!" Harriet exclaimed. "You are a complete goose to think I care a fig what those old Tabbies say."

"Giles will care, you may be sure of it," the viscount cut in firmly. "Mrs. Brooks has the right of it. However unfair you may think it, there are certain rules that cannot be broken. Any scandal attached to you must affect the Montague name as well as our own, Harry. So think well before you do anything foolish, dear."

Harriet knew it was useless to pursue the matter. She opened her arms to Ophelia and hugged her fiercely. "Promise me you will write the minute you get to Bath," she repeated, a catch in her throat.

The Beauty smiled tearfully. "You may count on it, dearest." And before Harriet had time to say anything more, Ophelia was gone, shepherded lovingly into the carriage by the taciturn Santa, who seemed in alt at having her lovely mistress all to herself again.

Long after the chaise had disappeared down the drive, Harriet wandered about the big house listening for the sound of the Beauty's footsteps and the music of her soft voice. How very painful it was, she thought moodily, to love two people and not be able to enjoy their company simultaneously. But Ophelia was right to leave, she finally had to admit. Giles might have relaxed his scruples enough to allow the Beauty to enter the sacred portals of his ancestral home, but it had been unrealistic of his wife to expect him to countenance her highly improper connection with his mistress. He had allowed the

visit only to please his wife, Ophelia had insisted. But Harriet
very sensibly refused to allow herself to believe such nonsense. In truth, thinking about the earl at all caused her head to
ache quite dreadfully, so Harriet sought the sanctuary of the
garden to recover her spirits.

By tea-time she was feeling pleasantly tired of pruning the
faded blossoms off the dozens of rose-trees that she had
planted in casual clusters in a wide swathe along the stone terrace. Next autumn she would tackle the front of the house, she
thought, pleasant images of digging up further sections of the
earl's pristine lawn making her smile. Perhaps masses of white
roses on one side of the driveway and red on the other might
be eye-catching, she thought, suddenly curious to know
whether the Montagues had been Yorkists, or had sided with
the Lancastrians in the civil war. She would have to ask Giles.

Thoughts of Giles made her pause to examine her plain
muslin gown covered by a practical apron tied neatly around
her waist. She remembered with a pang of nostalgia that afternoon last year when she had been surprised in her gardening
attire by her future husband, her curls tied back with a simple
ribbon, and her fingers pricked by thorns. Had she known then
what she knew now, would she have accepted him? she wondered, clipping one last dead rose and tossing it into her basket. Harriet sighed. She could not imagine giving up what she
had now, even if Giles did not learn to care for her, as Ophelia
had insisted he would.

Carefully skirting around such disturbing thoughts, Harriet
picked up her basket and joined her aunt on the terrace. The
scene was so reminiscent of that other time that Harriet could
easily imagine herself back at Lark Manor.

"I wonder how the new yellow roses are doing in the bed
Turpin dug for me before we left Sussex," she remarked idly
as Carruthers, accompanied by two footmen, brought out the
tea-tray and set it down beside her. She removed her gloves,
and her eye was caught by the wedding band Giles had
brought her from London. There was no getting away from
thoughts of the man, she mused. His presence was every-
where.

Peter joined them at that moment, distracting Harriet with
an account of a fox he had seen skulking across the south
meadow.

"I trust you did not harm the poor animal, Peter," Aunt
Sophy observed, passing around a dish of gooseberry tarts.

"You would not call them poor animals, Aunt, if you had lost a dozen prime layers as old Mrs. Hayes did last week, Mulligan was telling me. We should prevail upon Giles to arrange a hunt next autumn. That should rid the countryside of some of the pests."

"I shall raise my voice in opposition, you may be sure of that, you bloodthirsty rogue," Lady Sophronia countered with some heat. "And I am convinced that I can persuade Richard to join me," she added darkly.

"Richard?" the viscount repeated in astonishment. "Never say that Richard Montague is back from the wars. Where is he, Harry? I must see the rogue to believe it."

"Richard has been with us for some weeks," Harriet replied. "He is presently over at Green Oaks with Giles."

"Oh, no, he ain't," the viscount retorted, getting abruptly to his feet. "Speak of the devil, you old reprobate," he said, striding across to clasp the captain firmly by the hand. "Never thought to see you abandon your soldiering to dance attendance on the ladies, Dick. It is dashed good to see you again."

Harriet regarded the captain silently, his amazing likeness to the earl making her heart hammer uncomfortably. Richard slapped Peter on the back and winked at her shamelessly. She smiled and bit back the question that trembled on her lips.

"And where the deuce is Giles?" Peter demanded, asking the question in her stead.

Richard grinned and looked directly at her, his blue-gray eyes dancing with some secret amusement. "Oh, you know Giles, old man. Had to change his coat before presenting himself to the ladies."

The cup Harriet was handing to the captain clattered as her hand trembled. He reached to steady it, and his grin widened.

"What did you do at Green Oaks?" Harriet asked, anxious to hear what had transpired between the brothers. "We didn't expect you back for at least a week, did we, Aunt?"

"No, indeed," Aunt Sophy responded amiably. "But now that we are positively invaded by gentlemen, don't you think you might remove that dreadful apron, Harriet?"

Harriet colored to the roots of her hair. She had forgotten the gardening apron she always wore to protect her muslin gowns from the thorns, and quickly jumped up to untie it. She had barely settled herself again when she became aware that someone else had come out onto the terrace. She had purposely kept her eyes away from the open French doors, and now she busied herself with the teacups to cover her nervousness.

The footsteps stopped abruptly but no one spoke.

Curiosity finally drove her to raise her eyes. Her husband's tall figure stood as if rooted to the mellow gray flagstones. He had advanced halfway towards the tea-table, but his eyes were focused not on the group gathered around it, but on the expanse of park that dropped away below the terrace and rose towards the hidden gazebo in the distance.

Harriet saw at once that his expression was anything but pleasant. Even as she watched, paralyzed with apprehension, the earl turned slowly and met her gaze, his own filled with astonishment and anger.

"What in Hades have you done to my park, Harriet?" he said savagely, his voice ringing loudly in the silence.

Harriet felt her heart leap crazily before dropping to the soles of her half-boots. Slowly she got to her feet, the scene unfolding in her dazed consciousness like a particularly unpleasant dream. She heard her aunt gasp something unintelligible, the scrape of chairs as the other two gentlemen got to their feet, and way off in the distance a lark's burst of carefree song. She tried to focus on the lark as she turned and walked towards the door, away from that humiliating scene Giles was playing out for her.

Just as Harriet thought she might get away without further embarrassment, she heard his voice again.

"Harriet!" he exclaimed, raising his voice with the cold authority she hated. "I asked you a question. Didn't you hear me?"

Harriet stopped in her tracks and turned, as if in a daze. She felt light-headed and knew she must be pale. When she spoke, her lips seemed to have great difficulty in forming each sound. "Yes, my lord," she said deliberately, the words dropping like stones from her lips. "I heard you. Unfortunately . . . everyone this side of Petersfield . . . heard you, too."

She stood for a moment, eyes locked with his, conscious of bewilderment and chagrin replacing the scowl on his face. Then Harriet turned and entered the house, her anguish too great for tears.

In the silence that followed his wife's departure, Giles could hear his own heart beating. The disastrous scene had unfolded almost of its own volition. He could not recall consciously raising his voice—hadn't he sworn off such uncouth tactics with Harriet? Even as the angry words tumbled out, and he heard himself shouting, he could not seem to stop them. He muttered a few choice epithets under his breath and took a step towards the door.

"Whoa, old man!" he heard his brother exclaim harshly, and felt Richard grasp his arm firmly and jerk him back. "Where the devil do you think you are going?"

Giles turned to stare unseeingly at his brother, noting hazily that Richard was glaring at him, and that the blue-gray of his eyes was flinty.

Giles disengaged his arm and returned the stare bleakly. "I am going to speak to my wife," he said slowly and distinctly, for his tongue seemed suddenly paralyzed.

"*Speak?*" Richard repeated contemptuously. "I imagine you mean shout, don't you, brother? That is the only way I have ever heard you *speak* to Harriet."

Giles grimaced at the truth in these words.

"You are a reprehensible lout, you know," the viscount said between clenched teeth, appearing quite abruptly beside Richard. Giles had the fleeting impression that he stood in grave danger of having his cork drawn by his best friend, or his daylights darkened by his brother. He could not blame them.

"Yes, indeed," Lady Sophronia snapped from behind him, her voice quavering with anger. "What an insensitive, ill-mannered, insulting way to address a lady. No wonder the poor, dear girl has gone off in a pucker. I think I shall join her," she added, rising regally and sweeping past the earl, a grimace of disgust on her homely face. At the entrance she stopped and threw him a fulminating glance. "I trust you will not attempt to ring a peal over the poor girl's head. You have raised quite enough dust for one afternoon, thank you." She turned and disappeared into the house.

The earl gazed after the normally mild-mannered woman in astonishment. Never had a female dared to rip up at him as Lady Sophronia had just done. And there was no pretending that her indignation was not justified, he thought grimly. He deserved to be flogged, and if he were not careful, Richard and Peter appeared on the point of obliging him.

"Damnation!" he exclaimed softly, quite at a loss for words.

"Yes, and damn *you*, Giles," the viscount said explosively. "What in Hades did Harry do to deserve that blistering?" he demanded. "Plant a few rose-trees? Is that what you're making mice-feet about? Your wits have gone begging, man."

Giles took exception to this tirade. "A *few* rose-trees?" he repeated, his anger flickering again. "By God, Peter. The place is smothered with them! Do you realize that this park is over four-hundred years old? We are talking about four hundred years of tradition here, I'll have you know. And there have never been rose-trees in this park. Never!"

Two pairs of eyes glared at him in astonishment, and Giles sensed that he had committed another gaffe, although he could not imagine what.

"The devil fly away with tradition!" Richard burst out, his eyes glinting furiously. "What a numskull you are, Giles. Only a dashed gapeseed would concern himself with a few acres of bloody grass when he has a wife like Harriet. I do not understand you, brother. Cannot you see that four hundred years from now the Abbey will be famous for its roses, and it will be Harriet who planted them here. She is creating your cursed tradition," he muttered under his breath.

"And if I remember rightly," the viscount interrupted, "you promised my sister she might have her flowers. Was that not one of the conditions of the agreement?"

"And they are a great deal more pleasing than plain grass," Richard added belligerently, as if to settle the matter.

Giles remembered all too well, now that Peter had mentioned it, that Harriet had indeed demanded flowers about her. She could not live without them, she had said. He had paid little attention to her request at the time, being more concerned with his own convenience. But he had promised. And Richard was right, too. The colorful mass of roses did look rather lovely, now that he came to examine them more objectively. And they reminded him of Harriet.

The thought of what he had just done to his wife, to the Harriet he had been so eager to see again, to touch, to kiss . . . made him shudder. Giles shook himself and glanced towards the door through which she had so lately disappeared.

"Do not even think of it, old man," the viscount warned. "Harriet will bite your nose off if you go near her now. Only make things worse, you know."

Giles doubted things could get much worse between them. He had behaved badly; against all reason he had riled at Harriet when it was quite obvious—as Richard had made very clear—that he owed her a debt of gratitude for bringing beauty to his home. It was also abundantly clear, he admitted to himself, astonished that he had not seen it creeping up on him, that his wife meant more to him than his ancestral park. He had reacted on reflex, a conservative reflex built into him since his birth, a reflex he must needs modify if he was to have peace in his household.

Beset by these mixed emotions, Giles felt the need to get off by himself to think. Excusing himself hastily, he strode through the park until he reached the sanctuary of his secret place. But here more than ever Harriet's presence made itself felt. The mass of pink roses climbing exuberantly over the gazebo roof brought her vividly to mind. The soft perfume reminded Giles of the night he had buried his face in her hair tumbling on the pillow as he made love to her.

Richard had been right in that, too, Giles reflected. He had been a fool to stay away so long. But that was about to change, he thought, fishing in his pocket for the note Carruthers had handed to him barely an hour ago. He read it through again and realized with unfamiliar humility that Ophelia had been far wiser than he. She had seen that the arrangement he had imagined so convenient of keeping his new wife sequestered in the country while he lived his life in London was doomed to fail. Had he chosen another kind of female for his countess, one more attuned to the ways of the world, he might never have come to this. But Ophelia had been astute enough to see that sooner or later Harriet would take over his life, as she had already taken over his house and his park.

After a long while, Giles replaced the letter in his pocket and rose to walk back to the house. It would soon be time to dress for dinner, and at dinner he would see Harriet again.

But Harriet did not come down to dinner. Lady Sophronia offered a patently false excuse for his wife's absence, and left the table early with only the briefest of nods to the gentlemen. After drinking his port without much enthusiasm, Giles followed his guests to the billiard room, where the viscount challenged Richard to a lively game.

Giles could only think of Harriet's hair spread on her pillow.

When it came his turn to play against his brother, he lost miserably. His luck at hazard was equally abysmal, and Richard finally suggested—as the clock in the hall struck one—that the time had come for Giles to go upstairs and apologize to Harriet. One of the clock, he thought wryly. A little late to disturb a woman who had gone to bed with the megrim. It would have to wait until morning. By then he would be more himself, he argued.

But once in his chamber, Giles could think of nothing but Harriet. After pacing up and down for a half hour, he crossed to the connecting door and opened it softly. Perhaps she was still awake, he thought, knowing that—as on that other night he had come to her bed—if Harriet were sleeping, he would wake her. He could not wait till morning.

He saw instantly that the bed had been turned down, but Harriet was not there. Giles stood for a shocked moment, visions of life without Harriet flashing before his eyes. Had she run away? he wondered, but chided himself for a fool. That would not be Harriet's way. She would confront him and tell him exactly what she thought of him. Giles grinned at the notion, and it suddenly became imperative that he find her.

He was reaching for the bellpull to summon her abigail when a thought occurred to him. Of course, he reasoned. Where else would the chit seek comfort but with her aunt? A surge of emotion fired his resolve, and before he realized what he was doing, Giles strode out of his wife's room and down the hall. Without stopping to knock, he flung open Lady Sophronia's door and stepped across the room to stand beside the huge four-poster.

Aunt Sophy sat up abruptly and let out a shriek. Her nightcap, a modish confection festooned with pink lace, had slipped down to reveal a tangled cluster of crisp curls, and her voluminous night-rail, also trimmed with pink lace, was tied firmly beneath her chin. In the flickering light of the solitary candle on the dresser, Giles saw her ladyship's expression change from fright to hostility. She took a deep, indignant breath, and Giles hastily lowered his eyes to the other occupant of the bed.

His wife was curled in a tight ball under the covers, apparently asleep, her curls spread out invitingly on the pillow. She looked so like a frightened child that Giles paused, wondering if he had made a mistake. Then Harriet opened her eyes, and he saw that she had not been asleep at all.

Giles grinned. He caught hold of the covers and threw them back, revealing her huddled form in a light batiste night-rail. His eyes raked her hungrily.

"How dare you, sir!" Aunt Sophy cried indignantly, her voice quavering. "What scrambling manners are these? Leave this room immediately before I call someone to throw you out."

Giles laughed at the ridiculous notion of being forcibly ejected by his own footmen. He bent down to slip his arms beneath his wife's small body.

"Come on, sweetheart," he murmured close to her ear, as he scooped her up and held her against his chest. "We have some unfinished business to attend to, Harriet."

Ignoring Lady Sophronia's increasingly vocal protests, Giles strode out of the room and along the hall. The high-pitched screeches followed him as he carried Harriet into his room and kicked the door shut behind them. He stood for a moment, savoring the feel of her warm body in his arms. Then he carried her over to the empty hearth and settled into his favorite armchair, cradling his wife tenderly on his lap.

Harriet had uttered not a sound during this whole episode, but the trusting way in which she settled herself against him and laid her head on his chest spoke volumes to his anxious heart.

She was not going to fight him.

Giles could not remember ever feeling quite this happy before in his whole adult life. Happiness, like love, was a vastly overrated emotion. At least he had always thought so.

Until now.

Now he seemed to be in imminent danger of drowning in it.

# CHAPTER FOURTEEN

# Roses for Harriet

Harriet climbed into her aunt's bed and pulled the covers up tightly around her neck.

"Are you sure you want to do this, Harriet?" her aunt queried anxiously. "His lordship will not like it at all when he finds out that you are here, and not in your own bed where you should be."

"Pooh! A fat lot I care what his lordship likes," Harriet replied bitingly. "He will never know, in any case. He is still downstairs carousing with those other two reprobates."

Only after these words were spoken did Harriet wonder at her own perverse feelings towards her husband. Here she was claiming not to care about him, yet she had unconsciously been listening for his familiar footsteps on the stair. And what about those angry words he had used to greet her after a month's absence? Had they not convinced her that she held no place in his regard? She had wanted to throw her arms around his neck—something she had never yet dared to do—and he had berated her most unjustly about her roses. What further evidence did she require for her heart to recognize that it had made a dreadful mistake?

Harriet closed her eyes tightly. She was glad she had not gone down to dinner. In her present state, she might not have been able to control her tears had that infamous husband of hers dared to address her in that arrogant tone of voice he seemed to reserve solely for her. She willed herself to go to sleep, but her mind was full of speculation. What was Giles doing downstairs so long? What was he thinking? Did he regret his harsh words?

The sound of muffled voices distracted her. Then she heard the distinctive sound of male boots on the stair. More muffled laughter, and then the sound of footsteps passing her aunt's room. That could only be Giles, she thought, her heart leaping painfully. A distant door opened and closed, and silence descended once more upon the house.

Harriet turned over and closed her eyes. Aunt Sophy snored gently beside her.

Sometime later, she was startled out of a light doze by the noisy entrance of someone into the room. She heard Aunt Sophy sit up abruptly and utter a shriek. Harriet opened her eyes to see the tall figure of her husband looming over her. She drew in a sharp breath as his face broke into a wicked grin. Before she could react, Harriet felt the covers jerked off and his eyes traveling down her lightly clad body.

Harriet was vaguely conscious of her aunt's angry exclamations, but she was lost in the murmur of her husband's voice close to her ear as he scooped her up in his arms and strode out of the room.

He had called her *sweetheart*! And his voice had been as far removed from that angry growl on the terrace as it was possible to get. He had also mentioned something about unfinished business, and naive as she admittedly was, Harriet had a pretty clear idea of what he meant by that.

Dare she hope for a miracle? she wondered.

Once inside his bedchamber, Giles disconcerted her again. Instead of putting her straight into the turned-down bed, he carried her over to an armchair and settled into it, cradling her on his lap. Surprised and pleased at the unexpected discovery that her husband wanted to cuddle, Harriet snuggled against him and laid her cheek on his chest. She could hear the rhythm of his heartbeat through the fine lawn of his shirt, and found the masculine smell of him vastly tantalizing to her senses. On the whole, she had to admit, this was far superior to her Aunt Sophy's chaste bed.

Harriet closed her eyes and sighed contentedly, waiting for his next move, her mind alive with impossible fantasies.

After a considerable period of time, she heard the earl clear his throat and shift uneasily.

"Am I too heavy for you, my lord?" she murmured, raising her head to gaze at him.

"It is Giles, remember?" he corrected her gently, one hand cradling her head once more against his chest and stroking her hair. "And no, you are not heavy at all, Harriet." He paused for a moment, then continued awkwardly. "I want to tell you how much I regret what happened this afternoon, Harriet. I never intended to shout at you. I do not know what came over me. In fact, I had been looking forward to seeing you. There are several things we need to discuss, my dear."

Harriet digested this information cautiously. It was not exactly what she had hoped to hear, but at least it was an apology of sorts. No doubt, poor Giles was not in the way of acknowledging his errors easily. She hoped he would not start on his precious park again, and her rose-trees. He had promised she might have them, and although she admitted that her enthusiasm had carried her away a trifle, surely he could see how beautiful they were? The only other topic that he might conceivably have on his mind was his mistress, and Harriet hoped with all her heart that Ophelia had not mistaken the nature of his lordship's feelings for his London lady.

Her heart constricted at the very thought.

"I quite see how you must be wondering why Ophelia is not here, my lord," she said, steeling herself for the worst. "But you really have only yourself to blame that she has left you. Only a gapeseed could imagine that a beautiful woman like Ophelia would take kindly to being abandoned for a whole month? No doubt she feared you were replacing her in your affections, or something equally horrid. I'll never understand why you did not marry her when you had the chance, Giles," she added seriously.

"What nonsense are you talking, Harriet?" the earl demanded, his instinctive frown settling on his forehead.

"Oh, it is not as nonsensical as you think," she replied tartly. "If you had—and I cannot believe that the notion did not strike you, for Ophelia is amazingly beautiful—then the dear girl might even now be living a healthy, happy life here at the Abbey. With you," she added, feeling quite sick at the thought.

He was silent for so long that Harriet finally raised her eyes from her perusal of the black hairs escaping from the top of his unbuttoned shirt. His eyes had darkened to a slate color, and his frown had disappeared.

"And what about you, Harriet?" he murmured in a low voice. "What would have become of your life?"

"Oh, that is obvious," she responded breezily. "I would be living a healthy, happy life at Lake Manor, wouldn't I? Unless Sir James had prevailed, and I were married to him, of course," she could not resist adding. "Then I would be living a healthy, happy life at Rathbone Hall."

At her last words, Harriet noticed that her husband's frown showed definite signs of reappearing.

"Would you, indeed?" the earl said tersely. "And would you have preferred it so, Harriet?"

Harriet stared into her husband's gray eyes, wondering what lay in that smug, enigmatic male mind of his. She wished that she could lie and jolt him out of his complacency by confessing that she would have been equally happy and content with Sir James at Rathbone Hall. But she could not lie. Even to punish her husband for not knowing the perfectly obvious answer to his own question.

She sighed at the perversity of men. "Perhaps not," she hedged gracefully. "I rather enjoy being the mistress of Kimbalton Abbey."

The earl grinned lazily, and his gaze dropped suggestively to her lips. "And do you enjoy being my wife, Harriet?" he murmured, running one hand over her hip and down her thigh. There was no mistaking the immodest meaning of this seemingly innocent question, and Harriet felt herself blush.

"That is one and the same thing, is it not?" she hedged again, unwilling to give him the satisfaction of confessing the truth.

"Not exactly, my dear," he said with maddening perversity. "I am curious as to how you rate me as a husband."

Harriet gazed at him in astonishment. Did he really expect her to list his obvious attractions such as his rank and fortune? she wondered. Or did he want the truth? She doubted it, but some perverse quirk of her nature demanded that she give him a candid glimpse of the convenient arrangement he had established between them months ago under the disguise of marriage.

She smiled at him to soften the blow. "You must know that you are the ideal husband, my lord," she began sweetly, watching his expression relax. "For one thing, you are never underfoot to bother me; I have free rein to do as I please. And then, of course, you keep the most beautiful mistress in London. How many wives can boast of that? And furthermore, Ophelia just happens to be my very dearest friend. Now that is really a convenience, wouldn't you say?" Harriet observed that her husband's frown had returned, but she continued implacably. "It is true that you do occasionally suffer bouts of temper and shout at me, but no doubt that is to remind me of my wifely duties. And you did promise to let me plant all the rose-trees I wished in that wonderful park of yours. Very generous of you, my lord," she added, watching his jaw muscles jerk convulsively.

"Best of all," Harriet continued in a rush before she lost her nerve at her own daring, "you have promised to help me fill the nursery with little Montagues. What more could a sensible female wish for, my lord?"

In the silence that followed, Harriet wondered briefly if her husband realized that she had just bared her heart to him. Probably not, she thought glumly, given the earl's past record of obtuseness. But then perhaps she had been rather heavy-handed in her description of their relationship. Perhaps she should have been less concerned with her own honesty, and rather more considerate of her husband's tender male ego.

After an agonizing length of time, during which Harriet listened to the uneven rhythm of his breathing, and tried to convince herself that honesty was always preferable to subterfuge, even for a good cause, the earl spoke, his voice curiously gentle.

"So you consider yourself a sensible female, Harriet?"

She raised her head and looked at him in surprise. "Indeed, I do, Giles," she replied unhesitatingly.

"Something tells me that you are not nearly as sensible as you would have us all believe, my dear Harriet. No truly sensible female would have accepted my conditions. Am I not right?"

Harriet stared at him for a moment. Perhaps he was not as obtuse as she had thought, she mused. How else could he have guessed one of her most closely guarded secrets? During the past several months, it had become increasingly clear to her that where her husband was concerned, her common sense had flown out of the window. If Giles once suspected that his convenient wife harbored embarrassingly inconvenient feelings for him, he might go off to London again, or something equally unthinkable.

But how could she lie to him?

"Perhaps you are right, Giles," she said, carefully picking her words. "If I were really as sensible as I thought I was, I would certainly have accepted Sir James Rathbone's offer instead of yours. I might be leading a happy, useful life caring for my invalid mother-in-law. And by now I would have one, perhaps two, little Rathbones to give me joy."

The earl snorted derisively. "Perhaps," he growled deep in his throat. "That is if you were not too busy playing nursemaid to your mother-in-law to get that namby-pamby Adonis into bed."

Harriet smiled and laid her head back on his chest. "Did you know that Sir James has a passion for roses?" she asked mildly. "And since he has no four-hundred-year-old park for me to turn into rose-beds, he would have no occasion to shout at me, would he?"

Giles growled something unintelligible. "I cannot imagine that exquisite knock-in-the-cradle has enough starch in him to shout at anyone, much less a managing female who would doubtless lead him a dog's life tied to her apron strings."

He sounded decidedly put out, and Harriet smiled secretly. "You must admit that with a husband as stunningly attractive as dear James is, I would be guaranteed spectacularly beautiful children," she pointed out mendaciously.

"Not necessarily so," the earl protested with a chuckle. "Aren't you forgetting, my pet, that the poor little mites might favor you?"

Harriet took instant umbrage at this implied slur. She raised her head and glared at him. "I will have you know, sirrah, that Sir James thinks I am beautiful."

"Indeed?" her husband murmured in feigned astonishment. "Now I wonder why," he added, a teasing light glinting in his gray eyes.

"Because he loves me, of course, you great looby," Harriet explained in a voice heavy with sarcasm. "But I cannot expect you to understand that, of course."

"Why not?" Giles inquired mildly, placing a warm kiss on Harriet's nose.

Harriet brushed him away impatiently. "Because you are not the kind of man to understand these things," she said pityingly.

"I can understand perfectly, thank you, sweetheart," Giles murmured as he ran his lips down her cheek to her neck.

Harriet was momentarily diverted by the warmth of his mouth in the hollow of her throat. "Ha! I do not believe you for a moment," she said, picking up the argument with a vengeance. "Explain it to me, Giles."

"I thought you were explaining it to me, dearest," he murmured against her ear. "I understood you to say that moonling Rathbone thinks you are beautiful because he loves you. Is that correct, love?"

"Yes, that is right," she agreed, fascinated at the tingling warmth of his hand moving on her breast.

"Seems rather irrational to me," Giles remarked between the kisses he was trailing down her collarbone.

"It is." Harriet gasped as his mouth inched towards her breast. "Very irrational indeed, but that is what love is all about." She sighed wistfully. "Naturally you would know nothing of that."

He raised his head and gazed down at her, his eyes glittering with an emotion which Harriet had never seen in them before.

"I think you must be wrong, love. I am feeling definitely irrational at the moment. Perhaps I know more than you think about love."

Harriet opened her eyes wide and stared at him, mesmerized by the air of quite irresistible decadence that hung about him. What he had just said made no sense at all. Giles irrational? The notion was laughable. She doubted her husband had ever entertained an illogical thought in his entire life. Giles in love made even less sense. What could this unflappable, self-controlled man know of the irrepressible tenderness and anguish that roiled in her breast at the mere sight of him?

"That is quite the most nonsensical thing you have said tonight," she said severely. "I do not believe a word of it."

"What if I told you I find you beautiful, too, Harriet?"

"I would think you quite mad, my lord," Harriet answered breathlessly. But try as she might, she could not still the wild leaping of her heart.

Giles grinned and covered her mouth with his. "Isn't that the whole point, sweetheart? I *am* mad," he murmured against her open lips. He deepened the kiss until Harriet felt the room begin to spin around her. She wanted nothing more than to lose herself in the maelstrom of emotions that threatened to take her over the edge of sanity.

Much later, after Giles had demonstrated to his delighted wife what he had failed to during their first night of love, that Harriet could indeed lose herself in a maelstrom of sensations which left her deliciously dizzy and contented, a nagging thought returned to haunt her.

She raised herself up on one elbow and gazed down at the man lying beside her. "Giles," she murmured, nudging him gently.

"Yes, love," he said drowsily, pulling her down against him again.

"How long is this madness going to last, do you suppose?"

He nuzzled her neck and chuckled. "I am irrevocably, irreversibly mad, my love."

"Forever?" she insisted.

"Forever is a long time, sweetheart. Let us just think in terms of the next fifty years or so, shall we?"

"Then you won't be going back to London?" she asked tentatively.

"No," he said categorically. "I shall stay here and help you plant rose-trees, my sweet Harriet. Does that answer your question?"

"Oh, yes," Harriet said, quite overcome by this new development. "And speaking of roses, Giles, I have a wonderful idea for some new beds. That is if you—"

"I have a much better idea," the earl said, turning his talkative wife on her back and running his hand up the inside of her thigh. "Why don't we leave the roses until tomorrow?"

Harriet gasped as her body responded instinctively to her husband's touch. "Of course, Giles," she murmured happily. "Anything you say."

After all, she thought hazily as she felt herself begin to spin again. What more could a sensible female wish for?